Muffins and Moonlight

Witch Haven Cozy Mystery - book 4

K.E. O'Connor

K.E. O'Connor Books

MUFFINS AND MOONLIGHT

Copyright © 2021 by K.E. O'Connor

ISBN: 978-1-915378-31-6

Written by: K.E. O'Connor

Preface

The Witch Haven series has been created so you spend time with four amazing witches:

Books 1-3 tell Indigo's story: Spells and Spooks, Hexes and Haunts, Curses and Corpses

Books 4-6 tell Luna's story: Muffins and Moonlight, Cupcakes and Cauldrons, Pancakes and Potions

Book 7-9 tell Odessa's story: Hauntings and High Jinx, Hauntings and Havoc, Hauntings and Hoaxes

Book 10-12 tell Storm's story: The Case of the Screaming Skull, The Case of the Poisoned Pumpkin, The Case of the Cursed Candy

And there are two bonus origin stories to enjoy:
Fire Fang and **Silvaria**

Chapter 1

"These cakes taste like boiled socks." Mallory Ling jabbed a finger at the box of half-eaten iced cakes on the counter. "I want a refund."

I ran my critical gaze over the cakes and winced. I'd baked them two nights ago. I'd been tired and not concentrating, longing for my bed and to curl up with a romance novel. The cakes had looked fine when I'd taken them out of the oven, but I'd felt something had been off with them, despite being careful with the magic I'd used.

I should have trusted my instincts and made another batch, but Fandango's was backed up with orders, and there hadn't been time to do anything else. That included making sure my baking magic was topped up, so I didn't produce cakes that tasted like boiled socks.

"Mrs. Ling. Are you sure it was the cakes? You said you had an Indian banquet at your party. Maybe the flavors got mixed up."

"Everyone said they tasted strange. You ruined my special day." Mrs. Ling sniffed.

"Excuse me, where's my caramel latte and slice of pumpkin loaf?" another customer said. "I've been waiting ten minutes."

I waved a hand in the air. "Sorry! I'll get right on that."

"Not until you've dealt with this problem," Mrs. Ling said.

"How about a replacement?" I hurried along the counter where our delicious home-baked treats were laid out for customers to browse.

She followed me, her eyes narrowed. "Did you make any of these?"

I bit my bottom lip. "I did. No one has complained about them tasting strange."

"Actually, this scone is stale." Another customer approached the counter with a plate in his hand. "Can I have a fresh one?"

Mrs. Ling arched her eyebrows. "Give me a refund. I'll have to go elsewhere in the future."

"Don't do that. I'll get everything sorted." I nudged the furry butt of my snoozing familiar, Earl, under the counter with my toe. He shouldn't be in here during opening hours, but no matter how many times I told him, he still snuck under the warming cabinet for a nap.

"Where's your uncle? His baking is always perfect." Mrs. Ling's gaze lifted over my shoulder to the kitchen door.

"Uncle Albert is icing a wedding cake, and I hate disturbing him when he's in the middle of one of his creations. We want nothing to go wrong and spoil the bride's special day."

"Try disturbing him, unless you want more unhappy customers."

I sucked in a breath, aware of the sweat on my forehead as Mrs. Ling continued to complain and draw more attention from the crowded bakery. I always did my best, but baking didn't come naturally to me. Not like Uncle Albert. Anything you imagined, he could create. Fluffy meringues, no problem, feather light chocolate sponge, easy peasy, lemon drizzle bars that tasted like sunlight, done.

Me, on the other hand, everything cake-related I touched risked turning into a sludgy, tasteless mess. Well, it did unless I kept on top of things. And I hadn't been doing that lately.

My gaze lifted to the queue of people waiting to get in. It wasn't even lunchtime, and we were rushed off our feet. I should be pleased, but all I felt was a low level of constant panic and a desire to creep out the back door and run.

My gaze settled on a tall man with his shoulders hunched and a cap pulled down low over his eyes so I couldn't see his face.

I squinted at him. He was watching the bakery, and it wasn't the first time I'd seen him. He'd been here yesterday for about half an hour, standing in the same place. He hadn't moved. I'd considered going over to see if he was lost or needed help, but the next time I'd looked, he'd vanished.

Mrs. Ling slapped her hand on the counter. "Luna! I need my cake problem fixed."

A warm hand settled on my shoulder, and I turned, relief flooding through me as I saw Uncle Albert.

"Is everything okay?" His kind eyes crinkled at the corners as he patted my shoulder.

"Everything's great. I was just fixing a customer's problem."

"You were staring out the window, not interested in helping me," Mrs. Ling said. "Albert, do something about these cakes. Try one. They're terrible."

He looked at the box of cakes and frowned. He picked one up, sniffed it, then poked his tongue out and licked the top. "Did you get these from here?"

"Of course. I placed my order last week. They were for my birthday party. Luna made them, and they're not acceptable."

I scowled at her, not appreciating her loud voice or the fact she'd dropped me in it. "They can't have been that bad. You've taken a bite out of every cake."

"To see if I could find one that was vaguely edible."

I opened my mouth to protest, but Uncle Albert patted my shoulder again. "Let's look at what we've got in stock. You can have another box of cakes, free of charge, a refund, and a free donut every morning for the next month. How does that sound?"

Mrs. Ling finally smiled. "I suppose that's something. It won't make up for spoiling my birthday, though."

"Sorry, Uncle Albert," I whispered.

He winked at me as he led Mrs. Ling back to the tempting dessert counter.

I turned away, grabbed the order for the customer waiting for her caramel latte and pumpkin loaf slice, and then replaced the stale scone. I felt terrible for failing Uncle Albert. I had to make sure my magic stopped failing when I most needed it.

With Uncle Albert's help, we cleared the queue of customers in ten minutes. I sank against the counter and sighed.

He smiled at me. "You're too hard on yourself. You shouldn't take it personally when a customer isn't happy. Some people get out of bed on the wrong side or simply need a reason to moan."

"Those were my cakes. I thought they looked good."

"Did you taste them?"

I shook my head. "Sorry, I was tired. And there's only so much cake you can stomach in one day."

"Luna! You're a Brimstone baker. Desserts are in your blood. You should never tire of cake."

I hid a frown. The trouble was, baking magic didn't flow through my blood. And I'd never admit it, but I wasn't a fan of sweet things. They made my teeth ache.

"You've got this. One small bite at a time. And you can always call on me if you need help." He patted his chunky stomach. "There's always room for a little extra cake."

"I don't like to bother you. And you need your rest."

He chuckled. "I'm a long way from being dead. Although I wouldn't mind an early night.

The wedding cake is proving difficult. It's even challenging my magic."

Uncle Albert's surname was Black, and he came from a family with an excellent reputation for creating amazing desserts. I was a Brimstone, and my auntie married Albert when they were both eighteen, joining two powerful, magical bakery dynasties.

"Once the evening rush is over, you can put your feet up, and I'll deal with the cleanup," I said. "It's the least I can do after upsetting Mrs. Ling."

"She'll get over it. She got a deluxe box of treats and didn't pay a thing." He gave my cheek a quick kiss before heading to the counter where a customer had arrived.

I watched him with no small degree of envy. Uncle Albert was a natural with baking and the customers. And I owed him a lot. He'd taken me in when I was young, and I'd been raised by two loving people.

My auntie was no longer alive. She'd died during an unfortunate dark magic event involving my best friend, Indigo Ash, when she was a teenager. I didn't hold it against Indigo. She hadn't been in control of her magic, but I'd lost a much loved auntie during that dark time.

Uncle Albert had been amazing, though, and I'd never felt unloved or unhappy. He was also so patient with my terrible baking. It was a shame I couldn't pay him back by being better in the bakery and taking pressure off him.

Despite what he said, Uncle Albert was slowing down and wouldn't be able to work full time for much longer.

I did what I could to help, but the baking magic that ran through his veins was like treacle covering a warm apple pie alongside a dollop of delicious vanilla ice cream. His magic thrived in the bakery. Whereas my magic... Well, I wasn't sure where it fit. It wasn't great at making everyone's sweet dream treats come true.

But there was no way I was giving up on Uncle Albert or Fandango's Bakery, so I took each day as it came. After all, you never knew what was around the corner.

It wasn't so long ago that I'd been abducted and dragged into limbo. That had never been on my fun things to-do list. But I'd survived. And I'd survive my wonky baking magic.

The bakery door opened, and I looked up, my smile fading as Englebert Whistletop walked in. He was an attractive older man, and, unfortunately, he was also sort of my sugar daddy, with a difference.

I wasn't all in on the sugar daddy experience. There was no hanky panky between us, not that Englebert didn't do his best to get me in the bedroom. But he'd given me an apartment and looked after me. And, most importantly, he was a magical lifeline. Although I was thinking it was time to give up that lifeline. Englebert and his roving hands were more trouble than they were worth.

You might ask, what did Englebert get in return? Well, he got my amazing company, my skills at dealing with his bunions, and a willing ear and dinner companion when he wanted to talk.

"My dear girl." Englebert reached over the counter and took my hand. "I haven't seen you in days." He kissed the back of my hand with his thin lips.

"Fandango's has been busy, so I haven't had time for fun." I smiled and gently eased my hand out of his grip. "You're looking well."

"And you're looking delightful. You must come to dinner."

"Oh, I wish I could."

"Seven o'clock tonight." He raised a white eyebrow. "I can send the staff away."

"I can't tonight. We're so busy at the moment."

"Then tomorrow."

"You go if you want to," Uncle Albert said. "We're not busy tomorrow night, and I can handle the custom baking orders. We should almost be caught up."

I hesitated. Uncle Albert thought my relationship with Englebert was odd. Most people did, considering he was old enough to be my grandpa, but I couldn't give him up. Not yet. Not until I'd found a replacement.

"You see, your uncle approves," Englebert said.

"I just want Luna to be happy." Uncle Albert's smile was cautious as his gaze flicked to me. "Providing you make her happy, then I have no problems."

"I assure you, I make her very happy." A wicked gleam entered Englebert's eyes.

I had to repress a shudder and look away. I knew what he wanted, but there were lines I never crossed. There'd be no naked fun with my wrinkled sugar daddy. His bunions I could handle, but not his withered pink bits flapping in my face.

I was relieved when the bakery door opened again, providing me with a distraction, and my relief morphed to happiness as my three best friends, Odessa Grimsbane, Storm Winter, and Indigo Ash, walked in.

They strolled to the counter, laughing with each other.

Storm arched a brow as her gaze ran over Englebert. "Are you having a day out from the old folks' home?"

"Storm!" I shouldn't have been surprised by the comment. She hated my relationship with Englebert.

Englebert glared at Storm as a vein bulged in his forehead. "I'll leave you and your friends to gossip. Don't forget, dinner at my place tomorrow night. Wear something pretty. And bring that peppermint scented lotion." He turned and walked out of the bakery.

"Wear something pretty?" Storm sneered at Englebert's back as she flipped her dark hair out of her eyes. "I don't know why you put up with that wrinkled old prune."

"I'm more interested in what you're planning to do with the peppermint lotion." Odessa's large eyes sparkled with amusement. "What bits does he want you to rub? You need to be careful. If you get menthol in the wrong places, it can smart."

I grimaced. "His feet."

"Urgh! You're handling those bony old claws. It must be love if you do that for him," Storm said.

"Be nice," Indigo said. "There are valid reasons they're dating." Her expression suggested she was as puzzled as the others.

"The free apartment," Storm said.

Odessa giggled. "The heaps of cash."

"Or he could have a lovely personality," Indigo said. "One that smells of peppermint after he's had a thorough rub down."

They burst into laughter, and I stood with my hands on my hips, glaring at them and trying not to laugh. They didn't understand. Sacrifices had to be made to keep my magic stable. Dating Englebert was one such sacrifice.

"Seriously, Luna, ditch the old guy," Storm said. "He treats you like some doll to dress up and leer at. You must be bored with him."

"I don't know how many times I have to tell you, we're friends."

Odessa nudged Indigo. "Friends with benefits. You could do better. I mean, I know he's stinking rich, but..."

"But nothing. Englebert's got class, and he is good to me. He helped me when I needed a place to live. I like him. He's interesting." When he wasn't demanding inappropriate kisses after one too many brandies.

Indigo wrinkled her nose and shrugged. Out of the three of them, I was closest to her. When we were kids, we'd always hung out together in the bakery after school.

Odessa sighed. "There are so many eligible men in the village. You should try one."

"Point out these eligible men," Storm said. "I don't see any wandering around."

"They run away when they see you," Indigo said. "You terrify them."

"That's their problem, not mine."

"They're everywhere," Odessa said.

"I don't see you dating these eligible guys," Storm said. "And you scare no one, so they're not hiding from you."

Odessa rearranged the napkins on the counter. "I'm busy with the scarecrows and my pumpkins."

Indigo and Storm exchanged a knowing glance. We knew the reason Odessa didn't date. She'd had what she believed was her one shot at true love, and her heart got shattered.

"Anyway, this isn't about me." Odessa smiled brightly. "This is about making sure our friend doesn't make a terrible dating mistake."

"Englebert isn't a mistake. And I'm considering my options. I have everything under control." I glanced out the bakery window again. I didn't feel in control. And Englebert was getting restless. It wouldn't be long before I'd have to put out for my sugar daddy or kick him to the curb. And I wasn't ready for either of those things.

"Have you got time to stop for an early lunch?" Indigo said.

I shook my head. "I'd love to, but it's been busy all morning, and we haven't had the lunch crowd in yet. Another time?"

A huge, sleek leopard named Monty bounded through the door. His eyes shone with excitement, and his tail twitched as he bounced from table to table, greeting the customers, even though not all of them were happy to be sniffed by a huge leopard familiar.

"Monty!" Olympus Duke strode in. He scowled at the huge cat and clicked his fingers. "Get over here and stop bothering people."

Monty wagged his tail. He was the only cat familiar I'd ever seen do that, and I had experience with cat familiars, having my own incredibly lazy black one.

Monty bounded over to Olympus and leaped up, placing two giant paws on Olympus's shoulders. "Can we get cake? I mean, not that I like cake. I like meat. Do they sell meat-flavored cake?"

Olympus shook Monty loose. "We're not here to get food."

Indigo strolled over and kissed Olympus before ruffling Monty's head fur.

I grinned. They made an adorable couple, and I was happy for Indigo. She'd had a terrible few years, getting tangled up in dark magic and losing her family. She deserved all the joy.

"Are you sure you don't have time to stop for lunch?" Odessa said. "And we were thinking of organizing a night out. All we seem to do is work these days."

"I need help." A woman raced through the door and over to the counter. She slapped down a brochure in front of me. "I have to have this cake. It's for a party. My husband was supposed to place the order, but he forgot. I'm so angry, I should smite him with a hex. Useless warlock."

"Give me a minute," I said to Odessa before turning to the quivering customer.

The woman had a stripe of flour down one cheek and what might be powdered sugar covering her bosoms. "I need an eight layer, multi-colored unicorn cake with magic sparkles, edible glitter, and self-lighting candles. And I need it by the end of the week."

"I ... um ... That's a lot of baking. How about something smaller?"

"No! I was trying to make it, but it was a disaster. The layers were wonky, the icing was gray, and when I tasted it, it was disgusting. Please, you're my only hope. It's for my three-year-old daughter. She'll be devastated if she doesn't get her special cake." A tear trickled down the woman's cheek.

I hated letting anyone down, but an eight-layer cake would take a lot of magic, and mine was drained. I glanced at Uncle Albert, but he was deep in conversation with another customer as they looked through a cake brochure.

This was down to me. "I'm sure we can figure this out."

"I don't mind paying extra for the short notice. But it has to be perfect."

"We can make it happen." So long as I got a huge boost to my baking magic and a decent night of sleep. And the way things were going, I wouldn't have time to do either.

"You're an angel," the woman said. "And how about adding a glitter cascade?"

"I'll grab us some coffee, and we can talk options."

As I made the coffee, I glanced out the window again, and a shudder ran down my spine. The guy who'd been watching the bakery was gone, but someone equally unpleasant had replaced him. He was dressed in the familiar black clothing and wide-brimmed hat of Magic Council employees.

I grimaced and focused on making the coffee. The Magic Council oversaw all aspects of magic regulation, and they were pedants and a pain in the butt.

I looked at Olympus and caught his eye. "Is that a friend of yours?"

He glanced out the window and shook his head. "I didn't bring anyone with me. I'm not working today."

"You're always working," Indigo said, a smile on her face.

I bit my bottom lip as the Magic Council employee glared in the window at me. It was never good news when they came poking around your business, and I had a feeling he wasn't here for a chocolate eclair.

I settled the customer at a table with a mug of coffee and a brochure of our cake designs. "Look through this and pick out elements you want to add to your cake. We'll go from there. I'll be back in a few minutes."

She nodded, eagerly poring through the material.

I grabbed a tray of cake samples and headed outside. I needed to deal with the Magic Council head on and see what they wanted.

"Good morning. Can I tempt you to a free sample? Everything is handmade and fresh today." As I got nearer, the man looked familiar.

He peered at the cakes down a long, thin nose. "Did you make those?"

"Of course."

"Then I won't try them."

I sucked in a breath. "Don't you have a sweet tooth? We sell savory items, too."

"I'm here because we've had a complaint about the tainted food you're selling."

The tray shook as my hand wobbled. "Tainted food? You must be mistaken. Everything we sell here is fresh. We're always careful about storing our ingredients."

"You're not that careful. I'm here to investigate this complaint, and if I find anything amiss, I'm shutting you down."

Chapter 2

Don't panic! Everything will be fine. I was totally panicked. "I'm sure this is a misunderstanding. Why don't you come inside, Mr..." I tilted my head.

"Devlin Goody."

"Oh! Of course. I... um... I met you in the forest not so long ago." I gritted my teeth. Our last encounter had involved Devlin trying to arrest me and my friends for the misuse of magic. In our defense, it had been desperate times, but Devlin was a stickler for the rules.

"Yes, we have met before. And the Magic Council has had its eye on Fandango's for some time. We have concerns about the magic you use."

I pasted a smile on my face to hide my growing alarm. "We only ever use our legal magic, and we have thousands of repeat customers. We use nothing harmful."

His eyes narrowed, and he looked at the samples on the tray again. "Tell me about the magic you use in your food."

"A lot of it is simple enhancing magic. Standard, everyday spells to make things taste amazing. We ensure the baked goods are exactly what people want. Everyone has a different palette, so we make tiny adjustments to better suit their needs."

Devlin flipped open the folder he carried and ran his finger down it. "We've had three complaints in the last month. Each one mentioned the food tasted spoiled or stale."

I thought back to Mrs. Ling's complaint and the guy with his stale scone. I'd made those scones. "If the products aren't looked after once purchased, they can go stale. We don't use artificial preservatives, and I always suggest how to store cakes, but people don't listen."

"They listen. And the complaints came from people who ate at the bakery. This isn't to do with the way they stored their goods." His narrowed eyes flicked over me. "It's how the products are created."

I had to play this calm and cool. Even though I knew this day would come, I wasn't ready for it. This was all my fault. I'd been too restrained in keeping my magic topped up. But I could fix everything with magic. I just had to try harder.

"Miss Brimstone, do you do all the baking in your store?" Devlin asked.

"No. My uncle, Albert Black, owns the store. We do our share of the baking, although he's the expert. I'm his lifelong apprentice." Working in the bakery had never been my dream, but I wouldn't let Uncle Albert down. If I wasn't helping him, he'd have no one. And I didn't hate baking; I just didn't love it. Sugar and spice didn't run through my veins like it did his.

"Either of you could be responsible for the tainted food?"

"No! My uncle is an excellent baker."

"So it was you?"

"I didn't say that."

"We take these complaints seriously. Whenever magic is used in food products, all the rules need to be followed."

"We follow them. You'll find nothing odd going on at the bakery."

"And yet I have these complaints."

"Which I'd be happy to rectify. Whoever made this complaint—"

"Three separate complaints from three separate people."

My smile felt increasingly forced. "Maybe I had an off day. It happens to the best of us. I could have sold a cake that wasn't up to our usual high standard."

"Surely you use the same magic for every product."

"Oh, no. It differs. And my magic is different from my uncle's magic. It's what makes each baker unique."

"Or you're testing magic you shouldn't be using."

I jammed one hand on my hip. "We're a legitimate bakery. Everyone who comes here loves our food."

"Not everyone. Have people been complaining to you directly?"

"No. No complaints." I was such a liar, but customers could be pedantic. And as for Mrs. Ling, I was certain she'd simply been after some free food. "Devlin—"

"Mr. Goody."

I nodded. "Mr. Goody. Surely you have more important things to do than investigate a couple of reports of stale scones? There must be some big bad magic user who needs to be chased down. How about you come and enjoy a delicious bun on the house, and we'll sort this out?"

"Don't try to get out of this with bribes."

"I'm not." It seemed my pretending to know nothing act wasn't working. "What are you, head of the stale bun department?"

Devlin drew himself up to his insignificant height. "I've been promoted to head of magical compliance. And I'm concerned the magic you're using is inappropriate. If that's the case, I intend to make an example of you. I won't permit dangerous magic practices in Witch Haven. We're clamping down and must make sure unstable magic doesn't get out of hand again."

I failed to repress a sigh. I knew what he was talking about. Not so long ago, dark magic had almost ruined Witch Haven. If it wasn't for my awesome friends and Olympus, we'd be living in a very different village. And everyone was still jumpy, especially anyone who worked for the Magic Council. They'd messed up and missed the signs that a big bad darkness had infiltrated the village.

Now it seemed my uncle's bakery would pay the price.

"I'm taking this sample tray. I'll test the food to see if there are signs of odd magic."

I took a step back. That would be disastrous. Devlin would know I wasn't using my own magic to make the food. "There's no need. I'll get you fresh samples. These are tainted."

"Tainted! By what?"

"By being outside. After all, this is a magic-filled village. Anything could have gotten into the samples."

"That's unlikely. Hand them over."

I tried to dodge out of his way just as something slammed into my side. Monty leaped up, smashed the samples to the ground, and stamped on them.

Devlin scurried back, holding his folder against his chest, his eyes wide as he stared at Monty. "Does this creature belong to you? It violates the magical health code to have familiars in a food environment."

"You know Monty belongs to me." Olympus strode over. "Devlin, what are you doing here?"

The anger on Devlin's face vanished as his cheeks paled. "Olympus! I didn't know you were working today."

Olympus beckoned Monty over. After another quick stamp on the samples, Monty bounded over and accepted a pet on the head. He looked proud of himself.

Devlin pulled back his shoulders. "I'm here on official business. I'm investigating complaints about Fandango's. Is that what you're doing here? I didn't think the case had been assigned to anyone."

Olympus shook his head. "This is a reputable business. Fandango's has been here for decades."

"The complaints are legitimate," Devlin said. "We can't let anyone break the rules. You're aware of the new guidance issued by the Magic Council."

"Of course. I helped write it." Olympus glanced at me, his gaze full of curiosity. "Albert and Luna are respectable business owners. I can vouch for them."

I whispered a thank you and then looked over to see Indigo watching. She gave me a grin and a big thumbs-up. She was an awesome friend and had been getting me out of scrapes since we were kids.

"I still need to investigate these complaints," Devlin said. "I was planning on taking those samples to test."

"They'll be no good now," Olympus said.

"Clearly not. Can't you keep better control of your familiar?"

"Monty got excited. He meant no harm."

Devlin scowled at Monty. "You should have him on a leash."

Monty's ears lowered. "I hate being restrained. I'm a free living familiar."

Devlin turned to the bakery, but Olympus caught his arm. "I heard there's a problem at the Grimvale mines. Wouldn't you rather be involved in that case than an issue at a small family run bakery? If you pull off an arrest at the mine, you'll get a big pat on the back."

"I'm keeping an eye on the mines. I was there first thing this morning. Everything was quiet."

"You don't want to miss anything," Olympus said. "How about I monitor Fandango's, and you go check things out?"

Devlin looked at me. "If I get any more complaints, I'll be back, and I'll expect your full cooperation."

"You'll have it. We have nothing to hide. Now, if you'll excuse me, I need to get back to work. I have a customer waiting." I nodded a quick thanks at Olympus and Monty before hurrying to the bakery.

"I saw Devlin grilling you and thought you could do with a hand," Indigo said. "Is everything okay?"

I gave her a quick hug. "Not really, but it soon will be. I need to get back inside. I hope Olympus won't get in trouble for helping me."

"He can handle Devlin. Are you sure I can't help, though? You seem stressed."

I needed all the help I could get, but I couldn't bother Indigo or any of my friends. "No, I'll be fine. Thanks. It's just one of those days." I hurried inside.

This was a problem to solve on my own. And I had a plan to get things back under control as quickly as possible.

Chapter 3

"I'm sorry they're not pretty. I promise, they taste delicious." I handed over a large tray of misshapen white iced muffins. It had been another frantic day in the bakery, and I was frazzled.

Regina Highmore cast an eye over the tray and smiled warmly. "Your food is always perfect. Thanks for bringing them. I planned to make something, but the day got away with me, and I always like to have treats at our magic swap and share evenings."

I looked around the inside of the magic store. It was an enchanting place in the middle of Witch Haven. There were shelves on every side of the store, full of intriguing magical artefacts. Atherton Hart, a powerful warlock, ran the place. I'd always considered him arrogant, but that's what came with having an immense amount of power and running a successful business.

Regina placed down the tray of muffins and touched my elbow. "You're welcome to stay. Is there anything you need?"

There was, but there was no way I was telling Regina. "No, but thanks. And I can't stay. I'm meeting a friend for dinner."

Regina smiled again. She was a pretty, feminine witch in her early forties, with a sweet nature. Her shoulder-length hair was strawberry blonde, and her blue eyes sparkled. She'd worked as Atherton's assistant for years and always had time to share a kind word.

Regina's gaze lifted over my shoulder. "Excuse me. Someone's just arrived for the magic swap."

I rarely came into Atherton's store, so I was glad to have a couple of minutes to browse the shelves. There were candles, small charms, herbal mixes of ready prepared spells, and stacks of books. He even had a small case of preserved beetles.

I stopped by a glass cabinet containing several bones. There was a complete hand laid out, a lower jawbone, and what might have been an arm bone. I narrowed my eyes and breathed in deeply. There was an enchantment around them, but I could still feel magic seeping off the bones. And it wasn't friendly magic. These bones had a lingering trace of despair and rage.

"Don't mind those," Regina said.

I jumped and turned to face her. "Why does Atherton have them in the store? He doesn't sell human bones, does he?"

"Atherton sells many unusual things, but he doesn't deal in bones. Only dark magic users associate with that kind of thing." Regina grimaced as she looked at the bones. "I stay away from them. They give me the chills."

"Why keep them in the store if they're not for sale?"

"According to Atherton, these bones belonged to a powerful enchantress. I'm not sure whether he's pulling my leg, but he picked them up at a magic antiques fair. He said they were a reminder of what happened if you didn't look after your abilities. You have to show magic the proper respect, or you end up with your bones on display as a symbol of what not to do."

"That's quite a symbol." I moved away from the bones. "And what's with these little beetles?"

"They're another one of his fascinations." Regina leaned closer. "Don't tell him I told you this, but he's a hoarder. Anything that takes Atherton's eye, he has to have. But he's meticulous and likes his magic to be ordered and done properly."

"Which is why this store is so popular. Everyone enjoys coming here to see what's new."

"He knows what he's doing," Regina said. "I'll be back in a moment. More customers." She hurried away.

I took another look at the bones before sidling past them. They might belong to a powerful enchantress, but they weren't giving off a pleasant vibe.

The sound of someone sniffing had me looking around. I bit my bottom lip as I saw Jinti Calrook with her head down, standing by a stack of books. One hand was pressed against her stomach.

Jinti was as old as the hills and always dressed in at least six layers of clothing, no matter the weather.

She was a small, hunchbacked witch with a wild mane of unruly dark curls striped through with gray.

I was about to turn away when she lifted her head and stared at me, her small, dark eyes pinning me to the spot. "Luna, I've not seen you at a magic swap before. Are you looking for something special?"

I raised a hand in greeting, feeling guilty for trying to sneak away. "No, I'm not stopping. I brought the refreshments."

"Bella always loved Fandango's. She used to come in once a week to get one of your special treats. She'd always pick me up something. Bella was a good girl." Jinti sniffed again.

And this was the reason I felt uncomfortable around Jinti. Her daughter, Bella, disappeared several years ago, and although her body was never found, everyone assumed the worst.

"I remember Bella coming in." I patted Jinti's arm. "You must miss her."

A tear trickled down her cheek. "She was my only child. I have nothing left."

"You do. You have friends in the village."

"Just like you, they never want to spend time with me. I can't say as I blame them. I'm not fun company." Jinti picked up a book on magical herbal remedies and flicked through it.

I looked around for Regina, but she was occupied with a customer. "Are you looking for anything in particular?"

"Something to mend a broken heart or bring Bella back to me." Jinti sighed and put back the book. "Ignore me. I'm in one of my self-pitying moods. It'll pass. There's always sunshine after a dark cloud."

"Yes, of course. Um... enjoy your evening." I turned to leave and almost bumped into Atherton Hart and Ulric Ward.

Atherton shot a sharp look at Jinti as he adjusted the sleeves of his tailored black jacket. He leaned down until his mouth was level with my ear. "I thought you might need rescuing."

"Oh, I'm fine. Thanks." I took a step back to put distance between us. "I was just chatting to Jinti." I nodded at Ulric. He was a tall, broad-shouldered man in his mid-fifties, with tousled gray hair and a spattering of stubble across his chin. He was the opposite of Atherton looks-wise, who was short and stocky, and I was fairly certain dyed his hair because it was all one color.

"I hope you aren't pestering Luna," Atherton said to Jinti. "You must always be polite to anyone making or serving you food. You never know what they might slip into the treats."

I choked out a laugh. "I'd never do such a thing."

"Why not? It would be the perfect way to get someone," Jinti said.

"Hide the poison in the sweet. That's dark, Jinti." Atherton chuckled.

"Please, don't say that out loud about my food." If Devlin ever heard comments like this, he'd definitely have a reason to shut down the bakery.

"I'm teasing," Atherton said. "Everyone knows how good your food is. Although I heard a rumor the Magic Council was there today. What did they want?"

"You shouldn't listen to rumors," Jinti said. "You only find trouble."

"One of my friends at the Magic Council said they're doing an audit of every business, so don't be surprised if they pay you a visit," Atherton said. "And after that business with Indigo's family almost destroying the place again—"

"No, that's not true. Indigo helped save Witch Haven," I said.

"The Ash witches can be trusted," Jinti said. "Indigo has my respect."

Atherton steepled his fingers together and gave me a smug smile. "Of course, you're still friends with Indigo. You must have a powerful bond to remain loyal to her after everything she did."

I switched my opinion of Atherton from smug to rude. "Indigo saved my life. I'd never turn my back on her."

"Friends are as important as family," Jinti said.

I nodded. Jinti was growing on me. Atherton, not so much.

"Don't mind Atherton being sulky." Ulric's voice was warm and smooth. "He's annoyed because most of the village was invited to a last-minute party at Cornelia's inn. They all decided it sounded more fascinating than rooting around his tired old spells."

"That's not true," Atherton said stiffly. "Besides, these evenings are better if they're not crowded. The bartering and haggling is demeaning."

Ulric smiled and gave me a discrete wink. "I'm looking for a sleep spell."

"I can sort you out something if no one comes with anything to swap," Atherton said.

"Enjoy your evening. I need to get back to the bakery and shut down for the night," I said. "It was nice to see you all."

We said our goodbyes, and I hurried out. I returned to Fandango's and found Uncle Albert slumped in a chair, nursing a large mug of herbal tea.

"Is everything okay?"

He raised his head, his eyes bleary with tiredness. "It's been another non-stop day, just like yesterday. It didn't slow for more than a few minutes. I know I shouldn't complain, but I'm thinking of hiring an assistant, especially with all the custom orders we're getting."

I flipped the sign to closed and locked the door. "You go up and take a break. I'll clear up."

"Are you sure you've got time? Haven't you got a date with Englebert?"

"I do, but I can cancel if you'd rather I stay home."

"You need some fun. You work too hard, and you're always running around after other people. Enjoy yourself with your... I was going to say young man, but he's not that. Is calling him an old man disrespectful?"

"Don't you start about Englebert. You know we're just friends."

"And I know he's also a man, even if he has more wrinkles than me. He gets a worrying twinkle in his eye every time he's around you. Don't be surprised if he wants more than friendship."

"I've made it clear that I can't be with him in that way." I hurried around, wiping down the work surfaces and packing things under the counter, trying to ignore how hot my cheeks felt.

"Luna, you're a smart woman, and Englebert has given you a lot. Some men expect something in return for those gifts."

"He's got his apartment back," I said. "And I'm happy living with you."

"Only because you didn't want to live in a haunted apartment."

"It's not that." It totally was that. I'd adored that apartment, but after the ghosts took over and destroyed the place, I couldn't sleep. I'd tried staying there a few times, but then begged Uncle Albert to let me live with him above the bakery.

"If Englebert puts a hand in the wrong place, you tell me and I'll have words with him," Uncle Albert said.

"If he does put a hand in the wrong place, I'll have my own words with him. I know how to look after myself."

"You do, but I still worry about you. After everything that happened—"

"No, you don't need to worry. I'm fine. I'm back here with you, just like it used to be."

"And you are happy, aren't you?" Uncle Albert's face creased with worry. "I... I don't know what I'd do without you."

"Don't worry about that, because I'm going nowhere." I walked over and kissed his cheek. "Get up those stairs. I'll finish the clean-up in the kitchen, then bring you some leftovers."

He patted my cheek as he stood and headed out of the bakery toward the stairs.

After a quick tidy up, I made him a plate of savory leftovers and dashed upstairs with it. I left Uncle Albert eating, while I freshened my make-up, slipped into a black dress, and tidied my hair.

"I'm heading out now," I called from the top of the stairs as I stashed peppermint lotion in my purse. "I'm not sure what time I'll be back, so don't wait up."

"Have fun," Uncle Albert said.

I dashed down the stairs and out of the bakery, locking up behind me. It was time to give myself a magic boost, and Englebert was just who I needed to see in order to do that.

He lived on the edge of Witch Haven in a detached house with two vast white pillars surrounding an ornate doorway. Other than his staff, he lived on his own and had ten bedrooms to choose from.

I couldn't understand why he remained in such an enormous place, but it had been in his family for generations. I'd much rather part with the large heating bills than have ten bedrooms to drift around in.

I reached the front door and smoothed down my dress before knocking.

Bates, his tall, sour-faced butler, opened the door and peered down at me. "Yes?"

"Hey, Bates. I'm here for dinner."

"Is Mr. Whistletop expecting you?"

We did this every time I visited. Bates made no attempt to hide his disapproval of my friendship with Englebert and did everything he could to dissuade me from coming here.

"As I'm sure you're aware, Englebert arranged for us to have dinner together."

Bates simply stared at me.

"Should I find a window to climb through, or will you let me in?"

He stepped back but didn't open the door any wider.

I pursed my lips. "Any other night, I'd happily play this game, but I've had a long day. I've had to deal with the Magic Council, Uncle Albert is coming down with something, and I cleaned the bakery before coming here. I don't need you adding to my problems. Are you going to let me in so I can eat dinner with Englebert, or shall we have words?"

He looked like he wanted to have words.

"Bates, is that Luna?" Englebert's thin voice echoed along the hallway.

I grinned at him. "Sorry to disappoint, but it looks like I'm coming in."

Bates stepped back again and finally let me through the front door. I walked along the familiar hallway with its ornate coving and richly colored green and gold walls.

Englebert stood by the dining-room door, dressed in a red velvet jacket, dark pants, and a white cravat tucked in his shirt. "Good evening, Luna. I was thinking you'd forgotten our date." He pressed a kiss to my cheek.

"Of course not. I've been looking forward to this evening."

"As have I. And I've been making plans. This way. I've gotten us a delicious claret from the cellar. It's been breathing all afternoon, so will be perfect."

I wasn't a fan of red wine. I was more a sugary cocktail kind of woman, but Englebert liked red wine, so that's what we drank at his house.

Bates strode in, poured the wine, and gave a bow before leaving and closing the door behind him.

We sipped our wine in a companionable silence, but I was aware of Englebert's gaze fixed on me.

I smiled at him. "You mentioned something about plans?"

He smoothed a hand down the front of his shirt. "I've been thinking about your living situation. It doesn't do to have you back with your uncle in that pokey little apartment."

"It has three bedrooms," I said. "There's plenty of room."

"I also have plenty of space here and lots of empty rooms. They need filling."

"Are you thinking of opening a bed-and-breakfast?"

His smile was indulgent as he caught hold of my hand. "I'm not a young man, but I can provide for any woman. And I'd like that woman to be you."

"What do you want to provide?" This wasn't how I'd anticipated the evening to go.

"Don't concern yourself with the age difference. There's plenty of lead in my pencil. My doctor makes sure of it. And I need a family to carry on the Whistletop traditions."

I gulped and kept my gaze fixed on his face. I would not look at his leaded pencil. "That's nice."

"Luna, I'm not sure you understand me. I want you to be my wife and provide me with that family."

I staggered back and hit a china cabinet with my hip.

Englebert smiled. "It must be a shock to get such an excellent offer. And this will mean a big change for you. You can give up the bakery and become a lady of leisure or work if that's what you desire. But you'd be free to focus on me and the children."

I shook my head, panic ricocheting through me like a slinky on a caffeine high. "I'm not sure that's a good idea."

"I've given it a lot of thought. I'll look after you, and you won't want for anything."

I'd want for love! I liked Englebert, but there was no passion between us, and I didn't want to be anyone's breeding machine. When I finally had children, I wanted them with a man who'd be a strong father figure, who could play with them and go on adventures with them, not stare at them from his rocking chair under his cozy blanket while his false teeth sat in a glass.

"Englebert, this is... sudden. You've always been happy with our arrangement."

"I'm not. And I expect more from you."

I hadn't come here for a marriage proposal. I was here to take advantage of Englebert, but he'd just turned the tables.

Bates knocked on the door, and I breathed out a sigh of relief.

"Come in," Englebert said.

"Dinner is ready, sir."

"Thank you. We'll be in presently."

Bates glanced at me, a coldness in his eyes, as if he sensed something unwelcome was happening. "Very good, sir." He closed the door again.

"Shall we celebrate our union with a little kiss?" Englebert said.

I set down my glass. I couldn't marry Englebert, but he had something I desperately needed. It wasn't his money, his big house, or the remaining lead in his pencil. He had powerful magic, and it was why I'd kept him around for so long.

"It's charming. You're speechless," he said. "I can see you're going to say yes. Any woman would. You don't get an opportunity like this every day."

"I'm so flattered by your proposal." I took hold of his hand. "Englebert, I'd be lucky to marry you, and you would be kind to me. But it's best we stay as we are."

"Oh, no, that's—"

"But I will kiss you." I stroked a hand down his cheek. I wished I could keep him with the others, but Englebert was a key figure in Witch Haven. If he'd disappeared, people would notice, and they'd ask questions. It had been risky, leaving him to roam free, but so far, luck had been on my side. No one noticed I'd been draining his magic.

Well, Bates didn't trust me, but that was because he didn't want some gold digger getting her hands on Englebert's fortune. If only it was that simple.

"I'll change your mind," Englebert said. "But for now, I'll accept your kiss." He leaned closer.

There was no point being half-hearted about this smooch. I needed direct contact with another magic user to take their power. Although I'd always gotten away with holding his hand or giving his gnarly old feet a rub to get what I needed, a kiss would do the job.

I grabbed his head in both my hands and held on tight before smacking my lips against his and evoking my magic drain ability.

Englebert's power flooded into me. His magic was warm and spicy, and it trickled through me before looping around my spine and down my legs, making my toes tickle.

Englebert groaned, then swayed from side to side as I kept our mouths clamped together. There was nothing sensual about this kiss, but he tasted vaguely of peppermint and red wine, so it wasn't unpleasant.

His magic felt so good and filled me with energy and optimism. This was what I needed. If I didn't get my regular magic fix, everything fell apart, and it was already fraying at the edges, as the visit from the Magic Council proved.

Englebert tried to pull my hands off his face, but I held on, and he didn't stand a chance of getting free. I was latched onto him like a barnacle on its favorite rock.

He slapped against my arm, but I still wasn't ready to let go. I'd made too many mistakes recently and wasn't doing it again. I needed to be greedy and get my fill of his power.

Bates shoved open the door and strode in. "What are you doing?"

I finally let go of Englebert. "Do you mind? We're having a private moment."

Englebert sank to his knees and collapsed to the floor with a groan.

Bates rushed to his side and checked his pulse. "You've killed him."

Chapter 4

The burst of Englebert's energy that flooded through me gave way to an icy cold shudder as I stared at his crumpled body on the carpet. "He's not dead. He's just... overcome with emotion."

Bates's eyes glowed red, and he growled. "Keep away from him, witch. I've never trusted you. There's something unnatural about you. What are you, a siren in disguise?"

"No! And Englebert wanted this kiss."

"Because you bewitched him." Bates kept his fingers against Englebert's pulse. "I can feel something. You haven't succeeded in getting rid of him."

"Let me help." I hurried to Englebert's other side. "We'll get him up. He'll feel better when he's on his feet."

"I wouldn't be so sure. Don't move him. I've never seen him look this pale." Bates tapped Englebert's cheek. "Sir, can you hear me? Shall I call for a doctor?"

"No! No doctor, he won't want that."

"You mean, you don't. The doctor will figure out you've been up to something sketchy. I should alert the Magic Council, too."

Englebert groaned and his eyes fluttered open. "Where am I?"

"Don't worry, sir. You're safe. I'm with you." Bates grasped Englebert's hand.

His gaze flicked to me, and concern flooded his eyes. "Luna? How long have you been here?"

"Not long. Don't you remember me arriving?" I was so racked with guilt, I almost confessed everything. I hadn't meant to take so much of his magic, but it felt so good.

"I... vaguely. Why am I on the floor?"

"We both got excited after your proposal. You must have low blood sugar and fainted. Did you forget to eat lunch?"

Bates sucked in a sharp breath. "Proposal? You're getting married?"

Englebert waved a limp hand in the air. "Can someone help me up?"

"Of course, sir." Bates lifted Englebert under the armpits and held onto him.

"I feel so dizzy," Englebert said.

"You should lie down," I said. "It could have been the wine. You should never drink on an empty stomach."

"I do feel odd. And... I know I had plans to propose tonight, but I don't remember doing it. What did you say?"

I glanced at Bates, who looked like he wanted to throttle me. "We can talk about that another time. You need quiet and rest."

Englebert's hand went to his forehead. "I would like to talk to you before you leave. Bates, get me ready for bed and then send Luna up."

"She should leave now, sir," Bates said. "You don't want to stress yourself any further tonight."

"I can visit another day." I was already inching toward the door, longing to escape this horrible situation.

"No, we need to get this sorted." Englebert swayed, and Bates caught hold of him again.

"I'll take you up now, sir." Bates glared at me. "Wait here. Touch nothing."

I paced the room, my hands clasped. Although my magic reserves were topped up and firing on all cylinders, I wanted the ground to open up and swallow me. I should have been more careful with Englebert. He was old, and I'd taken advantage. Once I had the magic I needed, I should have backed off. If I'd done that, Englebert would still be drinking wine, and I'd be convincing him I wasn't the woman he wanted to marry.

A shiver ran down my spine as I stood in front of the open fireplace. How had I gotten into such a mess? If only my magic was more reliable, but I'd always struggled, even with easy spells. And although I'd never been tested, I was certain I was a magical blunt, the kind of magic user who'd only ever do basic spells.

And that was why I needed my support system. Englebert was one of four magic users I turned to when I needed a magic boost.

I glanced around the room, not noticing anything and wishing things could be different. But without my magic, I was no good to anyone and wouldn't be able to work with Uncle Albert in the bakery. I'd be a pointless witch. Not even a witch, just a failed magical blob with no value.

I waited another five anxious minutes before Bates returned. He strode into the room, his back stiff.

"How is he?"

"Not any better. And despite my protests, Mr. Whistletop has requested you visit him in his bedroom."

"I promise, I didn't mean him harm," I said.

"The man can barely keep his eyes open, he's confused, and he has memory loss. I don't know what was in that kiss, but don't try anything like that on him again, or he won't make it through the night."

The concern in Bates's eyes was genuine. He'd worked as Englebert's butler for years, and they were close. "I really am sorry. I'll speak to him for a couple of minutes and make sure he's okay. I won't touch him. And you don't have to worry. I won't be coming back."

"Make sure you don't. He's old and vulnerable. You shouldn't manipulate him."

I dashed out of the room, keeping my chin high. I felt like a fraud and a liar, and Bates had seen right through my attempts to conceal what I was doing. Englebert deserved better than me, and it was time to put an end to our relationship.

I tapped on his bedroom door and eased it open.

Englebert was sitting in bed, swamped by four large white pillows, a purple comforter pulled up almost to his chin.

His bleary eyes looked over at me, and he blinked. "Luna, I'm glad you're here. Come closer."

I walked to the bed but kept a safe distance away from him. "How are you feeling?"

"Tired and glad to be in my bed. I always feel better when I'm surrounded by my things."

"I'm sorry about what happened."

His gaze settled on my lips, and he frowned. "Your kiss was unusual. It wasn't what I expected."

"You remember the kiss?"

"It's the only thing I do remember. You say I proposed?"

"Yes. Do you remember my reply?"

He shook his head. "After our embrace, I've realized I might not be the man for you. You're a powerful witch, and you need someone who can keep up with you. I'm slowing down and like my early nights and my comforts. And that kiss..." His fingers went to his lips.

"I agree. I mean, you are a vigorous, handsome, charming warlock who'd give a woman everything she desired, but we're better suited as friends."

Englebert let out a relieved sounding sigh. "I thought having a young wife would make me feel younger. But after that kiss, I've aged ten years."

He looked like he had too, although the effects of my draining were temporary. After a couple of days, he'd be fine. "You get plenty of rest, and you'll feel better in the morning."

"My apologies this evening didn't go as planned." His eyes were already closing.

"Think nothing of it. Take care, Englebert." I headed to the door, walked out, and closed it behind me.

I let out a sigh as I headed down the sweeping dark wooden staircase and passed gilded oil paintings and antiques. All of this could have been mine, but I didn't care about the finery, fancy parties, or big house. I just needed my magic to work.

Englebert had been my magical meal ticket for a long time, but I couldn't have that anymore, and that meant I was in trouble.

Bates stood by the front door as I reached the foot of the stairs. He made a point of opening it and clearing his throat. "I don't expect to see you back here."

"Good evening to you, too." I hurried out of the house, too relieved to care about Bates's rudeness as he slammed the door.

Englebert was alive, I'd topped up my magic, and I'd be fine to work in the bakery for a couple of weeks until I needed more. By then, I was certain to have figured things out.

I was heading back to Fandango's when a shadow moved in a passageway I passed.

I slowed. "Hello, is someone there?"

There was silence, as if the air was holding its breath, then a scuffle and running footsteps.

I took a step into the alleyway, and my eyes widened. I recognized the man who turned to look at me. It was the guy who'd been watching the bakery. I hadn't seen his face clearly, but he wore the same clothes and baseball cap.

"Oh no, you don't. You don't get away." I threw my purse over my shoulder and raced after him. "Why are you following me?"

The man continued to run, pumping his arms as he tried to escape.

But I had a big advantage. Englebert's incredible magic meant I crackled with power. I cast a speed spell, flicking it at my feet, and turned from a sloppy jogger in heels to an elite marathon runner. I was flying as I chased the mystery lurker.

He looked back at me and shot a spell over his shoulder.

I dodged it. "Stop! I need to know what you want with me and the bakery. Why do you keep watching me? Is there something you need?"

He kept running, and I kept chasing him, gaining with every passing second. I was done with being bothered by strange men and interfering members of the Magic Council. I wanted answers.

The end of the alleyway drew near, and the guy scaled a twelve-foot fence and dropped over the other side with an agility that showed he had power of his own.

I slowed my speed and threw myself at the fence, scrambling up it with a lot less grace. I dropped over the other side, skinning my knee as I hit the dirt.

The alley ended by the local pet store, and then the route opened up to the forest at the edge of the village.

A sharp wind hit me in the face as I exited the alleyway. I had to catch this guy before he got to the forest, or I'd lose him among the trees, or get grabbed by a tree spirit.

I was considering another spell, when a blast of hot air shot by me, accompanied by a faint whiff of warm fur.

A huge, muscled guy with shoulder-length dark hair slammed the jerk I was chasing to the ground. He crouched over him, growling in his ear.

"Hey! That's my collar." I raced closer.

The mysterious attacker's gaze flicked to me, and I froze. I knew a lethal predator when I saw one, and this guy screamed werewolf. His muscles flexed, his teeth were longer than they should have been, and his eyes glowed amber.

I scampered back. This night was about to end horribly. "Um, or you have him. I don't mind. I'll leave now." Some werewolves were fine, but I didn't know this one and didn't want to risk him being the unfriendly kind of wolf that bit first and howled at the moon later.

"Wait!" His voice was a deep grumble in his chest. "You looked like you needed help, and I needed to burn off energy. I caught him for you."

"Err... you did?" A cautious smile spread across my face. "Are you a good furball?"

"I've not been called that in a while, but I figured this guy had done something wrong since you were determined to get him." His gaze flicked down me. "You're hurt."

"No. I mean, not really. I just cut my knee when I fell off the fence." Oh, darn. I gulped and hid my torn up skin with my hands. This werewolf could smell my blood. Would I be his next snack?

"You should get those wounds looked at." He glanced at my legs, and an appreciative smile crossed his face.

"I will. As soon as I've dealt with this guy." I inched closer. "I'm Luna Brimstone."

"I know."

"Okkayyy. And you're..."

"Cole."

"Just Cole?"

"For now. You want this jerk, or should I let him go?"

"I want him." I licked my lips, my heart thundering in my chest.

Cole's eyes shifted from amber to a deep chocolate brown. They were beautiful. "I'm safe. You have nothing to fear from me."

"Says the werewolf to the witch."

Cole's smile made him look a thousand times friendlier. "I reckon you can hold your own. You've got power fizzling beneath your skin." He lifted his nose and sniffed. "Although it's odd."

"I smell odd?"

"No, you smell like sugar and wine. But also of old guy and warlock. You can't have warlock magic in you. And there's something else, too—"

"How about we stop the sniff the witch game and focus on the guy you're squashing?"

Cole's eyes slid over me again, making me shake with fear and a little excitement. Werewolves were always so deliciously primal. "Sure. What's he done to you?"

"He's been stalking me."

"Huh? That's not a nice thing to do to a lady." Cole lifted the guy, then dropped him back in the dirt. "Explain yourself."

"How about we take it easy on him? I need him alive so I can get answers." I gestured for Cole to move back before he scared the guy to death.

"He's your capture." Cole stood smoothly.

"Thanks. And it's appreciated." I stepped closer to the guy in the dirt. "Why have you been watching Fandango's?"

He grunted and scrambled to his hands and knees, his glare on Cole. "Keep your mutt away from me."

Cole bared his teeth and snarled.

"He's not my mutt. He's... his own mutt. And an excellent one at that." I nodded at Cole, keeping my attention on the mystery man. "What do you want with me?"

"I'm keeping an eye on my assets."

"You have nothing to do with the bakery."

He stood and swiped dirt off the knees of his jeans. His cold gaze cut to me. "You owe the boss."

I flicked a glance at Cole, who had his arms crossed over his chest and was watching the scene with a cool interest. If this mystery man made one wrong move, I had a feeling he wouldn't be breathing for long. That gave me a nice sense of safety.

"I don't owe anyone," I said.

The guy reached inside his jacket, and Cole crouched, his hands balling into fists. "Easy, Fang. I'm getting my records. We have a lot of customers, and I need to get the details right." He eased a small notebook out of his pocket and flicked through it. "Here we are. Luna Brimstone borrowed one hundred and twelve hits of magic from Sylvester Mahoney."

Ice flooded my veins, and my gut pinched so tight I thought I'd puke. "That's wrong. I didn't borrow that much."

"Over the last year, you did. We record every transaction. And you used credit for twenty of those hits. The boss is calling in the debt."

A strangled breath rasped out of my lips. "I... are you sure it's that much? I figured I only owed a couple of hits."

"We're sure. We never forget a debt, and we always collect. Sylvester has been generous because you've been such a good repeat customer, and he likes your... sweet buns." The guy chuckled. "But your time's up, and he needs his money."

I did a quick calculation on my fingers. "I can give you the money, but it'll take me a while to get it together." If I sold a few things and scraped together my savings, I should have enough.

"He needs it by the end of the week."

I gulped. "I can't get it that quickly."

"And Sylvester expects six thousand."

"No! Five! That's what I owe."

"Angel, these credit hits ain't interest free."

Cole growled again.

The guy flicked a glare at him. "You could ask your lap dog for the money. He seems to want to help."

"I can handle this." I shook my head at Cole as his hands clenched and his teeth glinted in the moonlight.

"I can make this idiot vanish. It would buy you time," Cole said.

The guy's swagger faded. "Sylvester will just send someone else if I go missing. You need to pay up."

"What if I don't?" I hated bullies. I knew what I owed and had every intention of paying Sylvester back and never using his services again, but life had gotten hectic, and it had slipped my mind. Well, I'd deliberately let it slip my mind. Who liked to think about their debts?

The guy smirked. "If you don't pay, I'll reveal your secret all over the village. I doubt your customers will think much of a witch who—"

"Stop! I'll get you the money." I couldn't handle the embarrassment or the disappointment Uncle Albert would feel if he knew the truth about me. "Give me a few days, though."

"Good girl. I knew you'd see sense." He tucked the notebook back in his pocket.

"I've had enough of this idiot." Cole swung a fist just as the other guy vanished.

I pressed my fist against my chest, feeling light-headed and sweaty.

A warm hand rested on my shoulder as I bent over, sucking in air that seemed too thin for my lungs.

"Are you okay?"

"On top of the world," I wheezed out. "Is it hot in here?"

"Here happens to be outside, and the temperature is sitting in single digits. It's definitely not too hot for an attractive witch in a little black dress and no coat." There was the hint of a smile in Cole's words.

"Oh, sure. I forgot where I was for a second." I glanced up at him. "Thanks for helping. Although a part of me wishes I'd never found out what that guy wanted."

"Ignorance is bliss, huh?"

"I wouldn't say bliss, but I was feeling good until he came along." I forced myself to stand.

"Let me walk you back to the bakery, just in case our friend tackles you when you're on your own." Cole extended his arm for me to take.

His chivalry charmed me, and I almost forgot he was a lethal killing machine who loved the moon more than his mama, as I tucked my hand through the crook of his elbow.

"How do you know I live at the bakery?"

"You mentioned Fandango's. Everyone around here loves that place. And I've been by a few times. I recognize your scent."

"Oh! That's..."

Cole smiled. "Weird unless you're a werewolf."

"A little." We walked in silence for a moment. "You didn't have to help me."

"I did. I never walk away when a woman is in danger."

"I had the situation almost under control." I looked up at him. Cole was easily six-foot six, and his dark hair looked silky. What would it feel like to touch?

I blushed and wriggled my fingers. There was no time to add a delicious werewolf to the mix, although it had been a while since I'd dated someone I found attractive.

"Is something on your mind?" Cole asked.

I noticed we were taking the long way back to the bakery and was pleased, happy to spend more time with Cole. "Nope. I mean, other than where I'm going to get all that money from by the end of the week."

"Did you really get into debt with Sylvester Mahoney?"

"Um... yep. Do you know him?"

"I know of him. The guy's a sleaze."

"Yes, he is, but Sylvester had what I needed. I'm not proud of it, and I honor my debts. I just got a bit behind. I would have paid him."

"Why do you have this debt?"

I sucked in a breath. "It's best you don't know. You won't think much of me if you knew my dark secrets."

He gave a soft grunt. "That statement goes for most people. We all have secrets."

"Some are worse than others."

"That they are." Cole looked down at me, his dark eyes searching for something.

I looked away. "So... you're new to Witch Haven?"

"That's right."

"Visiting friends?"

"Nope."

"Family."

"Can't say I am."

"Is this another secret?"

His grin had a wicked gleam to it. "Do you know Atticus Farraday?"

"Sure. Atticus is the alpha wolf around here. He keeps the peace and makes sure all you furry guys and gals don't get crazy on the full moon."

"He's also an enforcer. We call on him when we have pack disputes."

"Is there trouble in fursville?"

He chuckled. "There is. It's not local trouble, but I'm the negotiator between three packs. Atticus will enforce whatever punishment is decided upon."

I wrinkled my nose. Werewolf justice could be brutal. "I don't envy you that job. Nor Atticus. I'll have to send him cake to cheer him up."

"He'd appreciate that. As would I."

"You have a sweet tooth?"

Cole patted his flat stomach. "I do."

I slowed as we reached the front of Fandango's. "Then the least I can do is invite you in for a slice of pie. Or a muffin. We have everything you could desire in the bakery."

Cole's gaze flashed hot for a second, and my cheeks responded with a matching flush of heat. "That's good of you to offer, but I have business to attend to. And I'm late for a pack meeting."

"Of course. Sorry, that was my fault."

He shook his head. "Don't apologize. I have no regrets about helping a beautiful woman who smells good enough to eat."

I swallowed. "I do?"

He hummed an approving note under his breath and stepped closer.

Before I had time to process what was happening, his lips brushed mine. I squeaked and leaped back, smacking my head against the door.

Cole chuckled. "Sorry to scare you, but I didn't want you to have a sour note to go to sleep on. I figured a kiss might make you smile."

I blew out a breath. "Shall we try that again? I promise not to squeak. Mouse noises aren't sexy."

"They are when you make them." Cole's hand clamped around the back of my neck, and his firm mouth landed on mine.

I didn't squeak, but it was a near miss, as heat and sparks sizzled through me. This wolf knew how to kiss. And his power, it was something else. His energy pulsed through him, straining to break free.

I couldn't help myself as I wrapped an arm around his neck, dragged him close, and feasted on that power.

Cole pulled back, his eyes wide and burning amber. "You've got something a little special to your magic. What is it? I know you're a witch, but..." His tongue traced across his lower lip as if tasting me to figure out what was unusual.

My knees were shaking, along with my head. "There's nothing special about me. My magic lies in baking. I'm from a long line of expert bakers. It's what we love to do, bake cakes and make people happy."

Cole touched his lips, a hint of amber still in his eyes. "That's not the full story, but I'm willing to take my time and hear it all."

"There's nothing to tell. I'm an open spell book."

He grinned. "There is, and I can't wait to hear the rest. I look forward to our next meeting, sugar witch." Cole turned and strode away.

Oh, boy! Werewolf power was insanely good. I had hot and cold shivers zooming up and down my spine as I unlocked the bakery door with a shaky hand.

I poked my head around the door once I was inside. Cole stood at the end of the street. He waved at me before disappearing into the night.

I dashed inside and shut the door. My limbs trembled, my heart raced, and I felt like I could bake the most incredible wedding cake for the Queen of England and she'd adore it.

I needed to test this power. Could this be what I was looking for? All I needed was werewolf energy, and my baking morphed into perfection.

A quick shrug and my jacket was off. I bounded into the kitchen, flicked on the oven, wrapped my apron around me, and pulled out the ingredients to make cinnamon chocolate caramel muffins. It was time to test this theory. And if I was right, I'd have to figure out a way to seduce this gorgeous werewolf and add him to my magical harem.

Chapter 5

I tapped on Uncle Albert's bedroom door at six the next morning. He was usually up by now, but I'd not heard him stirring.

I balanced a tray with almond croissants and a huge mug of steaming tea in one hand as I eased open the door. The curtains were shut, and Uncle Albert was gently snoring under his covers.

Creeping in on my toes, I set down the tray and opened the curtains an inch. "It's time to get up. Those cakes won't make themselves. And we need to finish icing all those fondant fancies for Juniper's sixtieth birthday party."

He stirred and groaned. "It's too early."

Settling on the end of the bed, I patted his feet. "I have good news." I flexed my fingers. I'd spent hours baking last night, and everything had turned out perfectly. And I hadn't even been tired when I'd gone to bed just a few hours ago.

"Do I get to sleep in some more?"

"I got a head start on the food. All the breakfast menu is done and most of the cakes."

He shifted about, and his bleary eyes peered over his duvet. "Everything is set for breakfast?"

"I had a productive night. And I've brought you an almond croissant to try."

Uncle Albert struggled up, his white hair fluffy around his head. He yawned and scrubbed his eyes.

I tilted my head. "Are you unwell? You said you were tired yesterday." I rested a hand against his forehead.

He removed my hand and patted the back of it. "I'll be fine once I get going. I'm just old. This will be you, one day."

I leaned forward and kissed his cheek. "You're not old to me. Are you up to having breakfast?"

"I can never resist a fresh almond croissant."

I settled the tray on his knees and waited in anticipation as he took a bite.

His eyes widened. "Luna! This is amazing. You've never made the pastry so light before. And the almond flavor. It's divine. Better than mine."

I laughed. "That's impossible, but I'm pleased with how they turned out."

"You should be thrilled." He ate two more bites and drank some tea. "What inspired you to stay up so late baking?"

A little of Cole's remaining werewolf energy tingled up my spine. "I just got the baking bug."

He nodded. "It gets me like that, too. I have an idea and I have to act."

"How about you take it easy today? I can serve the morning crowd. Everything's made, so the counter just needs setting up."

"I don't want to leave you on your own."

"Then don't, but there's no hurry. Come down when you're ready and have an easy morning." I didn't want him pushing himself when there was no need.

"You're an angel."

"If you need me, just call." I left Uncle Albert to his breakfast, feeling smug at how incredible my baking had turned out. The meringues I'd made were lightly golden and sweet, the cherry tart was the right side of tangy with a fresh zing, and the fruit cake was packed with sweet flavors. I'd finally found my baking mojo, and it felt amazing.

I fired up the coffee machine, opened the till, and flipped the closed sign to open. I was setting the tables when my first customer came in. I had a great feeling about today. And best of all, there was no sign of my creepy debt collector lurking about. Cole must have scared him off.

I grinned. Cole was my furry knight in shiny armor and possibly a permanent solution to my magic problem. Life was great.

The next few hours passed in a blur of coffee, donuts, small talk with happy customers, and smiles. I dealt with the morning rush with not a single complaint, and everyone complimented the food.

A tap on the window at the front of the bakery had me looking up. Odessa grinned at me and waved. I waved back and gestured at the counter.

She shook her head, tapped her watch, and dashed away.

Storm strode past a few seconds later, a look of icy determination on her face. Her new sort-of familiar, Fire Fang, shadowed her.

"I'm still in shock by it all." Gretchen Moonfall passed me with her friend, Ingrid, and they headed to the counter, their heads close together.

I followed them, always interested in the gossip. "Good morning, ladies. What will it be?"

"Something sweet to help Ingrid get over her shock," Gretchen said.

"You've had a shock?"

Ingrid nodded. "I'm surprised you haven't heard about the death. Such a prominent figure in our community. It's a real loss."

My happy vibe blinked out. Uh, oh! Had Englebert died in the night from my overly vigorous kiss? "Was it... Englebert?"

"No! I'm sure that wiry old warlock will live for another hundred years," Ingrid said.

"Especially with the young company he keeps." Gretchen raised a knowing eyebrow at me.

I ignored the jibe. "So who's dead?"

"Jinti Calrook!"

"But I saw her last night at Atherton's store. What happened?"

"We're not sure." Ingrid leaned closer. "Some say she died of a broken heart."

"It wasn't anything so melodramatic. It was just her time. Jinti hasn't been well," Gretchen said.

Ingrid shrugged. "It's not like she had much to live for. And Jinti lived in that tumbledown place, which I'm sure was damp. When I went there to get a remedy for gout, it smelled musty."

"Maybe that's what got her. She could have had a weak chest from living in squalor."

I frowned. I'd been to Jinti's a few times over the years and never thought her home was damp. It had an old-fashioned flair about it, but she'd kept the place neat, and it always smelled of lavender.

"She didn't look too bright when I saw her," I said, "but I didn't think there was anything seriously wrong. Jinti was browsing through herbal remedy books, though. Perhaps she was looking for something to help her."

"It would be the only reason she'd go to Atherton's store," Ingrid said. "She couldn't stand that smarmy warlock. There was bad blood between them."

"Because of the whole missing daughter thing?" Gretchen said.

"No! Well, that didn't help. Jinti used to clean for Atherton, but he fired her because she turned up late and refused to apologize." Ingrid's eyes glittered with delight as she shared the gossip. "And I heard Atherton only kept Jinti on because he felt guilty."

"Not that guilty if he sacked her."

"Guilty about what?" I asked.

"Bella!" Ingrid said.

"I don't see the connection."

"Girl, you need to listen to the gossip more closely." Ingrid adjusted her scarf. "Jinti's daughter, Bella, was Atherton's wife. Don't you remember the stink he kicked up to get the Magic Council to keep searching for her?"

"Oh! Of course. I'd forgotten. It was years ago."

"I haven't. Jinti always had her suspicions about Atherton. She didn't trust him with her only daughter. And, according to rumor, Bella was miserable being Atherton's wife. She'd even talked about leaving him. Then she disappeared."

"Did Jinti think Atherton had something to do with that?" I said.

"She was certain he murdered Bella."

Gretchen looked around as she tapped on the back of Ingrid's hand. "Shush! You never know who could be listening. Atherton might make you vanish too if he hears you badmouthing him."

"I'm not afraid of him. Besides, Atherton got away with it. The Magic Council found nothing on him. That warlock is so clean his butt cheeks squeak when they rub together."

The ladies chuckled.

"You think Atherton hired Jinti to clean for him because she was his mother-in-law?" I wiggled all the information into place.

"It wouldn't have been for her skills in domestic science," Ingrid said. "I reckon he wanted to make sure she had something to occupy herself, so she wouldn't keep looking for clues that he killed Bella."

"Or so he could keep an eye on Jinti and make sure she didn't keep bothering the Magic Council and pointing the finger of suspicion. Atherton's a sly one. I wouldn't trust him with any of my children," Gretchen said.

"Me either. Although I don't have children, I wouldn't let him pet sit any of my cats." Ingrid eyed the cakes. "I'll take a box of those cherry puffs."

"Add four Danish pastries," Gretchen said, "and two takeout peppermint teas."

"Coming right up." I boxed their order, my brain whizzing. I felt sorry for Jinti and wished I'd spent more time with her at Atherton's store. She'd been distressed, and I should have done more to help her. Now she was gone.

I handed over their order, took the money, and said goodbye to Gretchen and Ingrid.

This was the reminder I needed to never go back to borrowing Englebert's magic. He was a powerful warlock, but at least as old as Jinti. I'd been lucky not to have killed him. I'd been putting Englebert at risk, and that was selfish.

I needed a strong, healthy magic user to drain discreetly. I smiled as an image of a tall, handsome werewolf with amber eyes hit me. Yes, Cole was exactly what I needed. And he'd be much more fun to smooch than Englebert.

He also seemed interested and had made all the right moves last night, but I still had to be careful. Cole had sensed my magic was different, and I didn't want him to find out just how many sources of magic I called on to keep things stable.

I needed to get the kissing up and running without him getting too interested. A furry friend with benefits scheme would be ideal.

But for that to work, I needed to de-rust my seduction skills. All I'd had to do to interest Englebert was flash him an ankle and a hint of cleavage, and he'd get all hot and bothered. Cole would be different. He was a prime werewolf, and must have the lady wolves circling like he was a sirloin steak they wanted to bite.

I had my charms, but they were more sugar than spice. Maybe that was what Cole was looking for. He'd had enough snap and sizzle and wanted someone sweet. And I'd be happy to oblige. In fact, I'd insist on it.

With his werewolf energy fizzing through my veins, I felt like I could take on the world, and there wasn't a recipe I wasn't prepared to tackle. Bring on the souffles, the tricky cheese sauces, and the crème brûlée. I'd make them all, and everyone would love them.

William Warren the Third wandered to the counter, a small smile on his round face. His collar was flipped up, and a baseball cap concealed his features. It was a necessity to avoid direct sunlight when you were a half-vampire. But he was a cute half-vampire, and this was the perfect opportunity to see how my flirting skills shaped up.

I fluttered my lashes and gave him a sultry smile.

William's gaze remained on the iced buns.

"Hi! See anything you like?" I thrust out my chest, then realized my assets were hidden under my apron.

"Everything looks delicious."

"Has anyone ever said you remind them of a fruit?" I pouted my lips.

His puzzled gaze lifted to mine, and he tipped his cap back an inch. "A fruit?"

"Yes. You're a fine apple."

"Um... thanks. Can I have six pink iced buns?"

"Oh! Sure." This wasn't going so well. I boxed the buns but kept a firm grip on them as I handed the box to William. "You must be peanut butter."

He blinked rapidly. "Why?"

"Because my legs just turned to jelly."

His mouth opened. He slapped down some money, yanked the box out of my hand, and raced off.

"Wait! What about your change?"

"Keep it!" He slammed the door behind him.

Hmmm, food themed seduction was off the menu. I needed to try another angle. Maybe fewer pickup lines and more cleavage? No, that wouldn't work. I'd have to ditch the apron which would be a health violation.

I added a tray of pecan and dark chocolate cookies to the counter and looked around for a new target to test my flirting skills on.

My breath stuck in my throat when my gaze landed on Devlin Goody striding to the door. I briefly considered hiding behind the counter and scuttling away, but he'd already seen me.

I could do nothing but hope he wasn't back to accuse me of using dodgy magic in my baking again.

Devlin entered the bakery and stomped to the counter.

I forced a smile. "Good morning. What will it be? We have some delicious savory breakfast muffins. They contain one of your five a day, but you'd never know it."

"I'm not here for food. I'm here to question you about Jinti Calrook's murder."

Chapter 6

"Err... You think I had something to do with how Jinti died?" I looked around to see several customers interested in Devlin's loud proclamation.

"That's what I'm here to find out," he said. "What can you tell me about her death?"

My brain froze, then scrambled, and alarm bells clanged in my ears. "Jinti was an old lady. Maybe it was just her time. Um, why don't we talk about this somewhere else? We don't want to put the customers off their coffee and cake."

He glanced around. "Do you have a room in the back we can use?"

"Of course." The last thing I wanted was for anyone to hear this mortifying conversation. "Give me a moment. I need to get Uncle Albert to look after the counter."

Devlin gave a nod then crossed his arms over his chest, watching my every move as I dashed away. My heart thudded so hard, I felt dizzy. I had to get a grip on myself. There'd be a reason Devlin was here, asking questions about Jinti's... I couldn't believe it, her murder.

Maybe I'd been one of the last people to see her alive. Devlin would want to know if she'd been behaving oddly or had been worried about anything. That would be it. This had nothing to do with me.

"Uncle, can you keep an eye on the counter? Devlin Goody is here. He wants to have a few words with me."

Uncle Albert was sitting at the large table in the kitchen. He was supposed to be icing cookies, but the icing bag lay untouched. "So long as it's quiet. I'm still not feeling right."

"I can always put Devlin off if you're not up to it." I shouldn't be bothering him when he looked so pale.

Uncle Albert tilted his head. "No, I can manage. What does the Magic Council want with you?"

"It's a misunderstanding. I... I'll get it figured out." After setting Uncle Albert up behind the counter, I gestured Devlin to follow me and led him into the kitchen. "I'm sorry to hear about Jinti, but I'm not sure I have anything useful to tell you."

Devlin's hard expression didn't make me feel too hopeful. "What was your opinion of Jinti Calrook?"

I clasped my hands together. "Honestly, I found her a little scary and intimidating. I was never sure what to say to her. And she could be sharp if you caught her on a bad day. But she was excellent with her herbal remedies."

"You didn't like her?"

"I didn't say that. I just didn't know her well. What happened to Jinti?"

"She was murdered."

"You already said that. But how?"

"I'm asking the questions. When was the last time you saw her?"

"Yesterday evening. I dropped off some iced muffins for Regina. The magic store was holding a swap and share evening, and she asked me to bring refreshments at the last minute. I was looking around the magic store when I saw Jinti."

"Did you talk to her?"

I nodded. "For a couple of minutes."

"What did you talk about?"

"Nothing much. A little about her daughter, Bella, and what she was looking for in the store. Atherton and Ulric came over and were keeping her company when I left."

Devlin pulled out a notebook and flicked through it. "You were seen arguing with Jinti."

"Last night? No, we didn't argue."

"She came into the bakery and made a complaint."

"Oh! That!" It took me a few seconds to recall the incident. "It wasn't anything. Definitely not an argument."

"You remember having a problem with her?"

"I do," I said cautiously. "But it wasn't a real problem. Jinti wasn't happy with a pie she'd bought, so I replaced it."

"Several people saw you. They said the argument became heated."

"There was no heat involved. It was tepid. I was surprised when Jinti came in making demands, but it got sorted." I grabbed a cloth and twisted it in my hands. "I could have handled it better, but I wouldn't hold a grudge because Jinti didn't like something I baked."

Devlin made a note on his pad.

I leaned closer. "What are you writing?"

"Nothing to concern yourself with. Did you return to Atherton's store at any point yesterday evening?"

"No. Was that where Jinti was found?"

He nodded. "Can anyone confirm where you were last night between ten-thirty and midnight?"

"Was that when Jinti was killed?"

Devlin narrowed his eyes. "She was found dead this morning at the magic store. The last time anyone saw her alive was around ten-forty five yesterday evening. Can you account for your movements?"

"Not really. I was alone. We'd had a busy day in the bakery, so I came back here, put my feet up, and did nothing."

"What about Albert? Can he confirm your movements?"

"Possibly. He might have heard me moving around, but he was tired and had an early night. You're welcome to check with him, but he was most likely asleep. I'm always quiet when he's in bed, so I don't disturb him."

"Which means, you have no alibi."

"No, but I don't need one. I've done nothing wrong."

Devlin's lips thinned, and he made another note in his pad.

"Devlin, be serious! Do you really think I'm a suspect because I had an argument with Jinti over a pie? That motive is thinner than one of Uncle Albert's famous chocolate crepes."

"It's more than that."

"Then tell me what you've got. If I'm a person of interest, I have to know, so I can clear my name." I matched his sullen expression. "I had nothing to do with this murder."

He flipped through his notepad. "Your time away from Witch Haven wouldn't have been easy."

I tensed. "It was difficult, but I've moved on."

"Perhaps you haven't moved on. You were exposed to dark magic."

"I don't remember much about that, but I had no interest in the darkness. And I was taken against my will. Everyone knows that. I didn't willingly get involved with dark magic users."

"Why?"

I blinked at him. "What do you mean?"

"Why did the dark magic deviants select you?"

"Um... it's complicated. I suspect it was partly to get Indigo's attention. Her mom wanted her to join her, and taking her best friend got Indigo focused."

"Anything else?"

I bit my bottom lip. "Nothing comes to mind."

"Is it possible those dark magic users influenced you?" Devlin said.

I chuffed out a half-laugh of disbelief. He had to be kidding. "You think Indigo's mom and her demon lover manipulated me into killing Jinti?"

"We take a dim view of dark magic. It brings trouble."

"Which is why I never use it." I drew in a deep breath. "When I was taken, I was held in limbo, but

I was mainly left alone. The few times contact was made, it was to make sure I was still alive."

"So you say."

"I do! And my word is good. Even if I had been corrupted by dark magic, why would I target Jinti? She was good for Witch Haven. She healed people."

"Dark magic rarely has any logic. Perhaps you thought Jinti shouldn't have been helping others," Devlin said. "She was a positive influence in the village, and you needed to get rid of that."

"I'd never hurt Jinti. You need to look elsewhere for your killer."

Devlin lifted a hand. "There's something else. One of your iced muffins was found by the body. Jinti had partially eaten it. The autopsy showed she had cake in her stomach."

"You don't think she choked on it, do you?"

"Jinti didn't choke. But I have concerns someone poisoned her. Your muffin would make a suitable vehicle for such a toxin."

My vision dimmed at the corners, and I gripped the table. "Why would I poison Jinti?"

"That's for me to uncover. But add this murder to the reports of your dubious baking, and you leave me no choice. I'm closing this bakery, taking samples, and searching the building for illegal or dangerous magic."

"What's all this?" Uncle Albert stood in the doorway, his face pale and his eyes wide. "We don't use illegal magic."

"Don't listen to Devlin." I was still reeling from being accused of poisoning Jinti. "He's making a huge mistake. He thinks I had something to do with what happened to Jinti."

"I just heard the news she died." Uncle Albert hurried over and wrapped a supportive arm around my shoulders. "What's this got to do with you?"

"Albert, you don't need to be involved," Devlin said.

"If you're even thinking about charging my niece, I'm involved." Uncle Albert pulled a handkerchief from his pocket and wiped it across his brow.

"Are you feeling well?" Devlin said. "You don't look too good. Did you eat one of Luna's iced muffins?"

"Zip it! I'd never poison my uncle." I caught hold of Uncle Albert's elbow and guided him to a chair. "You should get back to bed."

"We have bigger things to worry about than my sore head. I can't have you accused of murder."

"We have evidence to suggest Luna is involved," Devlin said.

Uncle Albert shook his head. "She'd never do such a terrible thing."

"The proof suggests otherwise. And then there's her involvement with dark magic. You must—"

"Be quiet," I hissed at Devlin. "Can't you see my uncle is sick? You're stressing him out for no reason."

"What's making him sick? Are you sure you didn't leave your poisoned muffins out, and he ate one?"

"That's enough!" I grabbed an oven mitt and slung it at Devlin. "Uncle, you need to rest." I hurried him out of the kitchen before Devlin could stop us, up the stairs, and into his bedroom.

"Luna, what's going on?" He had a bemused look on his face as I eased him down on the pillows. "Devlin really thinks our muffins killed Jinti?"

"Devlin Goody is picking on me." I took off his shoes and tucked the covers around him. "He's got it into his thick skull that I've been tainted by dark magic, and it made me poison Jinti."

"The man's an idiot."

"He is, but let me deal with him. You rest. This will all be fixed as soon as I've talked sense into Devlin."

Uncle Albert caught hold of my hand as I was about to leave the room. "There is nothing wrong with your food. I ate one of your breakfast muffins yesterday and that croissant. Both were delicious. You're a good baker. Dark magic hasn't touched you."

I patted his hand. "Of course. We both know I had nothing to do with this." I hurried to the door, then stopped and turned back to look at Uncle Albert.

He had eaten my baking. Was that why he was unwell? Was there something wrong with my cakes?

I shook my head. It couldn't be that. I wasn't the reason Uncle Albert was sick and Jinti was dead.

When I returned to the kitchen, Devlin was poking his head into one of the large refrigerators. I caught hold of the handle and yanked the door back. "You need a warrant if you want to look around. And don't contaminate the food, or I won't be able to serve it."

He reared back, glaring at me. "I have every right to investigate. We need to find evidence you're a killer."

"Then you're wasting your time, because there's nothing here."

"You need to clear the bakery so I can begin my search," Devlin said. "I've called in backup. They'll be here soon."

"You have no right to do that. And have you even spoken to anyone else who attended the magic swap and share? If I poisoned the muffins, they'd all be sick."

"What's this about poison?" Cole stood in the doorway, his broad frame almost filling it as he glared at Devlin.

"Customers aren't allowed back here," Devlin said.

"He's not a customer. He's a friend." I hurried over to Cole. "How did you know we were back here?"

"I heard raised voices and wanted to make sure you were okay," he said. "Is this guy bothering you?"

Devlin glowered at me, his expression growing worried as he glanced at Cole. "I'm here on official Magic Council business, so you'd be wise not to get involved."

"My pop always said I had a dumb streak, so I'm planning on staying."

I was so glad he'd said that. Not the dumb part, but the staying part.

"Devlin wants to search the bakery for illegal magic," I whispered.

"Is that right? Do you have the paperwork to conduct a search?" Cole said. "If you find evidence and you don't have the right papers filed, it'll be inadmissible and you'll have wasted your time."

"That's right." At least, I hoped it was right. I had no experience of dealing with legal matters, other than binge watching a few cop TV shows.

Devlin let out a grating sigh. "It would be looked on favorably if you let me search the bakery without having to get a warrant."

"That's not happening." Cole's biceps flexed.

"What's to say she won't move incriminating evidence while I'm gone?" Devlin jabbed a finger at me.

"She won't," I snapped, "because that would be impossible. There's nothing incriminating here. And you need to come back another time. I have a business to run, and as you saw, my uncle isn't well. I have to juggle the counter and keep an eye on him. I can't handle you, too."

"You heard Luna. It's time for you to leave," Cole said. "The lady doesn't want you here." His hands flexed as he advanced on Devlin.

Devlin flashed me a fear-filled gaze. "I will be back. And you'll regret standing in my way. All of this is going in my report." He dodged past Cole and scurried out, his notebook clasped in his hands.

I shook my head and let out a slow breath, tension spiraling up my spine.

Cole gently squeezed my shoulder. "I hope I wasn't overstepping, but I've tangled with Devlin Goody a time or two. He can be a problem."

"You have?" I leaned into his touch, glad I had someone helping me.

"Devlin gets an idea in his head and struggles to shake it loose, even when everyone tells him it's the dumbest idea since the invention of the chocolate teapot."

"You didn't overstep, and I appreciate you chasing him off. Devlin was being difficult."

Cole was silent for three heartbeats. "He really thinks someone got poisoned from food made in the bakery?"

"You heard that?"

"I hear plenty. Werewolf hearing is a blessing and a curse."

I couldn't help but notice he was still holding my shoulder. It felt comforting. "Jinti Calrook was found this morning in Atherton's magic store. Devlin thinks she was poisoned by a muffin I delivered last night."

He snorted his disbelief. "You'd never do anything like that."

"I appreciate your confidence in me, but you don't know me that well. I could be a sneaky, dark magic wielding poisoner. I'm not, but..." I shrugged. With my past, people who didn't know me would most likely assume the worst.

"I know you well enough. My first impressions of a person are always right, and I got a good feeling about you when we met."

My hand went to my lips, and despite the awful situation, I couldn't help but smile. "I had a good feeling about you, too."

Cole reached up and touched my cheek, caressing his thumb across my cheekbone. "If there's anything I can do to help, just ask. Even if it means standing guard outside the bakery so Devlin can't bother you."

"Are we interrupting something?" Indigo stood in the doorway, alongside Odessa, who had a huge grin on her face as her gaze ran over Cole.

I stepped away, my cheeks flushing. "No, nothing. We were just talking."

"You need to talk some more. We just found someone who's been asking around about you," Indigo said.

"Was it Devlin?" I said. "If so, he's already visited."

"No, not Devlin. This guy." Indigo reached behind her and dragged a man into view. "We thought we should bring him here since he was so insistent he find out all about you."

The man's hands and feet were tied together, and he had a gag in his mouth.

I stared at him, and horror hit me right between the eyes. It was the guy I'd chased last night.

I flicked a glance at Cole. He was glaring at the guy like he wanted to tear his head off.

"Who is he?" Odessa was still ogling Cole.

My mind blanked. How was I supposed to hide my magic draining secret from my friends now?

Chapter 7

"Hey, earth goddess to Luna. Do you know this guy?" Indigo said. "He seemed certain he was friendly with you."

I'd been staring for too long without saying anything, but couldn't think of a reason my unwelcome debt collector would be here.

"We heard him asking around about you, so we pretended to be helpful. He had no idea what he was getting himself into," Odessa said. "It was hilarious."

The man made a muffled protest. He was most likely cursing from behind his gag.

I glanced at Cole, whose expression was full of curiosity and anger, although he hadn't spoken a word since Odessa and Indigo appeared.

This needed covering up, and I had to get the debt collector to play along to keep my secret hidden.

"Luna, what's going on? Who's this guy you were about to make out with?" Indigo jabbed a finger at Cole. "And who's this trussed up sneaker asking all the questions about you? I don't know either of them, and if they're in your life, I should."

My brain was on overdrive scramble. Think, Luna, think. I'd start with the easy. "This is Cole, he's... a new friend."

"Hey, Cole." Indigo remained focused on me.

"Cole Kellam." He reached out a hand.

Odessa and Indigo both shook his hand and introduced themselves.

I looked at the guy they'd brought in. He was sweating and his eyes were bulging. "And... that's my boyfriend."

"Your what?" Indigo shook her head. "That makes no sense. He wanted to know everything about you. He kept saying you must have secrets, and he needed to know them all."

"That's just his silly game." I hurried over, grabbed him by the front of his T-shirt, and yanked him away from Odessa and Luna. "It's something we do for fun. He keeps trying to find out my favorite things, and I make him guess, don't I, honey?" I pulled him further away and pressed my lips to his ear. "Play along and I'll double the payment. Do we have a deal? You keep the extra." I pulled back and stared at him.

For a second, fury blazed in his eyes, but it was replaced with amusement, and he nodded.

"I still don't get this." Odessa was pouting. "He's not the kind of guy you go for." Her gaze flashed to Cole. "And neither are you. Although you're handsome."

Cole nodded, his gaze on the debt collector. "I appreciate being noticed."

"I needed a change." I kept my focus on the trussed up guy. "Angel, will you behave yourself if I take out this gag?"

I didn't miss the surprised look that passed between Indigo and Odessa as I eased the gag out of the guy's mouth. I tensed, waiting for everything to crash down around my ears. What would he do?

The debt collector leaned forward and kissed me. "Hey, beautiful. Those are some friends you've got there. They threatened to disembowel me."

"They were only teasing." I removed his bindings, my hands shaking and my insides a riot of nerves.

The second the debt collector was free, he grabbed me and kissed me again. He tasted of cheese and onion toasty. I tried hard not to gag and almost succeeded.

"Wow! You two are close," Odessa said. "Why haven't you introduced us?"

I shoved the guy away. "It's not that serious."

"It's serious to me." He wrapped a hand around my waist and tugged me closer. "I'm Bram. I've been asking Luna to introduce me to her friends and family for ages, but she's shy. So I decided to do some digging and get to know her better."

"Huh! Does anyone else think that's weird?" Indigo said.

"Luna's a complicated lady," Bram said. "And I love complicated." He dropped his head to get another kiss.

I stepped out of his grip and forced a laugh. "This is my fault. I've been so busy."

"What about Englebert?" Odessa said. "You're not together anymore?"

"Who's Englebert?" Bram said.

"A friend." I shot a glare at Odessa, and she gave me an apologetic shrug.

"I hope you're not seeing anyone else," Bram said. "Should I visit Englebert and make sure he knows the score? I'm not keen on sharing my women."

Indigo snorted a laugh.

"There's no need," I said. "Englebert's a much older man, and you don't want to frighten him. He has a weak heart." I glanced over at Cole. Anger blazed in his eyes, his fury directed at Bram, who continued to leer at me.

"I should get going," Cole said.

"Good idea," Bram said. "I hope the door doesn't hit you on the way out."

Cole growled at him as he slunk off.

"How do you know him?" Odessa stared after Cole.

"I don't, not really. He helped me out when I had a situation to deal with." I shuffled away from Bram. "Shouldn't you get going, too?"

"I want to get to know your friends, sweet lips," he said. "We could have fun together. I've got so many secrets to share about Luna."

"Another time." I shoved him at the door. "I want to catch up with my girlfriends, and you'll only get bored when we gossip."

Bram's expression suggested he was having way too much fun torturing me. "I found out loads of interesting things about you while I was asking around." He smacked another kiss on my lips, then strode away. "Nice to meet you, girls."

I waited until Bram left, then slumped against the table.

"Um... What the heck was all that about?"

I looked up to find Odessa in front of me, with Indigo beside her.

"Yeah, that was super strange. That guy we tied up was all over you. Where did you meet him?" Indigo said.

"I forget. And Bram's a rough diamond, but you warm up to him once you get to know him."

"I didn't realize your tastes had changed that much," Odessa said. "Any reason why?"

"They haven't changed. I'm just trying something new. There's no harm in that."

"So long as it makes you happy," Indigo said. "Does Bram make you happy? He seemed a bit gropey."

"I wouldn't be with him if I wasn't happy." I strode to the fridge. "Does anyone want food?"

"I'm confused. Are you really dating Bram?" Odessa said. "And what about Englebert? Won't he mind?"

"And we can't forget the moody werewolf," Indigo said.

I turned away from the fridge. "I never officially dated Englebert, and I'm definitely not now. I had dinner with him, and we've decided to stay friends."

"You always told us you were only ever friends," Indigo said.

Odessa grinned. "Which we knew wasn't true."

I gritted my teeth. "We might have had a cuddle once or twice, but Englebert always instigated it. And before your filthy minds go into overdrive, it never got beyond cuddle stage. I could never marry Englebert."

"Now you're talking marriage?" Indigo shook her head. "You've been holding out on us."

If only they knew the truth.

"Bram seemed keen on you," Odessa said.

"I don't like him," Indigo said.

"I like Cole," Odessa said. "And I've not seen him around before. Is he new to the village?"

"Cole's just visiting," I said. "He's got business with Atticus. Something about pack disputes. Anyway, let's forget my men. I've got a big problem on my hands."

"Is there a fourth guy we don't know about?" Indigo said.

"It's got nothing to do with men. Well, it has to do with one man, and that man as good as accused me of murdering Jinti Calrook. That's my focus."

Both their jaws dropped.

I dumped a plate of cookies on the table. "I know! Devlin Goody left just before you arrived. Jinti was found dead with one of my muffins beside her body. Devlin is convinced I poisoned her."

"He has to be joking," Indigo said.

"Devlin thinks I've gone dark and poisoned her after a fight over a stale pie. He's determined to find something bad on me." The problem was, if he dug too hard, he'd find lots of dirt, and I couldn't have that.

"You proved you had nothing to do with it?" Indigo said.

"Not that we think you'd kill someone over your food." Odessa lifted a cookie and turned it over.

"Sure. That's what I meant," Indigo said. "What's your alibi?"

"It's bad. I was here."

"With your uncle?" Odessa said.

"He was asleep. He's not been feeling well, so he had an early night. Uncle Albert won't be able to say for sure where I was."

"He'll back you up. He'll know you had nothing to do with this," Odessa said.

"Yes, of course, but I don't want him to get in trouble by giving me a false alibi."

"You had no reason to kill Jinti," Indigo said. "You might not have a decent alibi, but you have no motive. Do you want me to get Olympus to have a word and make Devlin back off?"

"Hopefully, you won't need to. Once Devlin has calmed down and realized how little evidence there is, he'll go away," I said.

"Hey! I heard you back here." Storm strolled into the kitchen. "What's going on? And why is there some random guy making coffee behind the counter? There's foam everywhere."

I raced to the door. "Follow me! I forgot no one was serving."

It took ten minutes of frantic serving and help from my friends before order was restored.

I made thank you triple caramel lattes with cream and passed them around, making sure Storm got a strong black coffee.

She arched an eyebrow. "I'm still waiting for an explanation."

"Jinti Calrook is dead. And Devlin Goody thinks Luna murdered her with a dodgy cupcake," Odessa said in a hushed tone as we stood behind the counter.

"It was a poisoned muffin. And from what I could get out of Devlin, he's not even sure poison was used," I said. "I think he was fishing when he visited me."

Storm leaned against the counter. "I can tell you this, Jinti's death wasn't natural. It was definitely murder."

"How do you know that?" I said.

"From my sources." Storm ran a private detective agency, which she'd set up after her sister, Eden, went missing. After years of looking and not getting anywhere, Storm began taking private jobs and had built a network of useful contacts.

"You can help me clear my name," I said.

"I can ask around and see what else people are saying," Storm said. "You're sure you didn't accidentally poison Jinti? Some of your cakes have upset my stomach."

"You can leave if you're going to say things like that."

Storm grinned. "Just checking. The Magic Council will leave you alone when they get all the evidence. You know what they're like. They arrest first and ask proper questions later."

"I hope you're right. But Devlin has me worried."

"If he keeps hassling you, I'll set Olympus on him," Indigo said. "Don't worry about it."

"You should worry more about all the men in your life," Odessa said. "How are you going to juggle them?"

"What's this?" Storm said.

"It's nothing." If I wasn't careful, Storm would run background checks on all my guys, and then I'd have tricky questions to deal with when she discovered Bram's true identity.

"Luna's got a couple of new guys she's been keeping secret," Indigo said.

"And she's finally ditched Englebert," Odessa said.

I groaned and hid my head in my hands.

"Is that right?" Storm laughed. "You've been busy."

"I've not been busy. And I need to simplify my life, not complicate it."

"It's too late for that," Odessa said.

"We should go on a double date, so I can check out Bram," Indigo said. "And you can talk to Olympus about how to get Devlin off your back."

"That's a great idea," Odessa said. "Storm and I can come along, too."

"I'm not going as your date," Storm said. "You're cute, but you're not my type."

Odessa swatted her arm. "Not as a proper date-date, just as friends. Don't you want to meet the new man in Luna's life?"

"It's a bad idea." Sweat broke out on my upper lip. "Bram's crazy busy with work."

"What does he do?" Indigo said.

"He's... in finance."

"He works in a bank?" Storm said.

"Not exactly. But he handles money." I had to get them off the topic of my fake boyfriend. "And I don't know when he's next free, so we'll have to postpone the date idea."

"He seemed keen on meeting up with you again," Odessa said. "I'm sure he can shuffle things around at work so you can spend time together."

"And if he's really into you, he'll find the time," Indigo said. "Let's meet up tonight. Olympus is free."

"That doesn't work for me. And Uncle Albert isn't well. I need to be around to make sure he's okay."

"I can hang out with Albert," Storm said. "I've got nothing going on. I'll bring Fire Fang. He needs socializing, so he can hang out with Earl."

"Perfect," Indigo said. "Get in touch with Bram and make sure he turns up. Seven o'clock at the Chinese restaurant?"

I bit my bottom lip, then nodded. There was no getting out of this. "Sounds good." I'd figure out an escape later.

"It's sorted. I'll meet your guy and give him the once over, and Olympus will deal with your Devlin problem," Indigo said.

"I... err... yep. Great." What a disaster.

"Now the man problem and the murder problem are sorted, can you fix me lunch to go?" Storm checked her watch. "I'm meeting a new client in fifteen minutes."

"Of course." I fixed Storm a bag of treats and gave Odessa and Indigo more coffees to go before seeing them out.

Odessa hugged me. "Don't stress about Devlin. You have nothing to hide."

I closed the door and leaned against it. The trouble was, I did. And they might not be worried that Devlin thought my muffin killed Jinti, but I was terrified.

It was time to get my sleuthing hat on and figure out what happened to Jinti Calrook.

Chapter 8

I looked down at the tray of cherry Bakewell slices and gave a satisfied nod. Food was always a great way to people's hearts, and it often got them talking. A sweet treat and a delicious cup of coffee was all that was needed to make people happy and lower their barriers. And that was exactly what I hoped would happen when I visited the magic store.

I scooped up the tray, shut the bakery, and headed over to Atherton's store. I slowed as I got near and frowned. There were two large gray trolls outside, standing under the glow of the nightlight over the door. The Magic Council often used them as muscle, to keep people out of places they didn't want them snooping around.

Trolls were usually no trouble, but they weren't all that brainy. I might be able to persuade them my cakes were worth taking a break for.

I smiled brightly as I walked toward them. "What are you doing here?"

The troll to the left of the door grunted at me.

He clearly didn't want to talk. I turned my attention to the second troll. He was slightly shorter, with a thick neck and a bulbous nose. "Is the magic store still closed because of the murder?"

He nodded at me.

"Perhaps you'd both like a cake. I made them fresh today." I offered the tray.

Neither of them moved.

Hmmm, perhaps cake wasn't the way to a troll's heart. "Can you let me in? I'll only be a minute. I want to drop these off and make sure everyone's doing okay. It was such a shock what happened to Jinti."

The troll on the left closed his eyes as if he couldn't be bothered to look at me.

I took a step forward. "So... is it okay to get through?"

The troll's left arm shot out and blocked my way. He kept his eyes closed.

"Leave," the other troll said. "No one is allowed in."

"I'm not here to cause problems."

"Go away."

"Luna, is that you?" Regina's head poked around the side of the building. "I thought I heard voices."

"Hi, I was dropping off these Bakewell slices." I held up the cake. "You've probably been too busy to think about eating with everything that's been going on."

"Thanks. That's kind of you." Regina glanced at the trolls, then beckoned me over.

I smiled at the trolls, then hurried to her side.

"Don't mind those two. The Magic Council put them there, and they're not letting anyone inside the store until they finish their investigation. Not even Atherton can get in. He's not happy. I'm working in the back office if you want to join me."

"I don't want to get in the way, but I can't stop thinking about Jinti."

"Neither can I." Regina led me around to a door in the side of the building and then along a corridor and into a tidy office with a small desk and two chairs. She gestured at a chair.

I sat and placed the tray down.

Regina looked at the cake and pursed her lips. "Did you make these?"

"I did. Just today."

She chewed on her bottom lip. "Don't take this the wrong way, but the iced muffins you brought for our magic swap and share were... unusual."

I winced. "I promise these are much better. I was trying a new recipe with those muffins, and I guess it didn't work. These were made to one of Uncle Albert's secret recipes, so they're tried and tested."

Relief flashed across Regina's face. "I'll make some coffee. I won't be a minute."

I nodded, then settled in my seat and inspected the office. It looked like Regina shared this space with Atherton. There were framed certificates on the wall showing his distinctions in magical education and loads of pictures of him with prominent figures, including several people from the Magic Council. Atherton had his fingers in lots of magic pies.

There were also several feminine touches, including scented candles and a pretty floral throw.

Regina returned with two mugs of coffee and sat in the seat opposite me. She picked up a Bakewell slice, glanced at me, then took a tentative bite.

Her eyes widened. "Oh! This is wonderful. You really made these?"

"Don't sound so surprised." My magic boost from Englebert and Cole had done their job, and my baking skills were back on track.

"Sorry! That was rude. I've eaten lots of your cakes, and they've all been nice, but this is sublime."

"No, you're fine. Honestly, I'm still growing into my baking ability. Sometimes, the magic happens, and sometimes, you get those odd iced muffins I gave you."

"You've done an amazing job with these. I shall have to hide the tray, or I'll eat them all."

I selected a slice and took a bite. "I suppose you had muffins left over if the ones I brought didn't go down so well."

Regina shook her head. "They got eaten. And they weren't so bad. They just had a strange aftertaste. Sort of peppery."

"An aftertaste? That's worrying." I set down my Bakewell slice. "I'll come clean with you. I had a visit from the Magic Council. Devlin Goody came to the bakery."

Regina nodded. "He's been here, too. He's leading on the investigation into what happened to Jinti. Did he ask you questions about her?"

"Yes. And questions about the muffins I delivered."

"Why was he interested in those?"

I sucked in a breath. "Devlin thinks they were poisoned, and Jinti ate one."

Regina gasped. "That can't be right."

"It isn't. And I promise I didn't poison her."

"Of course you didn't. Why would Devlin think that?"

"He has a grudge against the bakery or, rather, me. He's been snooping about trying to cause problems." I leaned forward in my seat. "I have to ask, did anyone else get ill after eating those muffins?"

"No! I definitely didn't, and I shared one with Atherton. We were fine." Regina sipped her coffee. "Was there an ingredient in them Jinti could have been sensitive to? Would that have made her sick?"

"It's possible, but it would have needed to be a severe reaction to kill her. And if she had a nut allergy or anything like that, the effect would have been immediate. Devlin said she didn't die until later that night."

"That's right. Sometime around midnight, I believe." Regina ate another bite of Bakewell slice. "Jinti was in such poor health. Maybe she was sensitive to something, and it triggered a reaction."

"I hate to think my food made her sick."

"It can't have been your muffins. Everyone else was fine on the night, and I've heard nothing about customers being ill."

I let out a relieved sigh. "Devlin is still suspicious of me. He wants to shut down the bakery."

"I'm not suspicious of you," Regina said. "And Jinti was unwell. I think that's why she came to the event, to see if she could find a remedy for her stomach pain."

"She didn't look too good when I spoke to her. But Devlin seemed convinced Jinti was murdered."

Regina was quiet for a few seconds. "Jinti had a tendency to make enemies. She could be sharp with people and often argued with Atherton."

"About what?"

She looked down at her hands. "They had a difficult relationship. You might remember Atherton married Bella, Jinti's daughter."

"I do. And Bella went missing."

"That's right. Jinti always considered Atherton was to blame for chasing Bella away. Their marriage wasn't happy, and Bella was prone to depression and had a temper. Atherton did his best, but in the end, it wasn't enough."

"Jinti thought Atherton drove Bella away?"

"Or something worse," Regina said quietly.

"She thought he killed Bella?"

"It's not true. Marriages sometimes just end. People aren't right for each other and go their separate ways. And it devastated Atherton when Bella disappeared. He looked everywhere and arranged search parties to scour the woods. He also paid a private detective to find Bella. But she simply vanished."

"What do you think happened to her?"

"I believe she'd had enough of Witch Haven and Atherton and left the village."

"That's all?"

"I'm sure of it. Atherton is a good man, and he'd never hurt anyone. He loved Bella and was shattered when she walked out on him."

"You've worked for him for a long time, haven't you?"

"Seven years, and I enjoy my job. Atherton's always bringing fascinating things into the store. I get to do the research and find out their magical history. And I love helping customers. I can't imagine working anywhere else. I trust Atherton, and he'd never have mistreated Bella."

"But he could never convince Jinti of that?"

"No, but I don't blame Jinti for being so sharp with him. She was a heartbroken mom who'd have done anything to get her daughter back. Sadly, she was looking for a resolution to a problem that could never be solved." Regina shook her head. "But I didn't like it when she got angry with Atherton. She'd come into the store and start an argument with him. He always tried to keep her calm, but it seemed Jinti wanted to rage at somebody, and he was her target."

"Atherton must be relieved Jinti's dead."

Regina's eyes widened. "He wouldn't think like that. Some people see him as arrogant, but he's just confident. He has a knack for finding things people want."

"It sounds like Jinti could be stubborn if she wouldn't let go of her belief Atherton harmed Bella."

"She was stubborn. Maybe I made too many allowances for her behavior, but my heart went out to her because her daughter abandoned her."

Regina let out a sigh. "I was worried when I saw Jinti at the magic swap and share, but she was actually pleasant. She browsed the store, talked to a few people, and then left."

"Her body was found in the store, though, wasn't it?"

"Yes. Although I've no idea how she got back in. I was the last to leave that evening. I tidied up, sorted the register, and locked up. Then I walked home. Jinti left at least half an hour before that."

"Who has keys to the store? Maybe she met someone later."

"I have a set of keys, and so does Atherton. Jinti used to, because she cleaned the store."

"Used to?" Thanks to Storm, I knew about her being fired but was interested in Regina's take on it.

"Atherton had to let her go. Jinti turned up late a few times, and he was worried she was under the influence of some odd magic. She sometimes sounded slurred when she spoke, and he was concerned she was using something dangerous."

"Like what?"

"He didn't ask her but requested that, when she works for him, she be competent. It didn't do the store's reputation any good if it was dirty."

"What did Jinti think about that?"

"Not much. They had words. Then Jinti came to the store in a mess one evening, and Atherton had enough."

"There was bad blood between them?"

"Not from Atherton's side, although he was relieved to move Jinti out of his life. Even though she used to be his mother-in-law, they had a tense relationship."

"That's no surprise, if Jinti thought Atherton killed Bella."

"I really hoped she'd moved past that crazy theory. There was a good woman hiding beneath all that grief and anger. But Jinti let her depressing thoughts get in the way of moving on."

"Maybe you can't move on when you lose a child," I said.

"Perhaps not." Regina tidied a pile of leaflets on the desk. "And I don't like to say this, but I'm relieved Jinti will no longer be coming to the store. She frightened me. She was so intense and quick to anger."

"I found her intimidating, too. Now, I feel bad. I should have spent more time talking to her."

Regina patted my arm. "I don't think there was anything anyone could have done to help Jinti. And you're not to worry about your muffins. I'll make sure Devlin knows you had nothing to do with what happened to Jinti."

"Thanks. I'd appreciate that."

"I'm sure his questioning is a formality so he can remove you from the investigation."

I wished I was as confident as Regina about that possibility. "I'd better head home. I hope you get the store open soon."

"Me, too. Although having it closed gives me a chance to catch up on the admin." Regina walked me to the door and opened it. We said our goodbyes, and I headed out onto the quiet streets of Witch Haven.

The sharp wind that had been blasting through the village had died down, although I didn't like the look of the heavy bank of dark clouds overhead. I didn't think we were in for bad weather.

I got back to the bakery to find Uncle Albert snoozing in his easy chair in the lounge. I caught hold of his hand and gave it a squeeze.

He roused. "Sorry! I must have dozed off."

"No need to apologize. You stay there. Are you still not feeling good?"

Uncle Albert gave a long, loud yawn. "I'm just so tired."

"How about I perform a healing spell on you?"

"Don't go wasting your magic on me."

"I'm happy to waste my magic on you, anytime. Especially if it makes you better."

Uncle Albert mumbled something I didn't catch, but his eyes were already closing.

I kneeled beside him and cast a general healing spell, letting warm magic slide over him.

"That feels different." Uncle Albert yawned again. "Your magic is always changing. It's unusual for an adult witch to have such different styles of magic. You're a magical chameleon."

"Without the scales."

He chuckled. "Exactly. And your ability is unique. Different from any natural baker I've ever worked with."

"Does it really feel so different?" I was using a mix of warlock and werewolf magic, so it would feel odd.

"You must be one of the rare ones."

"I wouldn't be so sure about that," I said.

"You shouldn't be down on yourself. You have wonderful abilities, and you always make people happy with your food. That's what the Brimstone bakers are known for. You bring happiness and joy parceled in delicious sweet packages."

I repressed a sigh. I had brought little joy to Englebert, who was most likely still tucked up in bed recovering from my magic draining kiss. And Devlin always scowled whenever he got near me. Some people were immune to my attempts to bring joy.

"Is something on your mind?" Uncle Albert had opened his eyes and was studying my expression.

"No! Everything is great. It's a nice idea that I help people with my baking magic."

"It's more than an idea. It's what you do."

I lowered my gaze. I didn't want to spend my life draining others just so I could function, but what option did I have?

Uncle Albert was soon fast asleep and softly snoring, his breathing even and a healthy flush to his cheeks.

I left him sleeping, gathered up a huge box of food and drink, and headed out again. I never visited my farmhouse until the stores were shut and most people were at home, so I minimized the risk of anyone seeing me.

As I hurried along, I kept an eye out for any neighbors, but the nip in the air and the strong breeze meant the streets were quiet. It only took fifteen minutes before I was in the right place.

After another look around, I lowered the magic barrier and stepped through, then hurried to the door. There was a light on in the front parlor, and I could hear quiet voices as I headed along the dated hallway with its faded checked wallpaper and creaking wooden floorboards.

I tapped on the door and poked my head into the parlor. "It's just me. I brought you supplies."

Gloria Barkridge and Faye Calhoun looked up and smiled.

"Hello, dear." Gloria's round face lit up. "We're glad to see you. We're down to our last pack of cookies."

"I've brought plenty. Don't worry." I set the box on the table and looked around. "Where's Ridley?"

Faye patted her iron gray hair as she looked around the room. "Ah! We're not sure. He's gone missing."

Chapter 9

"He's missing! Are you certain? He could be in another part of the farmhouse?" I tried to keep my voice level, although my insides were doing a rapid tap dance of panic.

"Ridley left a while ago," Gloria said. "When was it, Faye?"

"He hasn't been here for some time. At least a day."

I gulped down my worry. It would be fine. Ridley had wandered off a couple of times before, but I'd always gotten him back.

I hurried to the long length of chain set in concrete in the floor. I didn't like chaining Ridley, but he needed careful handling. All of them did, which was why Faye and Gloria also had ankle chains.

My small harem of magic donors had murky pasts, and Ridley's was the murkiest. When he was a teenager, he'd killed a demon, and that demon's family and friends were still hunting him. He needed a safe place to hide, and I'd given it to him in exchange for a regular donation of his magic.

Ridley was powerful, so he'd been a welcome addition to my small group, although his magic made my cakes taste of lemon, so he wasn't an ideal subject, but needs must.

I studied the length of chain, frowning at the bent links. "Did you help him get out?"

"No, dear. And I can't understand why he'd want to leave," Gloria said. "You're so good to us."

"Thanks." I held the chain in my hand. I made their lives as comfortable as possible, and this was a good deal for all of us. They got a free place to stay, room and board, plus they stayed hidden from their pasts. Ridley never had to worry about facing off with an angry demon's family. And as for Gloria and Faye, they were happy to do a deal with me to make sure they stayed safe.

I paced to the window and peered outside. Where was Ridley?

"It's too dark to see out there," Gloria said. "And the wind has picked up again. Come sit with us and tell us about your day. I enjoy hearing about all your adventures in the village."

"I'll just check Ridley isn't upstairs or in any other room. Maybe he fell asleep." I headed into the large kitchen, but there was no sign of Ridley. There was another parlor, which was also empty.

I dashed up the stairs and searched each of their bedrooms. Gloria and Faye's rooms were neat and tidy, whereas Ridley's room looked like a teenage boy had held a frat party. But all his clothing was there, and everything in his bathroom, which suggested he hadn't run off with no plans to return.

I needed Ridley back. One condition of being in my harem was that everyone remained silent about our agreement. I didn't want anyone getting the wrong impression about me.

It was illegal to drain magic users of their power, but we were helping each other, and I wasn't holding any of them against their will. Some people might not see it that way, though.

I hurried down the stairs and into the front parlor. "Gloria, think back to when Ridley left. What happened?"

"I was knitting a scarf," Gloria said. "Would you like one, dear? You'd look nice in a red scarf. It would look striking with your dark hair."

"Thanks. That would be great. But think about Ridley. Tell me everything you can remember."

"He disappeared yesterday evening," Faye said. "We'd had lunch together, and he was acting strangely. He kept tugging his chain and saying he needed to get outside."

"And he seemed confused and said he needed to see his daughter because it was her birthday. It's the first time I've heard of a daughter," Faye said.

"Me too," Gloria said. "He's never been married, and I'm sure he doesn't have children."

I nodded. I was always careful to select members of my harem who didn't have big, influential families. Admittedly, I'd taken a step off the path with Englebert, but he was an exception, and I hadn't been able to resist his power.

"He definitely said he needed to visit his daughter?" I said.

"Ridley wasn't making any sense." Gloria bit her lip and focused on her knitting. "Although we were worried about him after you last drained him."

"Why? I didn't do anything different."

Gloria and Faye exchanged a glance.

"What? Did I do something wrong?"

"No, you're always good to us." Gloria tugged at her wool. "But the last few times you've visited, we've both felt the effects."

"I took too much magic? You should have said, and I'd have stopped."

"We... um... well, we did," Faye said. "And I'm not complaining, but I was in bed for two days after you drained me. You didn't want to stop. Do you remember I had to smack your arm to make you let go?"

"I didn't realize you were so unwell afterward." I dropped down beside Faye. "I'm so sorry."

She patted my cheek. "As you can see, I'm back to full strength. Ready for another drain."

"The last time I visited, I only drained Ridley," I said. "Did he start behaving strangely after my visit?"

"His odd behavior has nothing to do with you," Gloria said. "He's always been a strange one."

"Anyone who can kill a demon will have something a little warped about them," Faye said.

"Was he weak after I took his magic?"

Gloria nodded. "He seemed more confused than normal and was talking about his past. Ridley kept saying how sorry he was and that he needed to make amends."

"You don't think he meant the demon he killed, do you? He wouldn't go looking for the demon's family because he wanted to say sorry, would he?"

"Only if he wanted to wear his insides on his outsides," Faye said. "He's not that daft."

"Is he unhappy here?" I bit my lip. I didn't want to let Ridley go, but I'd never hold him against his will.

"No, he's fine."

"And you? If either of you is unhappy, talk to me." My gaze slipped to the chains around their ankles. They were necessary. My little harem had its issues, and those chains kept things under control when I wasn't around. They weren't prisoners.

Gloria and Faye exchanged another glance.

Worry swirled through me. I had to make sure my magic harem was happy, or everything would fall apart, and new recruits were hard to find.

"Let's go back to the evening Ridley escaped," I said. "He said he needed to make amends. Do you know what he was talking about?"

"Not a clue," Faye said.

"How did he break his chain?"

Gloria shrugged. "He's strong. When Ridley sets his mind to something, he doesn't give up. And he took one of my metal knitting needles. He bent it out of shape."

"He's been tinkering with that chain for a while," Faye said.

"Did he say where he was going?"

"He said he needed spell ingredients to fix his problem."

My breath stuttered out of me. "Spell ingredients? What time did he leave?"

"Ridley waited until it was dark, but he got loose from his chain before that. Once he was free, he seemed anxious, like he was waiting for something."

"I expect he was worried about leaving our paradise," Gloria said brightly.

"It's been a long time since Ridley has been anywhere," Faye said. "Perhaps he wanted an adventure."

"Did he mention wanting to go to Atherton's magic store to get his supplies?" My heart was vaulting in my chest. Ridley couldn't be involved with what happened to Jinti, could he?

"He didn't tell us where he was going," Faye said. "And he suddenly left. He didn't even say goodbye. He needs better manners."

"Ridley is young. We can teach him. And it's quiet without him here," Gloria said. "Will you bring him back, Luna?"

"Of course. I just need to figure out where he went."

"If you don't find him, can his replacement be female?" Faye said. "We're much tidier. I took a peek inside Ridley's room last week and almost fainted."

"I don't know about that," Gloria said. "It can get catty if it's just women. You need a man to calm things down."

"Speak for yourself," Faye said. "I'm always calm."

"Concentrate on Ridley leaving for now. I need to do everything I can to find him," I said. "He definitely didn't say where he was getting his supplies?"

They both shook their heads.

"Did he mention Jinti Calrook? She was the village healer."

"No, he said nothing about her. Why?" Gloria said. "What's she got to do with Ridley leaving?"

"Hopefully, nothing. But Jinti is dead," I said. "The Magic Council thinks someone murdered her in the magic store."

They inhaled sharply.

"And you kept this from us!" Gloria tapped the back of my hand. "We miss all the fun things."

"You don't think Ridley did it, do you?" Faye said. "He's always been odd, but a witch killer?"

"He killed that demon when he was a teenager," Gloria said. "Maybe he's moved on to witches." She cast a fearful glance at the door.

"Ridley would never hurt either of you." I was doing my best to sound calm, but I was freaking out. What if I'd damaged Ridley by taking too much magic? He got desperate and went hunting for supplies. When he was searching, he'd found Jinti in the magic store and they'd fought.

Devlin hadn't mentioned a struggle, and neither had Regina, but if there'd been a fight, it would have been obvious.

"Would you like some of my magic?" Gloria said. "You've suddenly gone pale."

"No, I'm good for now, thanks. I'd better go. I need to find Ridley and bring him back."

"Tell him we expect an apology," Faye called as I headed out the front door. "He can't just leave like that."

I closed the door, made my way through the magic barrier, and walked into Bram.

Chapter 10

He grinned as I staggered back.

"What are you doing out here?" I glanced behind me to make sure he couldn't see the farmhouse, but the magic barrier concealed everything.

Bram grinned and shook his head. "I'm more interested in what you're up to. And you don't think I forgot our deal, do you? I play along and be your guy, and you double the payment. And I plan to make good on that. Although getting a few more of those kisses would also be fun."

"No more kisses for you. That was just for show."

His grin faded. "I hope you haven't changed your mind. A deal's a deal."

I glanced over my shoulder again. "I haven't."

"I'm not so sure about that. I was stopping by the bakery, when I saw you sneaking out. Figured you were making a run for it."

"I wasn't sneaking anywhere." Bram's unexpected appearance flustered me, and I needed a few seconds to get my brain into gear.

"You were being careful when you left, though. Then you disappeared. I was just about to give up looking for you, but here you are." His gaze moved around as if trying to see through the barrier. "What are you hiding out here?"

I tried to tug Bram away, but he didn't move. "I thought someone was following me, so I hid. I didn't know it was you. I'd have stopped if I'd known."

"Yeah, so you say." He kept looking around. "So what gives? Why are you out here?"

"I came for a walk. It's been a busy day at the bakery, and I had a stressful visit from the Magic Council to deal with. I needed some quiet. Shall we..." I pointed away from the farmhouse.

Bram still didn't move. "What does the Magic Council want with you? Did you tell them about me?"

"No. Why would they be interested in you?" Oooh! That was an interesting idea. Could I get Devlin to arrest Bram? That would get rid of one big problem.

Bram shrugged. "I hate authority figures. And those guys give me the creeps."

"They're investigating a murder."

"Huh! That you're involved in?"

"No! I'm not involved. And I have to make sure the Magic Council knows that."

"Are you concealing evidence out here? I know you're up to something. What secrets are you hiding?" He rubbed his hands together. "You can cut me in on the deal. Did you kill this person for money?"

"No! And I'm hiding nothing. As you can see, it's just trees and pasture. This is a nice, quiet place to walk and clear my head after a busy day."

Bram shook his head. "You'll have to do better than that. I'm good at sniffing out liars, and I can sense lies pouring out of that pretty mouth of yours."

I tilted my head. Maybe my feminine wiles would work on Bram, and I could entice him away from the farmhouse with a hip wiggle and a wink. "I hate all this sneaking around and lying."

"I've not been lying. I've been straight up with you about what I want."

"You haven't been entirely honest. You spent days stalking me, and I had to chase you down with a werewolf to get you to talk."

"The job called for it."

I attempted to flutter my lashes, but felt like I was squinting. "So... How about we get out of here?"

His forehead furrowed. "Why?"

"This situation doesn't have to be uncomfortable."

Bram scratched the back of his neck. "I can't make this comfortable for you. You owe a lot of money. And I can't cancel your debt if that's what all the pouting is for. I don't have that kind of clout."

"No, but we could go somewhere and talk. Just the two of us." Even though my flirting had failed to get the desired result, I was still desperate to get Bram away from the farmhouse.

"You mean, like a date?"

"Um... sure. You're a handsome guy, and I imagine you're going places."

"Straight to prison if Sylvester learns I've been messing around with a client."

"It's better than fighting."

"I'd like to see you best me in a fight, witch. I know where you get your power. It's all borrowed and drains quickly." He smirked at me. "You should get that looked at."

"And you should learn some manners." I was done with being sweet. I blasted him with a spell, punching it into his chest and sending him flying.

Bram grunted as he hit the dirt. He rolled over and back onto his feet. "I thought you wanted to be nice to me?"

"You shouldn't have chased after me. No one likes a creeper."

He brushed dirt off the back of his jeans. "I'm only doing my job. The boss is worried you won't pay up."

"I will. But you need to leave." I flickered magic on my fingertips.

"I don't think I will. You're up to something out here on your own, and I plan to find out what that is. Maybe you'll end up owing me even more when I get to the bottom of your secret."

I spread my hands, the borrowed magic firing through me. A lick of flames shot out of the ground and circled Bram.

He yelped and cast his own magic, dousing the flames.

My throat burned with a power I had little control over. It felt unstable, like the magic wanted to destroy everything it touched. Maybe this was werewolf anger coming through, but I hadn't taken much from Cole, just a taste of his power.

The wind slammed into me, blinding me for a second with my hair.

Bram glared at me, his hands raised as he smashed a jagged arc of magic at me.

I threw up my arms, blocking the spell with a raging power that felt like it would break free any second.

Bram ran at me, and I lifted my hand. The power inside me faded as I thrust out a knockback spell. Well, it was supposed to be a knockback spell, but a ball of fire exploded from my palm and skimmed Bram's head, sending him sprawling to the dirt.

I backed away as Bram lunged at me again. I tried another spell, but it flickered and died.

Bram's hand wrapped around my throat, and I squeaked. I was out of magic juice and couldn't defend myself.

"You're like all the clients, always trying to get out of your debts. I bet you never intended to repay Sylvester." Bram snarled in my face. "And as for our little deal, I should have known better than to go along with your scheme."

"I will repay the money." I scratched his hands with my nails. "I need more time."

"That ain't my problem. The boss wants his money, and since you've messed with our plan, I deserve a little sweetener." He smacked his lips against mine.

The dash of werewolf magic I'd borrowed from Cole burst to life. I growled, and my muscles tensed as I slammed my foot between Bram's legs.

Bram roared as he dropped me and stumbled back, clutching his groin.

I bared my teeth at him as a hot, primal power fired through me. Where had this been all my life?

Bram's eyes widened, and he backed away. "You need to be careful, or you'll find your magic borrowing secret exposed. What will your friends think of you then, when they find out you're a magic thief?" He gently prodded at his groin and winced.

I threw myself at Bram and rammed him into the dirt. I rolled him onto his front so he was face down and grabbed his hair, yanking his head back as I straddled him. "You're telling no one. This is my business. Keep out of it."

Bram writhed beneath me, but I was operating on werewolf juice, so he was going nowhere. "What are you going to do if I don't?"

I snarled, my mouth opening as I lowered my teeth to his throat.

Bram froze.

The shock on his face stopped me, and I checked myself at the last second. I wasn't a killer. And as angry as I was, I wouldn't take this man's life.

I dropped his head and stepped away, the werewolf magic still fizzling through my veins, but quieter now.

Bram must have glugged down idiot juice, because he lunged at me. I flew off my feet and crashed through the magic barrier, taking him with me.

I landed on the ground with a gasp as the air flew out of my lungs.

Bram's head whipped up. "Where did this farmhouse come from?"

I squeezed my eyes shut for a second as I scrambled away. "This has nothing to do with you."

Bram gave me a sharp grin as he stood and stared at the farmhouse. "This is another one of your secrets. Let's see what you're hiding." He raced to the farmhouse and through the front door before I could stop him. But I was close on his heels, gasping out a breath as I found him in the front parlor.

Gloria and Faye stared at him, surprise on their faces.

"Is this a new addition to the family?" Gloria said.

"What have you been doing with him?" Faye said. "You're both covered in mud."

"The family?" Bram said. "You're related?"

Gloria smiled. "In a way. We share a lot. Luna looks after us, and she can look after you, too."

"Does she now?" His gaze cut my way, and that evil grin broadened.

"No more talking. You don't want this man to get the wrong idea about us." I stood in front of Bram, so he couldn't get any closer to Faye and Gloria.

"If he's joining us, he needs to know all about us." Faye peered around me and waved at him.

"Why are there chains around your ankles?" Bram said.

Faye jangled her chain. "Luna thinks it's for the best. She's had a few former family members leave when she wasn't expecting it. I don't mind the chain. It chafed a bit to begin with, but I put padding inside so it's comfortable now. And it's long enough so I can get all around the house. I do trip up on it sometimes, though."

"Why have you got these old biddies chained up?" Bram said. "What do you do with them?"

"We help Luna," Gloria said. "We make sure she has everything she needs. You must know the arrangement, or you wouldn't be here."

"Let's not talk about our arrangement. It's time to go." I grabbed at Bram, but he skipped out of my way.

"I'm not done. I'm still figuring out what's going on." He pointed to the empty chain that belonged to Ridley. "Who belonged in that chain?"

"Ridley. Aren't you his replacement?" Gloria said. "We need a strapping man around the house."

Bram's eyes gleamed as his gaze flicked my way. "You're taking their magic, aren't you? You greedy girl. What we gave you wasn't enough, so you took more. You're an addict."

"You're wrong. Let's just go. I'll explain everything."

"I'm right. What have these old biddies ever done to you? You can't hold them prisoner."

"They're not prisoners. They're here of their own free will."

He shook his head. "Those chains around their ankles say otherwise."

"Luna's right. We're happy here," Faye said. "We have a safe place. And other than those few days when she went missing, and we worried she was dead and we'd starve, we're always looked after."

"That's a story I need to hear," Bram said. "Where'd you go?"

"No, you don't."

"Welcome to the harem," Gloria said. "I'll knit you a lovely sweater."

Bram shook his head, grinning as I tugged him out of the farmhouse and slammed the door. "You're something else. You play little miss innocent and go begging to the boss to have magic on account, and all this time, you've got those old girls shackled so you can take what you need. Just how bad is your problem?"

"Gloria and Faye needed my help, and I needed some magic. We came to a deal."

"It's a lousy deal on their side," he said.

"It works for us all."

"It can't work that well, since you got into debt with us."

"I had some trouble and needed a magic boost when I came back from—" I bit my tongue. I wasn't sharing my abduction secret with this jerk.

He chuckled. "We do our background checks. I know you got taken by some crazy resurrected witch. Did she remove your power?"

"No. My magic is just different."

"Your problem is written all over your face. You're desperate for magic because you malfunction. If you think a couple of old biddies will keep you right, you need to rethink your strategy."

"My magic works fine." I staggered back as a blast of wind slammed into me and tugged my jacket around me. "Bram, you need to keep quiet about this."

He wobbled his head from side to side. "Maybe I will, maybe I won't. What's in it for me?"

"Please, I don't want other people to know about this place. Gloria and Faye need a safe place to stay. There are people who want to hurt them. I have to make sure that doesn't happen. That's why I concealed the farmhouse."

"You sound like a proper do-gooder, helping those in need." Bram smirked. "The way I see it, you're the one who's in real need, and this is for your benefit. Maybe those old girls needed help, but you're taking advantage."

"Are you going to tell Sylvester or the Magic Council?" My heart sank. I'd kept my farmhouse secret for a long time, and it was about to be pulled down around my ears.

Bram was quiet for a few seconds as he rocked back on his heels. "Nah, I can stay quiet."

I narrowed my eyes. "In return for what?"

"In return for you owing me."

"I can't give you more money. I've already agreed to double the payment."

"I don't want more money, but I often have things that need moving about or loose ends to tie up. I'm sure you could handle that for me."

"So long as it's nothing illegal."

He chuckled. "It's always illegal."

The wind howled around us as I contemplated the terms. There was nothing I could do but accept his offer.

"See you around, Luna." Bram leaned down for a kiss, but I shoved him away.

"Don't push your luck."

He laughed as he strode into the night.

I sank to the ground and rested my chin on my knees. The wind continued to kick through the trees like a hyperactive mule, and the branches groaned in protest.

The secret about my farmhouse was out, and I didn't trust Bram to keep his mouth shut for long. But I couldn't worry about that now. I still had to find Ridley.

I sat cross-legged, closed my eyes, and cast a locator spell.

Fix one problem at a time. Locate Ridley, deal with Devlin and his suspicions about me being Jinti's killer, and figure out a way to deal with Bram once and for all.

That was quite a to-do list.

Chapter 11

My locator spell was surprisingly successful, and I was soon on my way to the Witch Haven library to find Ridley.

I'd always loved this imposing gothic building with its tall spires and small, dark leaded windows, which meant the place always burned bright with electric light. It reminded me of something out of a Victorian novel. The bricks were a dark red, looking almost black in the gloom of the evening as I approached.

I tiptoed up the steps to the main door, which was locked. No surprise, given the place had been shut for two hours. I peered inside, hoping to see Ridley. There was no sign of him, but my locator spell showed this was where he was hiding.

Why he'd escaped to visit the library, I wasn't sure. Ridley wasn't much of a reader.

Although this place was stunningly beautiful, visitors needed to be on their guard, thanks to the library protector, a half-dragon, half-warlock, called Nazan Grizig. He was large, super intense, and terrifying if you got on his wrong side by misfiling books or returning them late. And Nazan tended to roast people who broke into his library. I was fortunate not to find Ridley thrown off the roof with his hair on fire for sneaking in.

I walked around the side of the building, peering in windows, trying to locate Ridley. I was worried about him and didn't want him to be unhappy in the farmhouse. But he must have escaped for a good reason.

If any of my magic harem wanted to leave, they could. They just needed to wait for me to find a replacement before I let them go and wiped their memories.

My thoughts went to Cole as I hunted for a way in. He'd be the perfect replacement for Ridley. Cole was magically robust, not to mention easy on the eyes. I wouldn't mind visiting the farmhouse more often if he was there to keep me company. We could share magic with a few sizzling kisses.

I shouldn't get ahead of myself. I knew little about Cole, other than how powerful he was. It wouldn't be easy to convince him to give up his freedom for a life helping me.

Checking around to make sure no-one was watching, I examined a small window that looked in on the basement. It wasn't locked, but it was narrow and the hinges stiff when I pulled it open. I'd only just fit through it, but once inside, I'd be able to unlock a door.

I squeezed through the narrow window, dropping on the floor in an inelegant heap and groaning.

Once I'd regained my dignity and determined no one had seen my spectacular entrance, I got up and looked around.

There were shelves on either side of the room full of sealed boxes, cleaning equipment, and a large generator standing in the shadows.

I headed out of the basement and found the stairs to the first floor. I crept open one door and peeked inside.

The only light in the room was from a green emergency sign by the exit doors. I risked casting a small light ball to help me find Ridley. There were four floors to investigate, so I could be here for some time.

I hurried along, peering down each row of books. I reached the end row and frowned. He wasn't here. I dashed back to the stairs and up to the next floor, completing the same exercise and still not finding Ridley.

Something flashed in front of my eyes. It was a quick moving shadow that left behind a scent of decaying roses. "Ridley? Is that you?" I'd never noticed him smelling of flowers before.

There was a quiet female giggle and a cold draft passed over my face, accompanied by the old rose scent again.

"You're not Ridley."

Everyone knew the library was haunted. The ghosts usually left visitors alone during the daytime, but perhaps they got lonely at night.

I continued my search. Giggling ghosts I could handle. I just didn't want to stumble across an angry half-dragon.

I crept up to the next floor, opened the door, and looked inside. Halfway along the book stacks, I spotted a light. Ridley must be in here.

Raising my light ball, I hurried along and turned the corner. There was nothing there, and the light was gone.

"Ridley," I whispered. "It's Luna. I've come to take you home. Gloria and Faye are worried about you. So am I."

There was no reply.

I crept back to the first book stack and started a methodical search of each one. Was Ridley hiding from me? Had he decided to leave but was scared I wouldn't let him go?

A light flickered three rows ahead of me. I dashed toward it and turned the corner. The light was just disappearing at the end of the row, so I raced after it.

"Ridley! You have nothing to worry about. I'm not angry. I understand if you need to leave. Please, talk to me, and we can sort something out."

The light kept moving.

Instead of chasing it, I dodged to the next row and ran as fast as I could, hoping to cut Ridley off before he turned the corner.

The light appeared in front of me, and I threw myself at it.

My hands met freezing air, and I landed on the red carpet with a grunt. I rolled onto my back and stared at the ceiling.

A pale face of a young girl appeared and looked down at me. "Boo!" She disappeared.

That was just what I needed. A library full of ghosts misleading me.

I completed my search of this level, getting more anxious by the minute that Nazan would show up and barbecue me.

There was only one floor left to investigate. Ridley had to be up there.

I hurried up the steps to the top floor of the library. I opened the door and let out a gasp of relief. There he was. Ridley sat at a table with a pile of books in front of him, his short, dark curly hair looking tangled as if he'd been running his fingers through it.

I hurried over. "Ridley, what are you doing?"

His dark gaze lifted to mine, and for a second, he appeared confused, then a smile spread across his broad, stubbled face. "I needed to study."

"You broke your chain and left the farmhouse without letting me know. I thought there was a problem. Gloria and Faye said you needed to see your daughter."

He waved a hand in the air. "Those two are always confused. Why would I say that? I don't have children."

I sat next to him. "Are you unhappy? Is there anything I can do to make life better for you? You know, you don't have to stay at the farmhouse. And I only keep you chained up for your own good."

He ducked his head. "I actually think it's for your benefit, but I understand why you do it. It can get intense when you take my magic."

"I'm so sorry. This is my fault. I'll try harder and make this right." I had to make sure my magic harem was happy. If they were miserable, I'd fail.

"No! It's not your fault. I sometimes forget myself and panic. I feel like I can't breathe when you drain me, and my survival instincts kick in."

"I never mean to frighten you. This arrangement has to suit both of us, or we can't go on."

Ridley turned to face me, determination in his eyes. "It does suit me. I'm grateful you took me in and kept those demons from finding me." He shuddered and rubbed his hands down his arms. "I'd be dead if you weren't watching out for me."

I looked around the silent library. "Aren't you worried you're exposed being in here on your own?"

"Nah. And I've only been gone an hour. Those demons can't find me that quickly."

"Ridley, you've been gone over a day. You left the farmhouse yesterday evening."

His mouth opened and closed several times. "I've been here all this time? I must have lost track."

"I found you with a locator spell. As soon as I realized you were gone, I came to get you. Why don't you come home? It's safer there, and the magic barrier will keep you hidden."

"Yeah, it does make me feel safe. Your magic is amazing. You're an angel."

I wasn't sure about that, but appreciated the compliment. "What about Nazan? Didn't he want you to leave when he closed?"

"The dragon guy?"

I nodded. "He protects the library."

"I've been staying out of his way. That guy gives me the creeps. His red eyes freak me out. They remind me of what I did, you know, to that demon.

He had red eyes, too. The light died in them after I killed him." Ridley's bottom jaw wobbled, and tears filled his eyes.

"Oh, Ridley. Let's get you home. I can make you soup, and we can listen to music if you like." I looked at the books he was reading. "What research are you doing?"

His cheeks flushed. "It's nothing. I'm just being dumb."

"I'm sure that's not true." I lifted a book off the pile. "Love Spells for the Lonely?"

Ridley chewed on his bottom lip. "I like Gloria and Faye, but I need company my age. You know, romantic company to get friendly with."

I pressed my hand against my mouth as I read through the titles. They were all to do with finding a partner and bringing love into your life. Ridley was lonely. I was the worst witch for not taking better care of his needs. Not that I would personally deal with those needs, not in that sense, but I should have done more to find him a companion.

"You can't find a girlfriend because I have you chained up at the farmhouse. I didn't think about that."

"I don't blame you. That house has been my haven, and I wouldn't change a thing. Well, I might not have killed a demon, but you found me when I needed you."

"But you're still lonely."

He shrugged. "Sometimes. It doesn't matter. Forget about this."

I couldn't. And I had to do something about it, but I wasn't sure how I'd fix Ridley up with his perfect woman if he couldn't leave the farmhouse. "We'll make things easier on you. And let me know if ever you need a break. I can even borrow books from the library and bring them to the farmhouse."

"Thanks. That's proper nice of you."

"Maybe we should start with fiction romance, so you can fine tune your dating skills."

He chuckled. "And show me what I'm missing out on? I'll stick to sci-fi thrillers."

I caught hold of his arm. "Before we go, have you seen Jinti Calrook while you've been out?"

Ridley shook his head. "I don't know many people around here. Obviously, I know you, and I've seen pictures of your uncle. And I know Gloria and Faye, but that's about it. Who's Jinti?"

"She was a witch who healed people with herbal remedies. She was elderly, with wild curls, and wore lots of layers of clothing. Does that sound familiar?" I studied his face to see if I could detect any lie. "Something bad happened to her, and I was concerned you might have seen something."

"I've not seen anyone other than a few people in the library, and I kept out of their way, so I didn't draw attention to myself. You taught me to do that."

"That's great. And you came straight here, or did you go to the magic store?"

"No, I didn't go to any stores. When I got here, it took me a while to figure out what I was doing. I've been... confused lately." Ridley scrubbed his forehead with his fingers.

"You left the farmhouse, walked to the library, and you've been here ever since?"

He nodded. "And I had no idea I'd been here so long. It doesn't feel like it. Although I'm really hungry. When we get back to the farmhouse, can I have something to eat?"

"Of course. Let's get you out of here." I didn't think Ridley killed Jinti. He seemed confused, not secretive. And he was looking for love, not hiding a murder.

A wave of guilt hit me. His confusion must be a side effect of all the magic I'd taken from him. I had to stop draining him so often. But I couldn't do that, not now Englebert was out of the picture. I needed more magic users. But with the Magic Council breathing down my neck, the last thing I could do was run a recruitment drive for magic users who needed a safe haven.

"Let's get these books back on the shelves and get out of here," I said.

"Of course. And Luna, I didn't mean to cause you trouble."

"You didn't. I'm just glad I found you in one piece." I scooped up his books and took a couple of minutes to find the right locations on the shelves before returning to his table.

As I rounded the book stack, my mouth dropped open. Ridley had taken off his shirt and was standing with his arms outstretched, revealing a toned torso with a spattering of dark hair.

I hurried over and grabbed his shirt off the table. "What are you doing?"

"Waiting for you to drain me. I figured you'd want some magic. You always take magic when you visit the farmhouse."

"Not every time." Or did I? Had I gotten too dependent on my little group and lost track of how often I drained them?

"Shall I take off my pants, too? We can try it naked again."

"No! Please, put on your clothes. The naked approach was a one-off, and we all agreed it was weird and uncomfortable."

"Not for me. And it worked." Ridley grinned. "It was kind of fun. Although I wasn't so keen on seeing Gloria's droopy bits. She's got a nice butt, though."

I grimaced. I'd been desperate when I'd suggested the naked strip and magic drain party. I'd needed a huge hit of magic, and lots of skin-on-skin contact worked best and was the quickest transfer method.

"I don't mind," Ridley said. "And if it's just the two of us, it won't be so weird. I've never had fantasies about having a foursome with a couple of old ladies. Not that Gloria and Faye aren't well-preserved, if you get me. They're just not my type."

"I get you. Put your shirt on. I'm fine for magic." I was drained after my fight with Bram, but there was no way I was using Ridley. "I recently got a boost off a new friend. He might even become a new friend to all of you if I can talk him into joining us."

"Another guy?" Ridley frowned.

"That's right."

"Are you sure you can't find me a hot female?"

I sighed. "I'll do my best."

"This new guy isn't old, is he?"

"No, although it's hard to tell with werewolves because they age slowly, but he doesn't seem that old."

"A werewolf!" Ridley whistled out a note. "That's a great source of power. You won't get super interested in the moon and go all hairy once a month, will you? That would not be cool."

"I haven't thought about that. I'm guessing no." Although I had almost bitten Bram when we'd fought. Maybe I would go faux werewolf if I took too much of Cole's power.

"I'd welcome someone else to the house. It'll be nice to have company. I love the old girls, but they repeat the same stories over and over. I've heard a dozen times about when Gloria won the Miss Peaches and Cream beauty pageant and was paraded all over her hometown while sitting on top of a giant peach pie. She tells it every time like it's the first time."

"I'll bring over more board games or maybe a deck of cards. That'll keep Gloria busy so she doesn't reminisce too much."

"That sounds good. How about—"

I slapped a finger over Ridley's lips as a low, rumbling growl echoed around the book stacks. "Nazan's here! We have to go."

Chapter 12

I grabbed Ridley's hand, and we raced to the door. I eased it open and looked down the stairs. I didn't know which direction that growl had come from, but it sounded angry, and the air was growing warm, suggesting someone with dragon blood was approaching.

I gestured Ridley to follow me and pressed my finger to my lips to make sure he didn't talk, then hurried down the stairs, peering through each door to see if I could spot Nazan.

"Keep up," I whispered. "We just need to get to the front door."

We got to the first floor, and I peeked through the glass window at the library stacks. I squeaked and scuttled away. Nazan stood with his back to me, his hands on his hips as his head swiveled from side to side.

I yanked my head back but not fast enough. "I think he saw me. Run!"

"Which way?" Ridley stared at the main door. "Isn't that the exit?"

"We have to get to the basement." My gaze ran over Ridley. He wasn't a small guy, and I had no clue if he'd get through the window, but it was the only escape option.

We raced to the basement, and I jammed a broom handle against the door, hoping it might slow down Nazan. He had dragon fire and dragon strength, so it was like using a cocktail stick against a skilled swordswoman.

I yanked open the window as wide as it would go. "Do you reckon you can get through?"

Ridley eyed the window. "You'll need to give me a shove. I don't want to get wedged."

"Jump. I'll help you."

Ridley launched himself at the window, grabbed the edge, and pulled himself up. He'd gotten halfway through when his pants caught on the latch.

I grabbed a chair, stood on it, unhooked his pants, and then shoved my hands against his butt, giving him a hearty push.

Ridley didn't move. "Push harder! I'm almost through."

I wedged my shoulder against his butt and leaned my weight against him as he wriggled and squirmed.

"Almost there," he grunted. "One more shove should do it."

"Find something to grab. You pull, and I'll push." I gave him another shove with my shoulder.

"Easy there, or I'll bruise."

I froze as the basement door handle rattled. "You'll have to put up with a few bruises. Move that peach butt!"

Ridley squirmed and bucked, getting out another inch. He needed an incentive. Or we'd both become dragon toast.

"Sorry, Ridley. This is for your own good." I sank my teeth into his right butt cheek.

He yelped and squirmed away just as the basement door opened a couple of inches.

I threw myself through the window, grabbed Ridley's outstretched hand, and propelled myself out of the basement.

Ridley stood in front of me, a hand on his butt cheek and a frown on his face. "You bit me!"

"It made you move, didn't it? Come on. We have a half-dragon after us. If you think my bite was bad, wait until Nazan gets hold of you." I grabbed his arm, and we raced around the building and onto the street.

My breath rasped out of me by the time we'd made it to the front of the library. I looked over my shoulder and heaved out a sigh. There was no half-dragon on our tail.

"You know, I didn't mind being bitten. It was a shock but a hot shock." Ridley winked at me.

I groaned and shook my head. "Desperate times, Ridley, desperate times." I turned to the front of the library, and my breath stuck in my throat. Nazan stood there, his red eyes glowing as he glared at me. "Let's get out of here."

"Hey, what are you doing?"

I tensed as I heard Indigo's voice. I turned to see Indigo, Odessa, and Storm hurrying toward me.

"Oh! Hey! I was just out for a walk." I glanced at Ridley, who was looking at my friends with interest. It was only then that I realized he was still shirtless, and I was holding his shirt. This conversation was about to get awkward.

"You didn't show up for our dinner date," Indigo said.

"Dinner date?" What had I forgotten?

"And I went to hang out with your uncle, but he wasn't expecting me," Storm said. "I left Fire Fang with him to keep him company. What's up?" Her gaze shifted to Ridley, and her eyes narrowed.

"Nothing. I...just got distracted." I'd spaced on the double date Indigo had forced on me. I'd been too busy keeping track of everything else.

"By what?" Indigo's eyes cut to Ridley. "Or should I say by whom?"

"Why is there a half-naked man standing beside you?" Odessa said. "And where's Bram? Have you already gotten bored with him?"

I looked up at Ridley, a pleading expression in my eyes, hoping he'd understand he needed to keep his mouth shut. "I'm taking my time making a decision on who to date."

"So you're dating this guy, too?" Storm said.

I caught hold of Ridley's arm and gave it a tight squeeze. "This is Ridley. We've been friends for a while."

"Okay." Indigo stretched out the word as her gaze kept flickering over Ridley. "Why is today the first time we're hearing about all these new men?"

"There's not lots of them. Only a few," I said. "And I wanted to keep things simple. I knew you'd all interrogate me about my dates."

"Uh huh." Indigo sounded less than convinced by my explanation. "You're not exclusive with Bram?"

"No. I don't know him that well."

"I'm glad. The guy gave me the creeps," Indigo said. "He had a shifty look about him. I reckon he's hiding something. Make sure you find out what that is before you go to the next level."

Storm's gaze ran over Ridley. "Don't I know you from somewhere?"

I shook my head before he could answer. "Ridley's not from around here. He's just visiting."

"How come you know him if he's not local?" Indigo said.

"Oh, you know, just from around. People come to the bakery, and we get chatting. One day, Ridley asked me out, and I said yes."

"You agreed to go on a double date with Bram, knowing you were seeing Ridley tonight?" Indigo said.

The hole I was digging myself kept getting bigger. "You didn't give me much chance to get out of that date. And I got my times muddled. Ridley showed up unexpectedly, so we took a walk. I'd have come and found you once we were done."

"It's too late for that," Indigo said. "Olympus got takeout. There's some left if you want it. Although I'm not sure you deserve it after standing us up."

"No, you're good." I was too tense to eat after having just escaped near death by half-dragon roasting.

"I could eat," Ridley said. "I haven't had a decent meal in ages."

"You can join us," Indigo said. "Although it depends on who Luna's supposed to be on a date with. What if Bram shows up and finds her with another guy?"

"It would be fun to watch Luna get out of that," Storm said.

"Bram won't be showing up." I kept a tight hold on Ridley.

"I'm more interested in finding out why you have no shirt on," Odessa said to Ridley. "Although the view is lovely, the wind is howling. You must be cold."

"Ridley, put your shirt on," I whispered.

He obliged but left the buttons undone, so his abs were on display.

I gave him a hand to do up his shirt. This was a mess. My friends didn't believe a word I'd just told them. And I never dated several guys at once. It was exhausting. I'd always been a one guy at a time witch.

"We'd better go," I said. "I'm walking Ridley home."

"Home? I thought you said he didn't live around here," Indigo said.

"Oh! I mean, of course he doesn't."

"Where are you walking to?" Indigo pursed her lips. "You need to explain what's going on."

"There's nothing to explain. Ridley, we need to go."

He hesitated. "We should tell them. It's not such a big deal if you trust them."

"Tell us what?" Storm said. "And I'm sure I know you. I've seen your face before. It'll come to me. I'm great with faces."

I didn't like the probing look in Storm's eyes. As a private investigator, she'd probably heard about Ridley after he'd killed that demon. It was also possible she knew the demons who were looking for him.

I had to get her off his scent and fast. "Let's go for a drink. The inn's just down the road. My treat, since I was late getting to dinner."

"Are you sure you don't need to walk Ridley home to wherever it is he actually lives?" Suspicion dripped off Indigo's words.

"We've got time. And it's not that late. Come along, everyone." I hurried away with Ridley clamped tightly beside me. "Stay quiet. Let me do the talking."

"Your friends seem nice," he whispered. "Do they know about the farmhouse?"

"No. And they're great, but our situation is complicated. They might not understand."

"You haven't told your friends about us?"

"There is no us. I mean, there is an us. Me, you, Gloria, and Faye, but not in that way."

"I don't mind if you want there to be an exclusive us," Ridley said.

"Please, stay quiet. And act like you like me."

"I do like you, so that won't be difficult." He grinned at me. "This could solve my problem. You could drain me of magic, and then we could—"

"Shush. My friends can't know about that, got it? And no sexy times in exchange for magic. We're friends."

"Got it. I'm your pretend, non-exclusive boyfriend, you don't have me hidden in a farmhouse, and you don't take my magic. And Gloria and Faye don't exist."

I looked over my shoulder to see my friends a short distance behind us. "That's it. Just be nice, keep the details vague, and everything will be fine."

We headed to the inn run by Cornelia Norwood. It was a squat, white building with huge fireplaces and the smell of fermented apples lingering in the air.

I went to the bar with Ridley to get drinks and gestured to a spare table. Indigo, Odessa, and Storm sat around it.

I took the drinks to the table with Ridley, along with a huge bag of chips for him, and we settled in our seats.

"How long have you been seeing each other?" Indigo addressed the question to Ridley.

He smiled broadly. "Ages. Years."

"Years? It's the first time we've seen you together," Indigo said.

"It's not years. He's kidding. This is new," I said. "Isn't that right, Ridley?"

"Oh, yeah. It's a new relationship." He nodded. "And we're not exclusive. We're just getting to know each other. Right?"

"Yes, that's right." I patted his knee, fanning my face with a beer mat.

"He's cute," Odessa said. "You need a nice man in your life. Someone to take care of you. After everything you've been through, you need stability."

"What's Luna been through?" Ridley asked.

"We don't need to talk about that," I said.

"Surely, you told your non-exclusive squeeze what happened?" Storm said. "He must have missed you while you were gone."

"Ridley doesn't need to know the details."

"Oh! Is this about you disappearing?" Ridley said. "Yeah, you had us all worried."

"Who are you talking about?" Indigo said.

"Oh, you know, I meant me... I was worried about her. Luna was gone for almost a week."

"That doesn't matter now. I'm back, and I have more important things to worry about."

"Like what?" Storm raised an eyebrow.

"Like the Magic Council. They're still on my back about Jinti's murder. Devlin Goody seems determined to bring me down." I sipped my cider. "I visited the magic store and spoke to Regina this morning."

"What did she tell you?" Storm's gaze slid away from Ridley.

"I found out a few interesting things about Jinti and Atherton. They didn't get along. Jinti thought Atherton murdered Bella."

Storm nodded. "When she went missing, there were rumors flying around that Atherton was involved."

"Was there evidence to suggest he killed her? I thought she walked out on him," Odessa said.

"She did," Storm said. "I kept an eye on the investigation. There was no evidence to suggest Atherton did anything to Bella. Although I'm not surprised she left him. I don't trust that guy."

"You don't trust anyone," Indigo said.

"If you don't trust, you never get disappointed."

"What's not to like about Atherton?" Odessa said. "He's always friendly to me."

"He's always friendly to a pretty face," Storm said.

"You have a pretty face, too. You just need to scowl less," Odessa said.

I squeaked and almost leaped out of my seat when Ridley pressed a kiss to my neck. "What are you doing?"

"Being nice," he said.

"Not in front of my friends. This isn't the right place."

His smile faded. "Sorry, I thought you'd like it. And you smell good."

"Let Ridley kiss you if he wants to." Odessa grinned at him. "You don't have a local accent. Where are you originally from?"

"He's from all around," I said. "Getting back to the murder, I need to find other suspects for Devlin to focus on, so he isn't poking around in my private business."

"Why should that matter if you have nothing to hide?" Indigo looked pointedly at Ridley.

I ignored her question. "Atherton is an obvious suspect because Jinti was killed in his store. Maybe they had an argument about Bella and things got out of hand."

"And I know Atherton fired Jinti," Storm said. "They could have argued about that."

I nodded. "Regina told me that Jinti turned up late and did a bad job a few times, so he let her go. Atherton only hired her because he felt guilty about Bella."

"Probably because he killed her," Storm said.

"Whatever the reason, there was bad blood between them," I said.

"What about Regina as a suspect?" Storm said. "She's worked in that store for years. Maybe she had a run-in with Jinti."

"I wondered about that, but I got no sense she had a problem with Jinti. She seemed intimidated by her, but I don't know many people who weren't. Jinti could be abrasive."

"She didn't bother me," Storm said.

"No one bothers you," Odessa said.

Storm lifted a shoulder. "So you have Atherton and maybe Regina as suspects?"

"Regina's at the bottom of this short list. Although she doesn't have much of an alibi. She closed the store after the magic swap and went home alone."

"No one can vouch for her?" Indigo said.

"You need to keep an eye on that one. She's too nice to be true," Storm said.

Odessa swatted the back of Storm's hand. "People can be nice and not have an ulterior motive. I'm always lovely to people."

"Yeah, but you usually have an ulterior motive," Storm said. "You get information out of people or get them to do stuff for you by fluttering those lashes or feeding them pumpkin treats."

"That's not true." Odessa grinned at me. "But I always find a little sugar incentivizes people."

"That would work for me." Ridley tried to catch hold of my hand, but I tugged it away and shook my head.

"Is there anyone else you need to think about for Jinti's murder?" Storm said.

"When I visited the magic store that evening, Ulric was there. He talked to Jinti."

"The shaman?" Indigo said.

"Former dodgy cult leader turned shaman," Storm said.

"That's right. I'd forgotten he used to run a cult. What was it called?" I said.

"The True Magic League," Storm said. "He got women enthralled, then took their money, got them into bed, and trapped them in his cult worship. He stopped doing that a while back, though."

"It wasn't long after Bella went missing that he shut down the cult," Odessa said. "Although I think he'd been winding it down for a while. He disbanded the group and became a shaman, offering free guidance and magic to those in need."

"That's a huge turn around," Indigo said.

"It's another scam," Storm said. "He's got to be conning people who go to him for help."

Odessa shook her head. "No, I've seen him working. He's legit."

"I often get Earl's catnip from him. It's powerful stuff," I said.

"I had to stop Nugget using that catnip. He slept all day," Storm said.

"I have the same problem with Earl, even without the catnip." My cat familiar was adorable, but kind of useless.

"Ulric won't have had anything to do with this murder," Odessa said. "He's so chilled out."

"I didn't know you were friends with Ulric," I said.

Odessa focused on her drink. "Our paths cross from time to time. He's good to do business with."

Storm's grin was wicked as she looked around the table. "You must have heard about Ulric and Bella."

My eyes widened. "What about them?"

"They were having an affair. Right under Atherton's nose."

My jaw dropped. "How do you know this?"

"Through my sources. I hear all kinds of useless information when I'm on a job." She glanced at Ridley again. "Which is how I know you. Have you ever been in trouble with the Magic Council?"

He glanced at me, his hand in the bag of chips. "Nope. No charges were ever brought against me."

"And they won't be," I said. "Ridley is law-abiding. You won't find dirt on him."

Storm's eyes narrowed. "If you say so. Although I can find dirt on everyone."

"Tell us more about Bella and Ulric." I was keen to shift the focus from Ridley. "How long was the affair going on? Was it serious? Did Atherton find out?"

"They were seeing each other for months, so I guess it was serious. It would be a good reason for Atherton wanting Bella dead," Storm said. "He found his wife cheating, so got rid of her."

"And if Jinti knew the truth, she wouldn't have been able to leave it alone," I said. "What if she threw that in Atherton's face and he snapped? He killed Jinti because she goaded him about Bella being in love with another man."

"There was also a theory floating around that Bella was depressed because she couldn't choose between Atherton and Ulric," Storm said. "She didn't want to break up her marriage, but she loved Ulric."

"It sounds like you've found your number one suspect," Indigo said.

"Be careful around Atherton if you poke about in his business. He's a slippery customer. And he has influential friends," Storm said.

"Including connections with the Magic Council," Indigo said. "Olympus knows him, although he doesn't think much of him. He doesn't trust him."

"Shall I get more drinks?" Ridley said. "Although don't say anything too interesting while I'm gone. This conversation is better than Faye's telenovelas."

"Yes, thanks," I said.

Ridley patted his pockets. "Luna, could you... I didn't come prepared."

"Why doesn't your date have money?" Storm said.

"Um... He left his wallet at home." I shoved my purse at Ridley.

"You're being super strange," Indigo said, the second Ridley was out of earshot. "And I've never known you to date more than one guy at a time."

"You're turning into Bella," Odessa said. "Too many men and not enough time to enjoy them all. Look what happened to her!"

"There's no harm in playing the field." I took a long sip of my drink.

"I doubt Bella would agree," Storm said.

I had to put my many men problem on the back burner. Once I got Ridley safely back in the farmhouse tonight, I had a plan to clear my name. Tomorrow, I was tackling Atherton about Jinti, and I'd show Devlin Goody he was wrong about me and my muffins.

Chapter 13

The sun was rising over the horizon as I left the bakery the next morning. The fun at the inn last night hadn't lasted too long, and I'd snuck Ridley back to the farmhouse with no trouble. Gloria and Faye had been delighted to see him.

I crept out so as not to disturb Uncle Albert. He was still not up, so I guessed he wasn't feeling great again.

I hurried along the quiet streets, breathing in the chilly morning air. There was still a strong wind blowing, but it was less intense than yesterday. I carried a plate of buttery breakfast scones. They were my secret weapon, all part of my plan to speak to Atherton and see what I could find out about his involvement in Jinti's murder.

There were no trolls barring my way when I arrived at the magic store. I peered through the glass and tapped on it when I saw someone moving around in the back.

A moment later, Atherton appeared. He was in a dark red and green dressing gown, but that didn't stop him from opening the door. "What have I done to deserve such a delightful early morning visit from my favorite baker?"

I smiled at him. "I've gotten myself in a little trouble, and I was hoping you could help. I've got fresh breakfast scones if you haven't already eaten."

"How delicious. And we can't have you in trouble. Come in and tell me about it. I can never turn away a damsel in distress." Atherton opened the door wider, and I passed under his arm to get into the store. He shut the door, locked it, and then followed me to the counter.

I turned to find him standing too close for comfort. I pushed the plate of breakfast scones into his hand. "Shall we have these with tea or coffee?"

His smile widened. "These will be perfect with a strong mug of English breakfast tea. Come through to the kitchen." He led the way through the store and into a smart, glossy black kitchen. "Tell me about your problem. Let me see if I can work my magic and fix things for you."

"It's all rather embarrassing." Atherton seemed to enjoy playing my rescuer, so I played up to it.

He brewed the tea and set mugs, plates, cutlery and preserves on the table, gesturing for me to sit on one of the chairs. "An embarrassing problem? This gets more interesting. Does it involve a man?"

"In a way. I had a visit from Devlin Goody after Jinti died."

He shook his head. "That was such a terrible thing to happen. I still don't feel comfortable going into the store."

"I imagine you won't. Where was Jinti's body found?"

"Slumped on the counter." He glanced at me. "Is this visit about your food? Regina mentioned you'd spoken to her about the muffins you brought to the magic swap event."

"It is. I—"

"You have nothing to concern yourself about. I shared a muffin with Regina, and neither of us had any ill effects." He winked at me. "I'll put in a good word for you with the Magic Council. They leap before they look. I hope Devlin wasn't a nuisance."

"I'd appreciate that, but I have a feeling he'll still be interested in me. I need to make sure he doesn't consider me a suspect."

"He'll only be interested if you have something to hide," he said. "And I can't imagine a charming witch such as yourself would have secrets."

I kept my expression neutral. "We all have a few secrets, but mine have nothing to do with Jinti."

Atherton joined me at the table and poured the tea before handing me a mug. He selected a breakfast scone and took a large bite. "This is excellent. Did you make them?"

"I did. And thank you." I took my own scone. "Can you think of anyone who could have gotten into the store to kill Jinti?"

"It's a mystery to me, and the magic swap ended early because so few people turned up, so Jinti didn't stay long. I remember you speaking to her."

"That's right. You and Ulric joined us." I dabbed crumbs off my plate with my finger. I wanted to ask why he was even talking to Ulric, since he'd had an affair with Bella, but I needed to tread carefully, or Atherton would shut down.

"We did. I was worried things looked tense between you and was concerned you might have been fighting."

"No, we weren't fighting, although it was awkward. We were talking about your late wife, Bella."

Atherton's face tightened for a second before he smiled again. "Jinti often talked about her. She struggled after Bella disappeared."

"You must have struggled, too. It must be impossible to get closure if you're not sure what happened to her."

"It is, but I manage. And the store keeps me busy. But we're not here to talk about Bella, are we?"

"No, but I would like to know your thoughts on who'd want to hurt Jinti. And you must be curious about how she got in to the store. Did she have keys?"

"She used to, but she gave them back a few weeks ago."

"Was that after you fired her?"

His eyes narrowed. "I see what you're doing. You're looking for other suspects. You're snooping so you can pin this murder on someone else and get Devlin off your back."

"I'm not snooping, but I want to get to the truth. And I definitely don't want the Magic Council considering me a suspect."

He refreshed my mug of tea. "I'd want the same if I was in your uncomfortable situation. But you must have an alibi. You live at the bakery, don't you?"

"I live with my uncle, but he was asleep."

"No one can say where you were at the time of Jinti's murder?"

"I know where I was, and it was nowhere near here. And I wouldn't have been able to get in. I don't have a key. Who does?"

Atherton smiled. "I'll indulge you, but only because these scones are so delicious. I have keys and so does Regina. That's it."

"Have your keys gone missing? Or maybe someone damaged the lock so they could get in after you closed."

"I haven't lost my keys, and I checked with Regina. She reported no key loss. And as for lock damage, the Magic Council checked the security. There were no signs of a forced entry."

"Could Jinti have made herself a spare set of keys? She let herself in, and her killer found her here?"

"It's possible. I asked for all the sets back, and she gave me what she had. I had no reason to believe she had more. And why would she want her own set? Jinti made it clear she wanted nothing to do with me. Which was why I was surprised to see her on the night of the magic swap."

"You didn't like her?"

"Much like you, I wasn't comfortable around her. But we weren't enemies."

It was also clear they hadn't exactly been bosom buddies.

"Jinti seemed in discomfort when I talked to her," I said.

"She most likely was. And I was certain her death was from natural causes. Jinti was an old, sick woman. She was asking about my herbal remedy books when she was here, and I suggested several we had. But as we both know, magic isn't a cure for everything."

"You think Jinti was looking for a cure for an illness?"

"She must have been, but she refused to give me the details of what was wrong, so there was little I could do to help. Jinti was always secretive. Bella didn't like that. She said her mom was always keeping things from her."

"The Magic Council is certain this was murder," I said.

"Because of the way they believe she died," Atherton said.

"Do you know what killed her?"

He sipped his tea, an amused look in his eyes.

I tried hard not to scowl. Atherton was enjoying having one over on me.

"They believe it was poison," he said.

"There are hundreds of poisons and toxins that could have been used. When Devlin talked to me, he didn't seem certain what killed Jinti."

"He wouldn't have been. An autopsy and test results take time. I got the information from a friend in the Magic Council."

"Does Devlin now know what it was?"

Atherton set down his mug. "The Magic Council thinks Jinti was poisoned by a mixture of deathcap rose and hemlock. They still have a few more tests to run, but that's what the initial findings show."

"I don't use those in my baking, so the poison couldn't have come from my muffin."

"So you say."

"So I know!" I pushed away my plate. "Don't you sell those herbs in this store?"

"Sometimes. But I keep any herbs or potions strong enough to cause harm in a secure cabinet."

"Who has access to that cabinet?"

"I do. And only me. If anyone requests anything from it, I do an assessment to make sure I know what they need the herbs for. You have to be careful when handling magic used on others. Your baking magic must be the same. It needs a careful balance to ensure it's perfect. Get it wrong, and things taste odd. Much like those muffins you brought to the swap and share."

"I have apologized to Regina about those muffins. I was having an off day. And I brought over replacements."

Atherton waved a hand in the air. "That's not important. And these breakfast scones show you have a natural talent for baking. I've also eaten food your father made, and it was exquisite. When is he back in the village? It must be over a year since I've seen him."

"Both my parents are busy. They go around the world on business. They barely see each other, let alone me."

"That's a shame. But it's only right they don't deny the world of their treats. I shall have to have dinner with him the next time he visits."

"Sure. I'll mention it to him when he calls." Which wouldn't be for weeks. Dad was obsessed with his baking. It was his one true love, much like my mom. "Could I have a look at your poison cabinet?"

Atherton stared at me. "Why do you want to do that?"

"To make sure nothing is missing. Maybe you overlooked something."

"That's impossible." He glanced down at his hands. "Besides, the cabinet was damaged."

"What happened to it?"

"Whoever killed Jinti must have smashed it and ruined the contents."

"Was anything taken?"

"I'm not certain. I do a weekly stock inventory and am comparing records. As far as I can tell, Jinti wasn't poisoned by anything I own."

"What about the herbs that poisoned her? None of that is missing?"

"It'll take some time to pick things over. But the herbs that poisoned her can be gathered from nature. If the killer knew what they were looking for, they could have harvested the plants themselves."

"How were they given to Jinti?"

"Orally. In food or drink. Maybe in a muffin." Atherton's eyes narrowed at me, but he was smiling.

"Jinti would have put up a fight if someone forced her to drink poison."

"You'd think so. But Jinti was old and frail, and her magic wasn't what it used to be. She'd have had difficulty fighting anyone off. And maybe she didn't even know what she was taking. Her killer could have put poison in a drink."

"Or my muffin." My mouth twisted to the side. No wonder Devlin was so keen on putting me in the firing line. A sweet muffin would hide the tang of poison.

"You said it." Atherton placed another scone on my plate.

"Jinti must have known the person she met with that night."

"Why do you think that?"

"She wouldn't be eating or drinking with a stranger or an enemy."

Atherton shrugged. "That's logical."

"And why did Jinti meet them here? I still don't understand that."

"The only person who understands this mystery is Jinti, and she can't tell you anything."

I stared into space as I juggled the information I had, trying to find an order. "Somehow, Jinti got into the store without keys, met with someone she knew, and they gave her a poisoned drink."

"Or a tainted muffin." Atherton raised his chin, an unpleasant smile on his face.

"Not tainted by my hand."

"Not directly, but what's to say someone doesn't want you to go to prison?"

"Me! I don't have enemies. You think someone is setting me up?"

"I doubt it, but you do have unusual friends. Friends with dark pasts," Atherton said. "And I heard about your confrontation outside the bakery. It involved Devlin."

"My friends are perfect, just as they are. And my confrontation with Devlin was a misunderstanding."

"These things are so often misunderstandings." He finished his scone. "As is the confusion surrounding what happened to Jinti and why she was killed here. I'm sure there's an explanation, but so long as my name is in the clear, I'm not concerned about it."

"Surely, you want to know who killed Jinti. She used to be your mother-in-law and your employee. You must have had a bond."

"There was a connection of sorts, but what I felt for Jinti was more pity. She was an old, bitter woman who couldn't move on from her tragic past. I was as generous as I could be, but she tried my patience."

"You're glad Jinti's gone?"

Atherton inhaled a slow breath. "I'm glad she's at peace."

"Don't you want to find out who killed her?"

"Maybe there is no mystery. I simply made a mistake and left the door unlocked, which was how Jinti and her killer got in. It could have been carelessness on my part, and the killer exploited the opportunity."

I shook my head. "Regina told me she locked up."

"Ah, did she? Well, perhaps I left the back door open. Jinti returned because she'd left something here, and the killer followed her in. That's as good an explanation as any." Atherton stood from the table. "I think we're done here, and I have a store to get back in order."

"I'm not done. I must clear my name and make sure the bakery reputation doesn't suffer because I've been associated with a murder." I remained at the table. "Aren't you concerned the magic store won't be as popular after what happened?"

"No, I have an excellent reputation for getting people what they want. If you focused on that in the bakery, instead of creating your... unusual tasting recipes, you'd find your customers are willing to overlook something like this."

"Willing to overlook a murder? I doubt it."

Atherton gestured to the door. "I must get on. And you should run back to the bakery and not trouble yourself with this murder. The Magic Council will deal with it."

I walked back through the store, slowing at the broken poison cabinet that sat close to the bone collection.

"There's nothing here for you to see." Atherton nudged me gently to the door. "Stick with the baking, or you'll only find yourself in even more trouble."

That sounded like a threat. "One more thing. Where were you when Jinti died?"

He scowled at me. "Luna, you can't think I'm a suspect."

"If you're innocent—"

"I am. I was at home, on my own."

"Thank you." I smiled and walked out the door. It was slammed behind me and the lock turned.

I didn't trust a word Atherton had said to me. And how could he be so callous about a frail old woman's murder?

He was hiding something. And I was determined to find out what that was.

Chapter 14

Uncle Albert flipped the closed sign on the bakery door as I cleared out the last of the dessert trays and wiped crumbs into the trash.

He staggered to a table and slumped into a seat. "I'm done in."

I set down my cleaning cloth and joined him. "You shouldn't have worked this afternoon. I didn't think you were up to it."

"I thought you could do with a break. You were out early this morning. And there were those custom cupcakes to deal with."

"You heard me leave? I didn't mean to disturb you, but I had something to do before work."

"What was that?" Uncle Albert's expression was full of kindness.

I shifted in my seat. "Jinti's murder is on my mind. I went to see Atherton to find out more about what happened to her and if he had any idea about suspects."

"There'll be other suspects. I'm certain Devlin can't seriously think you were involved. You're a wonderful girl, well, young woman, and you'd never hurt anyone. What did Atherton have to say?"

"He wasn't concerned that Jinti was found dead in his store. And he couldn't tell me much, other than that she was a burden to him. I got the impression he was glad she was dead."

"The Magic Council will come to their senses about you," Uncle Albert said. "We run a professional operation here. I'm still amazed Devlin had the nerve to poke around."

"I'd like to know what happened to Jinti. It seems unfair. She had so many troubles, what with losing Bella and then being fired by Atherton. It's a horrible thing to happen to her, especially when she was already unwell."

"I didn't know Jinti was sick. What was wrong with her?"

"I'm not sure. Atherton seemed to think she was on her last legs. Jinti even asked him for some herbal remedy books to find a cure."

"She knew everything there was to know about magical herbal cures. Jinti had been around for such a long time, helping others who were sick. Her loss will be felt by many."

"She must have been desperate to go to Atherton."

"That poor woman." Uncle Albert's smile was sympathetic. "I don't want you worrying about this. We need to focus on cake. We've got several large custom orders. That woman you spoke to the other day placed an extra order on top of the birthday cake. She needs three-hundred cupcakes, so you'll have your hands full here. You don't want to get tangled up in Jinti's murder and get distracted."

"I'm already tangled up, thanks to Devlin."

"Devlin Goody is young and trying to make a name for himself. I've met many magic users like him. He's just being extra thorough. I expect by tomorrow, the killer will be caught."

"I hope so. I won't let this get in the way of my work." The thought of tackling three-hundred cupcakes sent a shudder down my spine.

Uncle Albert studied me for a few seconds. "Is everything okay? I thought you'd be excited about the cupcakes, but you seem unhappy."

"That's hardly a surprise. I'm a murder suspect."

"Are you sure that's it? Is there anything I can help with?"

I took hold of his hand and gave it a gentle squeeze. "Everything is fine. I've just got a small complication I'm dealing with."

"Is it to do with a boy? I'm no expert in matters of the heart. Your auntie always talked to you about relationships, but if I can help..."

"Uncle Albert, I don't date boys. I date men."

He chuckled. "I know, but you'll always be a child to me. I still remember you with pigtails as you cast your first baking spell."

I grimaced. "And the contents of the bowl splattered all over the kitchen wall. I haven't forgotten."

"We all have to practice to excel at our craft. There's no shame in that. And never struggle with a spell; just ask me. I'm always happy to add some of my magic."

I looked down at our joined hands. Uncle Albert's magic pulsed beneath his skin. It always felt so warm and welcoming and had a faint hint of sweet spices to it. With a hit of his magic, I'd become a baking superstar.

I yanked my hand back and set it on my lap. For the briefest second, I'd wanted his magic. I'd never drain Uncle Albert, especially not when he was sick.

"You can talk to me about anything." The worry was clear in his eyes. "Even if it's about men friends. I'll always try to help. I don't promise to have the answers to your questions, but I'm here. I expect I'm a poor substitute to your auntie, but—"

"No! I love our chats. And I love living here and helping you. But this isn't something you can help me with." I dug my nails into my palms. I wouldn't take Uncle Albert's magic.

A tap on the window had me turning, and I stiffened in my seat when I saw Cole outside.

"Is that a friend?" Uncle Albert said.

"Kind of. A new friend. We met the other evening when I was out for a walk."

"Let him in. He looks like he's got something serious to talk to you about. Oh, unless that's the reason you've been preoccupied." Uncle Albert stood. "If you don't want to speak to him, I'll tell him to go. I won't have a man bothering you."

I smiled at his sweet overprotectiveness. "Cole isn't a problem. I'll see what he wants. You head upstairs and get started on dinner."

"If you're sure. Although I'll take a bath before we eat. My shoulders are aching."

"That's just what you need. There's no rush." I waited until Uncle Albert left the bakery before heading to the door and unlocking it. "Hey, Cole. I wasn't sure I'd see you again."

His brow was furrowed, and his hands stuffed into the pockets of his jeans. "We need to talk."

"About what?" I gestured him into the bakery, then shut the door behind him. Cole was giving off an annoyed vibe, and I wasn't certain why.

His eyes glittered amber for a heartbeat. "I want to know why you lied to your friends."

I licked my lips. "When did I do that?"

"When that other guy showed up. The one we chased down. The one you owe money to. Why did you tell them you were dating?"

"I don't recall saying that exactly. You must have misheard." I turned away, but he caught my arm.

Cole tapped the side of his head. "Werewolf hearing. I don't miss much. You whispered to him to play along and you'd pay him double. Why?"

I pulled my arm away and fixed him with my fiercest glare. "Why is that your business?"

"Because we hunted together."

"And that's important because..."

"It means something when you share a hunt."

I wasn't up on my werewolf etiquette, but maybe it was a big deal to Cole. "I didn't know that. And, technically, I was chasing Bram, and you joined in my hunt. You didn't get an invitation. Perhaps I didn't want you barging in when I was having fun."

"I didn't need an invite. The guy was running, and he needed to be chased down. We did that together. You couldn't have done it without me."

"I was doing fine on my own."

"He was getting away."

"Nope. I was catching up."

"And what would you have done when you caught him? Bram isn't a small guy. And he has strong magic."

I hadn't planned that far ahead. "I'd have worked something out. What's the big deal? We're now hunt buddies, so we have to share everything?"

Cole rumbled a growl deep in his chest, and my heart did a strange flip-flop. "Something like that. And I'm interested in you."

"Um... you are?"

"Of course." He said it like it shouldn't be a surprise. "I need to know what mess you've gotten into and why you can't tell your friends what's going on."

"I didn't ask you to be interested."

"Yet here I am, being curious about you and wanting answers." Cole's lips quirked. "You can either tell me the truth or keep adding to your list of people you're lying to."

It was a growing list. And I was a terrible liar. "You don't need to know."

"I want to. I could help."

I pressed my hands against my closed eyes. I was so tired of hiding everything. Until a few days ago, I had a handle on it all. Now, I couldn't be further from that. My farmhouse had been discovered, Ridley had escaped, Bram was closing in and demanding money, and the Magic Council had me on the suspect list as a murderer.

Cole's hand settled on my shoulder. "Hey, it can't be that bad. And even if it is, we can figure this out."

My shoulders slumped. "I'm not so sure about that."

"Take a seat. You can tell me all about it. And I won't judge. I've been in plenty of messy situations over the years. I know how easy it is to get in over your head."

"I doubt you've been in a mess quite like this." I accepted the seat he pulled out for me and sank into it. Maybe it would be better if I unburdened to someone I didn't know. And Cole was leaving soon, so he could take my secrets with him.

He settled in the seat opposite me, rested his elbows on the table, and looked at me, his gaze steady and intense.

I sucked in a deep breath. "I'll start with Bram, since you've met him. He's been watching me for a while, and I didn't know who he was at first. I'd see him outside the bakery, and he wasn't doing anything, simply seeing what I was up to, but I got a bad vibe off him."

"You had no clue what he wanted?"

"No. And I was heading back to the bakery that night when I saw him. I gave chase, and that's where you joined the party."

"You owe this guy money?" Cole said.

"That's right. I got in trouble and needed a quick fix of magic."

"What kind of trouble?"

"It's complicated."

"Try me. I have to deal with uptight werewolves all the time, and they love complicated."

I glanced at the empty counter. "My magic is supposed to be ideal for creating magic filled treats. I'm a Brimstone baker. We're a big deal in the baking community. It's what we're known for."

"I've never heard of you, but I love your food."

"You probably love Uncle Albert's food. He's a Black, but he married my auntie. The Black bakers are also awesome at making desserts. Anyone who eats anything he makes is instantly in love with his food."

"I've been by a couple of times and tried the food. It's amazing. I'm sure it was made by your hand."

"That's nice, but most likely not true."

He smiled. "I'd eat anything you made. Go on."

"Baking is different for me. Sometimes, my magic won't cooperate, and my food can be questionable."

"So practice more," he said. "Isn't that what magic is all about, refining your craft until you become a super witch?"

"I've been refining my craft since I was a kid. I'm always practicing, and things never turn out right. Baking spells feel unnatural to me." I gulped down the lump forming in my throat. I'd never voiced my fears to anyone. "I'm worried my magic might be... blunted."

"Blunted? I've heard of that. Some spell casters have trouble with their natural energy, is that right?"

I nodded. "Magical blunts achieve nothing other than basic spells, and our magic stays in a childlike state. We get stuck and can't progress to the next level."

"You think that's happened to you? That's why you went to this guy to get a top up of magic?"

"Yep. And it helps. I only went to Sylvester occasionally, when I could afford it. But we had several huge rush jobs, and Uncle Albert was relying on me. I hate letting him down, so I had to get more magic."

"All from this Bram?"

"From his boss. Bram is the muscle. I have other sources who help, but I'd used them and couldn't risk taking any more of their magic in case I hurt them."

Cole's eyes narrowed, but he didn't question me further about that. "You went to this guy, and he gave you a magic boost on account?"

"Several boosts on account," I said. "They weren't cheap, and there's interest to pay. I got behind with repaying the debt and missed two payments. That's where Bram comes in. Sylvester got tired of waiting for his money."

"And you added to your problems by getting Bram to lie about who he was. You doubled your debt to keep this from your friends? Why hide this from them?"

"I panicked. They don't know about my magical blunting problem. I'm not sure they'd want to be my friends if they knew the truth."

"I call bull. True friends don't care about things like that. Did you grow up together?"

"Yes. We've known each other for years, since we were children."

"They must have seen you struggling with your magic when you were younger."

"Sure, but we all struggled. I always hid my trouble."

"I reckon they still know something is wrong. True friends cut through the fake and get to the truth."

I didn't speak as I considered this. "Maybe, but we don't come into our full powers until we're older, so it was never a big issue. And when I realized I was still having problems, I figured out a way to deal with it."

"You're not talking about paying for magic boosts from that Sylvester guy," Cole said.

"No, I'm not. You don't need to worry about that. It's under control." My gaze flickered over him. It would be even more under control if I could convince Cole to join my farmhouse. Werewolf energy was exactly what I needed.

"You need Bram off your back."

"I don't have all the money. I have some savings, but I have plans for that."

"Are you working on expanding this business? I'm guessing this will be yours when your uncle retires."

I couldn't stop from grimacing. "Most likely. But when Uncle Albert stops baking, the truth will get out. This business will fail because my magic is messed up."

"Who says it's messed up? It's just different. Maybe it's not meant to be used for food magic. Your talents could lie elsewhere."

"That's impossible. My magic must have a connection to baking. I come from a long line of magic users who specialize in this kind of magic. It's in our blood. It should be in my muffins."

"I love your muffins." Cole chuckled, and my cheeks flushed.

"You know what I mean. Werewolves must be the same. You have your alphas and betas and... the other ranks, don't you?"

"Roles are determined by more than just brute strength, but also your skills as a negotiator and a diplomat. Everyone sees werewolves as blunt instruments who force their way into positions of power, but it's more complicated. And we have magic." Cole leaned back in his seat. "Now and again, a werewolf is born of an alpha and has no interest in leading. Maybe you should do the same and explore your options. Food magic isn't in your blood."

"It is. And if I explored my options, I'd let down Uncle Albert. This business is his life. I won't walk away from it."

"Then you need to let me help."

"How do you plan to do that?" I arched a brow. "Can you bake?"

"Nope. But I can get Bram out of your way."

I leaned across the table. "By eating him?"

Cole's expression tightened. "I don't eat people. Even scum like Bram."

"Oh! No, of course." I shook my head. "You don't need to help me. You owe me nothing. I barely know you."

"You know me well enough. And I haven't forgotten that kiss. It was unique."

"You liked it?"

His grin appeared. "I did. Have you got any more?"

I stopped myself from leaning closer. "Before we get to that, there's something I need to tell you about that kiss."

"What's that? Don't stamp on my heart and tell me you're taken."

"No, I'm single." I let out a soft sigh. Was it too much to hope for that Cole would join the farmhouse? "And maybe you can help me, but we have to be discreet."

"I can be discreet. What is it you need?"

There was a rap on the door, and I turned to see Devlin Goody and two other enforcers from the Magic Council standing outside.

I groaned and stood from my seat. "What does he want?"

"Nothing good if the sour look on his face is anything to go by," Cole said. "Shall I make him go away?"

"No, I'd better see what he wants." I walked to the door and opened it. "The bakery is closed if you're looking for something to eat."

Devlin shoved a piece of paper in my face. "I have a warrant to search these premises."

"Why?" I grabbed the paper and inspected it. It was legitimate.

"Because you're a suspect in Jinti's murder."

I stepped aside as he walked in with his colleagues. "My muffin didn't poison her. I've already spoken to Atherton, and he told me what poisoned her. We don't have deathcap rose and hemlock here."

"Is that so?" Devlin said. "We're still investigating several possibilities. Your poisoned muffin included."

I gritted my teeth. "It wasn't poisoned."

Devlin pointed around the bakery. "Inspect the cabinets and look through everything. Then deal with the kitchen. Make sure you're thorough."

His colleagues marched off and rooted around behind the counter.

Cole came to stand beside me. "Is there a problem?"

Devlin eyed him warily. "I'm here on Magic Council business. I'd advise you to stand aside."

Cole growled, and Devlin shrank back.

"It's okay," I said to Cole. "Devlin won't find anything incriminating to link me to Jinti's death."

"Is that because you've disposed of the evidence?" Devlin asked.

"There's no evidence to find." I spoke through gritted teeth.

Cole continued to glower at Devlin. I was glad to have him here. After the day I'd had, I didn't think I could face the Magic Council on my own.

"Hey, keep the noise down." I gestured to one of Devlin's colleagues who'd knocked over a pile of metal trays. "My uncle isn't feeling good. I don't want him disturbed."

"I found this." He held up Earl, who was sleeping in a large mixing bowl.

Devlin smirked. "That's a health violation."

"Not true. That's my familiar."

"He still sheds fur and uses his tongue to clean himself."

"He sometimes uses the shower." Why couldn't Earl have been hiding on top of a cabinet? He had to be wedged inside a bowl. He was as wonky as my magic.

"If that's the best you've got, you're wasting Luna's time," Cole said.

"Perhaps we'll find something in your apartment," Devlin said.

"Is that necessary?" Cole said. "The lady told you she had nothing to do with this murder."

"The lady could be lying."

I patted Cole's arm to stop him lunging at Devlin and ripping his head off. "Have you spoken to Atherton?"

Devlin glanced at me. "Of course."

"He has a strong motive for wanting Jinti dead. She thought Atherton killed Bella."

"Bella Hart? She isn't dead," Devlin said.

"That you know of. She went missing, and Atherton was questioned as a suspect in her disappearance."

"Unless you have access to confidential Magic Council records, you don't know that." Devlin rifled through a cabinet before shutting it.

"It's logical to assume, though. Bella was Atherton's wife, she was unhappy in her marriage, and—"

"That's enough speculation. Atherton has been spoken to and eliminated from the inquiry. He's a respected member of this community. He wouldn't murder his former mother-in-law."

"Atherton has no alibi. He was home alone." I glowered at Devlin. "Or does his elimination have to do with his friends in the Magic Council?"

"That wouldn't influence my investigation." Devlin turned away. "I need to concentrate on this search. I don't want to miss anything."

"Atherton Hart is a slimy jerk and a womanizer," Cole muttered.

"How do you know him?"

"I've met him once, and I know his reputation. I wouldn't trust the guy as far as I could throw him, and I'm strong."

I glanced at his bulging biceps. "What makes you say he's a womanizer?"

"It's the way Atherton looks at women, like he thinks he can own them."

"When I visited his store to ask about Jinti, he was overly friendly. It made me uncomfortable."

"Did he hurt you?" Cole growled. "If he overstepped the line—"

"No! And I had everything under control. But he was flattering me and getting in my personal space, as if testing the boundaries to see what he could get away with. I didn't like it."

Cole's eyes burned amber. "The guy's been in my territory a few times, hunting out herbs and artefacts to sell. I've heard several women complain he hassled them. Although the woman I saw him with the other night didn't mind being hassled."

"What woman? Atherton's not seeing anyone."

"He came out of his store with her. He put his arm around her and kissed her. And it was more than a friendly goodbye kiss."

"What did she look like?"

"She was pretty, petite, with a friendly face, and blonde hair. They walked off together."

"That sounds like Regina," I said. "But she's not with Atherton. They just work together."

"What I witnessed wasn't a professional relationship."

This was interesting information. If Regina and Atherton were together, had Jinti found out and thought they were betraying Bella's memory? Perhaps they were both in on killing her. They lured Jinti back to the store and poisoned her. Atherton could have replaced the missing herbs from his cabinet. Then they left Jinti's body with my muffin beside her, hoping to muddy the investigation.

My forehead wrinkled as I considered this option. Why pick the store as the place to kill Jinti? It automatically put Atherton and Regina in the spotlight. Unless Atherton thought his reputation would protect him. What about Regina? If she was dating him, maybe he assumed he could keep her safe.

Cole smoothed a finger down the middle of my forehead. "I lost you a couple of minutes ago. What's on your mind?"

"Murder. And trying to figure out why Atherton killed Jinti in his store. It makes no sense."

"You're a smart witch. You'll figure this out. And if you need my help, you only have to ask."

I grinned up at him. I was glad to have my new werewolf friend by my side. "Thanks, hunting buddy. I'll keep that in mind."

"How about I wait with you until the Magic Council is done tossing this place?"

"You don't have to do that."

"I want to. And it gives me more time to get to know you better." His grin was wolfish as he settled back at the table. "And weren't you about to show me your kissing technique?"

I laughed. "We can circle back to that another time." I grabbed carrot cake and coffee and set it in front of Cole. "Give me a minute to let my uncle know what's going on. He'll worry when he learns what Devlin is up to."

Cole nodded as he bit off a chunk of cake.

I dashed up the stairs to find Uncle Albert opening the bathroom door. He was in his dressing gown. "Don't panic, but the Magic Council is searching the place."

He startled and tightened the belt on his robe. "Does this have to do with Jinti?"

I nodded. "Devlin has a search warrant, so I can't stop him."

Uncle Albert headed for the stairs. "I'll stop this." He paused at the top, and his hand went to his head.

I rushed over and caught hold of him. "You're still unwell. You need a hot meal and then bed."

"But Devlin shouldn't be here. It's wrong." Uncle Albert didn't protest for long as I led him to his bedroom.

"I'm sure he'll leave us alone once he comes up empty-handed. I'll make sure he doesn't cause problems. And I won't let him disturb you." I settled Uncle Albert in his bed. "I'll bring a tray of dinner in later. You rest."

After making sure he was comfortable, I hurried back to the bakery. Devlin and his team were still working through the cabinets, so I settled in with Cole, and we chatted for the next hour while keeping an eye on the Magic Council.

Devlin emerged from the kitchen with a sealed bag in his hand.

"What are you taking?" I said. "You can't have evidence against me."

"I was unable to test your food the last time I was here," Devlin said. "I might as well take some away."

I let out a relieved sigh. "Those samples have nothing to do with the murder. Did you find anything incriminating?"

Devlin's lips thinned. "Nothing suspicious. But don't leave the village. I still have questions for you." He left with his colleagues, and I was happy to shut the door behind them.

I turned to Cole. "I'd better check on my uncle. He'll be worried."

"I'll leave you to it. But don't forget what I said. Any time you need my help, you ask. I'm around for another couple of weeks."

"Thanks, I'll think about it."

He rested a hand on my upper arm just before I opened the door. "And you were going to suggest a way I could help with your magic. We never got back to that."

"Oh! No, forget about it." I opened the door. I had to focus on Uncle Albert and sorting out the mess the Magic Council had left behind. "Thanks for being here. I'd have attacked Devlin with an industrial mixer if you hadn't been around to keep me steady."

He chuckled, then brushed a soft kiss against my lips. "See you around, sugar witch."

I closed the door and sighed. Before I got to grips with Cole, I had to find out more about Atherton and Regina's relationship and if it could be linked to Jinti's murder.

Chapter 15

"Are you sure you've got everything?" I settled a thick beige blanket over Uncle Albert's legs and placed a tray of food on his knees.

"I'll be fine. Do you have to go out, though? You don't think the Magic Council will come back again tonight?"

"No, they're gone. As we both knew, they found nothing." I decided not to mention the food samples Devlin took. It would only make Uncle Albert worry.

"I can't believe they burst in here demanding to look around. They even went through my underwear drawer."

"They're clutching at straws. I suggested Devlin take a closer look at Atherton. After all, Jinti was found in his store."

Uncle Albert huffed out a breath. "They can't keep hassling us."

"If they do, I'll ask Olympus to have a word," I said. "He carries influence at the Magic Council. Although I get the impression Devlin and Olympus aren't friendly."

"Olympus needs to remind Devlin it's rude to poke about in a man's Y-fronts."

I repressed a smile. "I'm sure he can do that."

Uncle Albert patted the bed, and Earl bounced onto the comforter.

"Hey, Earl. Keep guard over Uncle Albert while I'm gone."

"I'll be happy to help him eat his dinner." Earl yawned. "What are we having?"

I ruffled his fur. "No eating. You're a ruthless protector."

He licked a paw. "If you say so. I call dibs on that fat sausage."

A groan slid out of me. Why was Earl so useless? If it wasn't food or catnip, he had no interest.

"We need to put this behind us," Uncle Albert said. "We've got a busy day of baking tomorrow."

"And I'll be here to help, I promise." I kissed his cheek, then headed down the stairs and out of the store.

Indigo, Storm, and Odessa were waiting outside.

"We got the SOS call," Odessa said. "What's going on? Have you got another man you need us to grill?"

"This has nothing to do with my men," I said. "I need help on a stakeout."

"Who are we staking out?" Storm said.

"Atherton and Regina."

Odessa grinned. "Murder suspects! What fun. I should have brought snacks."

We walked along the street, turned the corner, and headed into a small residential area, where the houses were pressed together in tight terraced rows.

"Do you think Atherton or Regina killed Jinti?" Indigo said.

"I do. And I found out something interesting. They're in a relationship."

Storm shook her head. "I'm not surprised. Atherton looks at Regina like she's his property. When I go in the store, he's always lurking around and getting in her personal space."

"And Regina never objects?" Odessa said. "Some guys have zero clue about boundaries."

"She seemed comfortable being pestered by Atherton the last time I was in there."

"Do you think Jinti found out and confronted them?" Indigo said.

"That's what we need to figure out. I want to watch Regina's place and see if Atherton shows up."

"And then what?" Storm said.

"And then... I don't know. Confront them? I wondered if they were both involved with what happened. Did Jinti get angry because they were in a relationship, so they killed her, and now they're covering for each other?"

"Remind me of their alibis," Storm said.

"Regina said she was home alone. Atherton said the same."

"He lives in that big pad on the edge of the village, doesn't he?" Odessa said. "I pass it every time I go to my farmhouse. He always has lights blazing."

I nodded. "That's right."

"If I was Regina, I'd want to hang out there," Odessa said. "Not in this tiny place. These houses are cute, but they're made for hobbits, not witches."

We stopped outside the terraced house owned by Regina.

"Let's find somewhere to wait and see if they show up," I said.

"Sure, but you're still missing the next step," Indigo said. "If they show, how are you going to get them to talk?"

"Confront them and shake the truth out of them," Storm said. "Your freedom is at stake, so you can't mess around."

"I have no plans to mess around. I want to know if what I heard is true. First, we find out if they're dating."

"And then?" Storm arched an eyebrow.

"The rest will be figured out shortly."

"Let's head to the bench down the road," Indigo said. "We can see Regina's house from there, and it'll look less suspicious than lurking on the street."

We walked to the bench, and all squeezed on it.

"Where did you hear about their relationship?" Storm said.

I glanced at her. "From a friend."

"One of your male friends?" Odessa said. "Was it Bram or the werewolf? Or someone else?"

"It was the werewolf," I said. "And his name is Cole."

"And how does he know about Atherton and Regina?" Storm said.

"He saw them outside the magic store. They must have thought no one was watching, so they had a quick make-out session. And Cole knows Atherton's reputation and isn't impressed by it. He called him a womanizer."

"You must think Cole is a reliable source of information if you're chasing suspects based on what he told you." Amusement danced in Indigo's eyes.

"There'd be no reason for him to lie to me."

"Cole must want to get on your good side," Odessa said.

"Or he wants to get in your pants," Storm said.

"It's not like that. He's helping me out. We're... buddies."

"Werewolves don't make buddies with just anyone," Storm said. "Why pick you?"

"Why not her?" Odessa said. "Luna needs a break on the boyfriend front. She's had a complicated time recently, you know, with the... vanishing."

"You don't have to pussyfoot around what happened," I said. "I know you all think I came back different after Indigo's mom and her boyfriend abducted me, but I'm the same old me."

Indigo caught hold of my hand. "We don't think you're different, but it must have had an effect. And you don't talk about it. I understand if you don't want to discuss it with me. After all, it was my messed up family who stole you away."

"No! That's not it. And I don't talk about it because I don't remember much." The guilt on Indigo's face made me sad. "It took me a few days to stop jumping every time a strange shadow moved in the corner of the bakery, but I'm fine. I don't blame you for anything that happened."

"I hope that's true," Indigo said. "We care about you. If you've got problems, you can tell us. We're here to help."

"Maybe she doesn't need her friends now she has her delicious new werewolf buddy looking out for her," Odessa said.

"I can never be doing with werewolves," Storm said. "They're too possessive. If another guy looks at you, they're ready to pound him into the ground."

I grinned as I remembered how Cole had behaved around Devlin.

"Oooh! You like this werewolf," Odessa said. "Does he give you the tingles?"

"I don't know Cole well, but I like having him around. But there's no point in getting serious. He's only here for a couple of weeks."

"Maybe he'll come back," Odessa said. "You could give him a good reason to return."

I stifled another grin. "Let's concentrate on this stakeout."

Indigo had kept hold of my hand. She gave me a nod and squeezed it. I could tell she was worried about me, but I couldn't share everything with her. Being abducted by her mom had been a shock, but I wasn't lying when I said I felt okay. And the problems with my magic hadn't started after I'd been abducted. They'd been with me for years.

"We're wasting our time," Storm said. "Let's just confront Regina. We'll knock on her door and tell her we know about her dating Atherton and see what she has to say. She could panic and spill her guts."

"Or think we're weird and never speak to us again," Odessa said.

"I'm going. You can stay here if you want to." Storm marched to Regina's front door.

After a second, we all hurried after her.

She grinned as she knocked on the door. A moment later, it was opened.

A short, middle-aged woman with dark hair looked out at us. "May I help you?"

"Hi, we're looking for Regina. Is she in?" I said.

"Regina? You mean my landlady?"

"Oh! She doesn't live here anymore?"

"She did, but Regina moved out a while ago. I'm renting the house. I've got her contact details if you need to see her."

"I've got a good idea where she is," Storm said. "Shall we go to Atherton's house?"

"Thanks. Sorry to bother you," I said to the woman.

"No problem." She closed the door.

I turned to the others. "It must be serious if they're living together."

"And you said Regina claimed she was home alone the night of Jinti's murder," Indigo said.

"So did Atherton. Which means they lied if they're living in the same place. But why? They must be hiding something bad."

"There's only one way to find out," Storm said. "How about we take a walk to the posh side of the village?"

We took a few shortcuts and arrived on the most exclusive street in Witch Haven ten minutes later. Atherton's penthouse was lit from the inside and sat in the middle of a row of white buildings.

"Atherton has to be the killer," I said.

"Why not Regina?" Odessa said.

"She's too nice."

"She could be covering for her lover," Storm said. "Regina doesn't want him getting in trouble."

"They're both in trouble if that's the case," Indigo said. "Do you want me to grab Olympus so he can hear what Atherton has to say?"

I nodded. I was certain I was right about this. Atherton had every reason for wanting Jinti dead. She was found in his store, and he had access to the poisons that killed her.

"Do it. Let's get this over with. All we need is a confession."

Indigo raced away, and the rest of us headed to Atherton's apartment complex. We walked into a plush hallway with an elevator in one corner and a wide set of steps leading up to the penthouse.

A locked door prevented us from getting any further, so I pressed the intercom.

"Who is it?" a female voice sing-songed.

"That's Regina," Odessa said.

"Say something." Storm nudged me.

"Err, hi! It's Luna. Can I come up?"

"Luna! Of course. Is Atherton expecting you?"

"Sort of." I shrugged at the others. I could hardly say I was here to accuse him of murder.

"Come on up." The intercom buzzed, and we headed to the elevator and took a smooth ride to the penthouse.

Regina opened a door in front of us as we stepped out.

"Are you doing some evening admin?" Storm said, a smirk on her face.

Regina's cheeks flushed. "No, I was just having dinner with Atherton. He doesn't have an appointment in the diary to meet with you, Luna. Or your friends."

"I don't expect he does. I need to talk to Atherton about why he lied about his alibi on the night of Jinti's murder," I said.

Regina's tongue traced across her bottom lip. "He lied? What makes you think that?"

"You're both lying," I said. "What are you covering up? Did you murder Jinti?"

"Who is it?" Atherton walked toward the door, slowing when he saw us. "What are you all doing here?"

Regina glanced at him. "You'll want to hear this. Luna thinks we murdered Jinti."

Atherton shook his head. "You're still on that? Haven't you got something more interesting to focus on?"

"I'll keep focused on Jinti's murder until my name is cleared."

"You should all come in," Regina said. "We need to sort this out."

"This is a waste of time," Atherton said.

"We can listen to Luna. Neither of us has anything to hide." Regina opened the door wider, and we walked into a high-ceilinged entrance hall with sumptuous thick gray carpet and gleaming white walls. She led us into a luxuriant living room.

I remained standing, along with Odessa and Storm, while Atherton and Regina sat on the couch.

"Why have you brought back up?" Atherton nodded at Storm and Odessa.

"Because people know your reputation," Storm said.

"I'm sure they do. I have an excellent reputation around here."

Storm glowered at him.

I took a few seconds to get my thoughts in order. "Regina, we just visited your house. You've rented it out."

She glanced at Atherton. "That's right. It's not a secret."

"How long have you been renting it out?"

"A few months. I've been spending so much time here, it didn't seem worth having a place of my own."

"How long have you been seeing Atherton?"

"That's not important," he said. "It's also none of your business."

"I think it is important. You both lied to me," I said. "Regina, you said you went home alone on the night of Jinti's murder. You couldn't have gone back to your house, so you must have come here."

She smoothed her hands over her skirt. "That's right. I came here."

"So why lie?"

"I didn't exactly lie. This is my home."

"But Atherton also said he was home alone. You were alone in the same house?"

"Oh! Well, yes, he did say that." Regina sighed. "I don't want people knowing I'm dating the boss. This village loves gossip, and I don't want to be the source of this week's scandal. Not that we were doing anything wrong, but I still felt uneasy. I'm a private person."

"I keep telling you you're being ridiculous," Atherton said. "And I'm a single man. I can date if I want to."

"Technically, you're still married," Odessa said. "Bella's only missing. You could be cheating on your wife by seeing Regina."

Atherton rolled his eyes. "Bella's been gone for years, which shows she has no interest in keeping this marriage going. What am I supposed to do, live like a monk because my wife decided she couldn't stick around?"

Regina caught hold of his hand. "We talked about going public but decided to keep things between us. It really is no one else's business. And even though Bella has been gone for some time, I was worried it looked disrespectful."

"It does," Storm said.

"We deserve to be happy," Regina said.

"So you lied about your alibi to conceal this relationship?" I said. "Is that the only reason?"

Regina nodded. "I was here that night. I left the store about eight o'clock, locked up, and then came back and had a late dinner. I went to bed about ten o'clock."

"And what about you, Atherton?" I said. "You told me you were home alone."

He shrugged. "I respect Regina's wishes for privacy. I didn't say I was with her that night because the truth would have come out."

I didn't believe him. He had to be hiding more than that.

"You should tell them everything." Regina's voice trembled. "It makes me uncomfortable thinking about what happened to Jinti. I don't feel safe."

"You're safe here," Atherton said. "And there's nothing else to share."

"I think there is. What else do you have to tell us, Regina?" I said.

"She has nothing else to say," Atherton said. "And I had nothing to do with Jinti's murder. It couldn't have been me."

"Darling, tell them where you were," Regina blurted out.

"I was here!"

She clasped her hands so tight the whites of her knuckles showed.

Atherton forced a laugh as he stared at her. "This is ridiculous. These witches have nothing to do with the Magic Council, and they can't force me to answer their questions."

"That's true," I said. "But I had a visit from Devlin Goody, and he searched the bakery. He still thinks I'm involved."

"That's not my problem."

"We're making it your problem," Storm said. "You look guilty."

"I'm not, but maybe Luna is," Atherton said. "Devlin will have solid reasons for pursuing you as a suspect."

Regina sighed. "Please, I don't like concealing information."

Atherton frowned. "What are you talking about?"

"You... you went out that night." Regina kept her gaze lowered.

I bit my lip. We'd gotten him. Atherton had lied and snuck out.

He shook his head, a disapproving look in his eyes as he glared at Regina. "What if I did?"

"Perhaps you took the opportunity to return to the store and kill Jinti," I said.

His disapproving gaze slid to anger as he focused on me. "I had an opportunity, but it wasn't the reason for me leaving."

"You told me Jinti was looking for a cure for her illness. Maybe you arranged for her to come back when there was no one else around."

"That didn't happen." Atherton pressed his lips together, then sighed. "I admit, I went out late that night, but it's not what you think." He looked at Regina again and frowned. "I didn't even realize you heard me leave."

"I'm sure you weren't doing anything wrong," she said. "But since we're revealing truths, they should know everything. And..."

"What's wrong?" Atherton said.

"I was worried you were seeing someone else," Regina said.

"Or killing someone else," Storm said.

Atherton shot her a filthy look. "I had a good reason for going out. I also have an excellent reason for keeping quiet about it. You should take my word for it. It would have been impossible for me to murder Jinti."

The intercom buzzed.

"Who's that?" Regina said.

Atherton glared at me. "I hope you haven't done something stupid, Luna."

"No, I haven't." I felt pretty smart at that moment. I'd figured out who the killer was.

Regina hurried out of the room and returned a few seconds later with Indigo and Olympus.

"Has he confessed?" Indigo said. "I filled Olympus in as we came over."

Atherton stood and held out his hand for Olympus to shake. "I'm sorry you've been dragged into this charade. Luna's gotten it into her head that I had something to do with Jinti's death. This is a waste of your time."

Olympus didn't shake Atherton's hand. "What have I missed?"

"You should tell him, Regina," I said.

Olympus raised his eyebrows and looked at Regina. "Does this have to do with Jinti's murder?"

"No, I'm sure it doesn't. As I was explaining to Luna and the others, I was keeping my relationship with Atherton a secret. After all, he's my boss. It wouldn't look professional if people discovered we were seeing each other. Atherton was all for telling everyone, but I wanted to take my time."

"So you can alibi for each other on the night of the murder?" Olympus said.

"No, they can't." I was too excited to stay silent. "Regina revealed Atherton crept out in the middle of the night. He killed Jinti."

"No one other than you has said that," Atherton said. "I simply didn't want the reason for me going out to be revealed."

"If this is important to a murder investigation," Olympus said, "you should reveal what you were doing."

A slight smirk crossed Atherton's face, and his gaze settled on me. There was an amused gleam in his eyes.

My stomach flipped, and my confidence wavered. Was he playing with me?

"Rather than me telling you where I was, why don't I show you? Then you can see my real alibi, and we can put an end to this."

"What do you have to show us?" Olympus said.

"It won't take long. We can walk there in fifteen minutes." He looked around the room at everyone. "And we'll make it a group activity, so Luna and her band of witches can see this for themselves and finally leave me alone."

Olympus gestured to the door. "Take us to your alibi, and we'll go from there."

"With pleasure." Atherton caught hold of Regina's hand, and they headed out of the room.

A few minutes later, we were striding along the road, heading toward the edge of Witch Haven.

"What's he going to show us?" Indigo whispered to me.

"Whatever it is, it won't convince me. We've caught our killer, and I'm getting my name cleared."

"Don't be too sure," Storm cautioned. "We're dealing with a slippery warlock. If he wasn't certain about this, he'd be deflecting or name dropping to weasel his way out of it."

"He's still deflecting. But we've got him. I just know it."

Chapter 16

Atherton strode ahead of us with Regina by his side, his walk confident as he strutted along as if he owned the entire village.

"He thinks he's got us," Storm muttered. "Look at him. I can't wait until we pull him down a peg or two."

"What's that building he's heading toward?" Odessa said.

Storm squinted at the building. "Oh! Why is he going there? Not many people know about this place."

"What is it?" I studied the small dark gray building. It had no house number or building name. I'd assumed it was empty every time I'd passed it, but I could see the paintwork was fresh and the flowerbeds tidy.

Storm glanced around. "It's kept on the down low for a good reason. I've been here a few times when I've been investigating a case. This is a reform school for gremlins."

"They're sending badly behaving gremlins into Witch Haven?" Odessa said. "Is that safe?"

"Have you had any gremlins attacking you or raiding the farm?" Storm said.

"Well, no. But they could if they're all living here."

"That's the reason this place is kept so quiet," Storm said. "People jump to the wrong conclusions. They think the worst about the gremlins and won't want the place here. But it's well run, and when I've visited, the project manager is always accommodating. The gremlins I've spoken to are never any bother. It's a good place."

Odessa's gaze ran over the building, guilt on her face. "I'll bring them a gift basket. I'm sure they'd like some of my pumpkin spiced muffins. Maybe I could offer them some work experience on the farm. Would the gremlins like that?"

Storm grinned. "You do that. I'm sure the gremlins will appreciate it."

"Why is Atherton bringing us here?" I said.

"We're about to find out," Indigo said.

Atherton walked up to the main door and knocked. Regina stood beside him.

We all stopped behind him and waited.

"This had better be good," Olympus muttered. "If he's dragged us here on a wild gremlin chase, I'll arrest him for wasting my time."

"I assure you, I'll explain everything in a few minutes." Atherton turned as the door opened. A taller than average middle-aged gremlin with a tuft of white hair on the top of his head stood in front of him, wearing dark jeans and a black sweater.

"Atherton! We weren't expecting you, were we?"

Atherton shook his head. "No, but I could do with your help. Sinbad, this is Olympus Duke from the Magic Council and his... associates."

"Good to meet you all," Sinbad said. "If you're here for a visit, you'll need to make an appointment. Although, if you're friends of Atherton's, we can make an exception. The residents are just finishing their evening meal."

"No, we don't need a look around," Atherton said. "Could you tell this group when I last visited?"

"I don't like where this is going," Indigo muttered. "Atherton is looking way too smug."

"He's bluffing," I said. At least, I hoped he was, or I was in big trouble. The temperature around me plummeted, and I looked around, half-expecting a ghost to appear.

"You came by two nights ago," Sinbad said.

"Thank you." Atherton turned to the group. "You see, I was here."

"What time was Atherton here?" Olympus said to Sinbad.

"He came by late. That's when the gremlins are most active. He was here at ten-thirty and left just after midnight."

"Why was he visiting?"

"He brought supplies for the gremlins. Food parcels and study materials. Atherton also provided calming magic. The residents have troubled pasts and often have difficulty controlling their abilities. Atherton has been wonderful since he learned we moved to the village. He's made the place a sanctuary for those with difficulties."

"How long has he been doing this?" I shivered against the biting cold.

"Several months."

"I don't believe you." I poked a finger at Atherton. "You weren't here. You were at the store with Jinti. You had to be."

Atherton's smile was annoyingly self-righteous. "I can't have been in two places at once."

"Atherton was here." Sinbad glanced out at the sky. "He's a wonderful warlock. So giving and generous."

"I... I don't understand," I said. "Why hide this? You said you went home on the night of Jinti's murder."

"What's this about a murder?" Sinbad said.

"It's nothing to worry about." Atherton focused on me. "There's a simple explanation for why I didn't say anything. I don't brag about my charity work."

"There's a first time for everything," Storm muttered.

Atherton ignored her. "I picked this reform school because they do amazing work, and I have the resources to help them do more. It's something I like to do in my private time. And something I didn't want anyone else knowing about."

"Oh, Atherton! That's wonderful, but you could have told me," Regina said. "I was thinking all kinds of terrible things, and I'd have liked to help. I feel awful for doubting you."

He caught hold of her hand and kissed the back of it. "That's sweet of you, but this is something I do on my own. Besides, you're busy with the store."

I grimaced. Atherton had to be using this place as a cover. Was it a front for something dubious? It was too convenient he snuck out without telling Regina on the night Jinti was killed. Had he set this up to give himself an alibi?

"Are you certain about the timeframe?" I said to Sinbad.

"Yes. Atherton is as regular as clockwork. He brings gifts and then spends time with the gremlins. Everyone needs to sign in their arrival and departure time. I can double-check, but I'm right."

"Do that." I glanced at Olympus.

He nodded. "We'd appreciate you checking."

"I'll be back in a minute." Sinbad disappeared inside.

"Am I getting sick, or is it suddenly iceberg cold out here?" Odessa stamped her feet.

Storm flipped up her collar. "I can't feel my toes."

"Why?" I addressed the question to Atherton, ignoring the icy chill in the air. "What do you get out of this?"

"Luna, I'm disappointed. Why can't I have a cause I support for no other reason than it gives me satisfaction to help the less fortunate?"

"Because you never do anything unless it serves you," I said.

"Luna, maybe you shouldn't," Odessa muttered.

"He killed Jinti!" I said. "It has to be him."

"It doesn't have to be me," Atherton said. "It could just as easily have been you. I recall you telling me you had no alibi. You could have left your bakery, used magic to conceal the break-in at my store, and murdered Jinti."

"You're making this up," I said. "Olympus, can't you do something? At least take him in for further questioning."

There was a regretful look in Olympus's eyes. "I'm sorry to say, I can't. Since Atherton was here, he couldn't have killed Jinti."

"He lied about his alibi. Can't you charge him with something relating to that?"

"Don't waste your time trying," Atherton said. "I didn't hamper this investigation by not revealing my altruistic ways."

"You didn't help it, though." Olympus shook his head at me. "I'm sorry, Luna. It looks like Atherton's in the clear."

"As I've been telling you all along," he said.

Sinbad returned and held out a book to Olympus. "Here's the sign-in sheet for that night. Atherton was here."

I looked at it alongside Olympus. There it was, Atherton's name printed out neatly and the time he arrived and left. He couldn't have been at the store.

"My apologies for disturbing your evening, Sinbad. We'll leave you to it," Atherton said.

"I hope I've been helpful. I look forward to seeing you here next week."

"Absolutely." Atherton turned to us as the door closed. "Are you happy? Will you leave me alone now? I had nothing to do with Jinti's death."

"No, I'm not happy." I'd been certain Atherton was behind Jinti's murder.

His fake smile slipped. "Olympus, you should take a closer look at this witch. She's protesting too hard about her innocence and looking for other people to pin the murder on."

"Don't worry. I know how to do my job," Olympus said.

"Oh, that's right. You're the wrong person to inform about this shambles. I'll let Devlin Goody know what's going on." A sharp look crossed Atherton's face. "I keep forgetting you associate with Indigo and her friends. Did your girlfriend try to have me arrested?"

Olympus glowered at him. "I assure you, my personal relationships don't get in the way of my work. Perhaps I will look into you faking an alibi, after all."

Atherton chuckled as he walked away with Regina. "You do that. Good luck with the outcome. I'm having dinner with Commissioner Brody next week. I'll mention this matter to him. He won't appreciate his employees wasting my time."

"Don't." Indigo caught hold of Olympus's arm as he went to march after Atherton. "He's not worth it. He's goading you so you'll do something reckless."

I shuddered, feeling hot and cold at the same time, despite the icy air. "Atherton knew he had an airtight alibi, yet he hid it. He made this investigation more complicated. I know he's hiding something."

"What?" Olympus gestured at the reform school, a snap in his tone. "His good deeds?"

"This isn't real. He must get something out of helping the gremlins," I said.

"This is a game to Atherton," Storm said, as we all watched Atherton and Regina walk away. "He's the kind of guy who plays with people because he can get away with it. He thinks he's untouchable."

"I plan on touching him. A lot. And I'll keep touching him until—"

Storm's laugh cut me off.

"What's so funny?"

"The idea of you touching Atherton." Storm cackled. "He's not your type."

Odessa grinned and looked away, while Indigo smiled and shrugged.

"You know that's not what I meant. What does Regina see in him?"

"Power, wealth, influence, a good job, and free accommodation." Odessa tapped a finger against her chin. "It reminds me of your relationship with Englebert."

I huffed out a breath. "I'm nothing like Regina."

Olympus turned to me, his expression stern. "Luna, you aren't to keep pursuing Atherton. He has influence, and he'll use it if you get in his way."

I glanced at him. "Sorry for bringing you into this. I really thought Atherton killed Jinti. When I found out he'd lied, I assumed it was because he was hiding the fact he was a killer. I didn't expect this." I gestured at the gremlin reform school. "He looked guilty, and he had good reason for wanting Jinti out of the way."

"Especially now he's in a relationship with Regina," Indigo said. "When people find out, they won't be happy. He still has a wife out there somewhere."

"Assuming Bella's still alive," Storm said. "I've been doing some digging. She vanished off the face of the earth. There's no record of her anywhere. No financial transactions, no rental agreements, nothing."

"She must be staying somewhere and have resources to live on," I said.

"I don't know how she's doing it, but Bella's living below the radar," Storm said.

"There was no evidence of murder during the investigation into her disappearance," Olympus said. "I remember the case, because Atherton was such a nuisance. He turned up at the Magic Council at least once a week, demanding a progress report. But there was little we could do. There was no evidence of foul play, simply a suggestion of an unhappy wife who walked out on her husband."

"He must want a resolution over Bella walking out," Odessa said, "especially now he's moved on with Regina. What if they want to marry?" I said.

"Atherton might be able to have Bella declared officially dead," Olympus said. "But that's not easy to do. She needs to have been missing for at least seven years before he can start that process."

Indigo looked at me. "What do you want to do now?"

"I want Atherton to be guilty of Jinti's murder. But it can't be him. And it wasn't Regina."

"Are you sure? I always say be careful around the sweet ones," Storm said.

"Regina seemed shocked about Atherton's secret. I think she was being truthful," Odessa said.

"So do I. And her motive is thin." My tone was glum as I tugged my jacket around me.

"Let's go back to my farm," Odessa said. "It's not far from here. We can warm up, talk things over, and figure out your next move."

"I wish I could join you, but I need to get back." Olympus kissed Indigo. "Luna, I'll let you know if I hear any updates." He hurried away.

We walked to Odessa's farm as a wind kicked up and buffeted us around, adding to my bone cold chill.

"What's with this weather?" Indigo pulled up her collar. "It's been weird for days."

"Just like us, the wind is angry with Atherton," Odessa said. "If this keeps up, I'll need to shelter my boys in a barn, or they'll get hurt."

I studied the scarecrows on display as we neared her detached farmhouse. "These look new. You've been busy."

She looked around and smiled. "I've had so much energy lately, so I figured I'd put it to good use. I made all of these last week."

"There are sixty scarecrows in that field," Storm said.

"And they're all magnificent," Odessa said.

"Are they all, you know, active?" Indigo shuddered.

"Not all of them. I haven't added my magic touch yet. Most of them can move around on their own, though."

Her scarecrows were huge and intimidating. They were giants with big pumpkin heads and fierce expressions on their faces. "Why do they all look so mad?"

"I'm not sure. I give them their initial expressions, but they change as the magic grows through them. Most of them are coming out on the intense side of the mood spectrum. I've already had to chain a few in the barn and arrange for them to go for re-education."

"Are you sure your magic is okay?" Storm said. "You don't want to create a bunch of killer scarecrows that rampage through Witch Haven when your back is turned."

"My scarecrows never rampage. They just get overexcited, especially when they first get their freedom."

"One is heading this way," I said. "Should we run?"

"No, that's Shamrock." Indigo raised a hand at the scarecrow as he loped toward us.

"And he's still crushing on you," Odessa said. "Even though I keep telling him you're taken, he's besotted."

"He needs to get un-besotted," Indigo said. "I like the guy, but I can't date two men. Well, one warlock and one scarecrow."

"Why not?" Odessa said, a grin on her face. "Luna does."

"I don't, not really," I muttered. I needed to get my relationship situation in order, but I couldn't think about that while I had this murder looming over my head.

Shamrock stopped in front of Indigo. He knelt before her with one large hand outstretched.

Indigo patted him on the shoulder. "It's good to see you, too. I hope you haven't been causing trouble for Odessa."

He stood and grinned at Odessa before attempting to plant a kiss on Indigo's cheek.

She backed away and shook her head. "We've talked about this. You need to get Odessa to make you a girlfriend. Then you'll be happy."

Shamrock looked at Odessa with a hopeful glint in his gleaming eyes.

"I'm not good at creating female scarecrows. I always get the bust wrong, so I turn them into strapping men."

"That's your subconscious telling you something," Storm said.

"What's that?" Odessa said sharply.

I exchanged a glance with Storm and Indigo. Odessa's relationship history was tragic, and we never talked about it because she got a wild look in her eye and changed the subject.

"Let's get inside before this wind blows us away and icicles form on our noses." Odessa raced up the steps of the farmhouse and shoved the door open.

Indigo waved goodbye to Shamrock, then followed the rest of us in.

A few minutes later, we were seated around Odessa's large table in the middle of a cozy kitchen, two huge plates of iced pumpkin muffins in front of us, along with steaming mugs of hot chocolate.

I took several sips of my hot chocolate, but it didn't soothe me. I was worried and annoyed at Atherton, and I couldn't see a way out of this tangle.

"Don't look so concerned," Odessa said. "We know you're innocent."

"We also know the Magic Council makes mistakes. My muffin is still in the mix when it comes to this murder, and Devlin Goody has it in for me."

"Devlin is a career ladder climbing sneak," Indigo said. "You don't have to worry about him."

"I do. He took away samples of my baking. What if he finds something odd?"

"What do you think he'll find?" Storm flinched as wind slammed into the side of the farmhouse. "There isn't something dodgy in your baking, is there?"

"Of course not. But you know I occasionally struggle with my baking magic."

"Sometimes, you do," Indigo said. "Other times, it works perfectly. Why does that happen?"

The contents of my mug suddenly got fascinating. "I wish I knew."

"Are you sure you don't know?" Odessa said. "I mean, it's unusual, isn't it? We should all excel in our family magic. And the Brimstone baking ability goes back generations."

"Longer than that," I said. "The Brimstones have been creating amazing food for hundreds of years. I don't know why it skipped me."

"It hasn't skipped you," Indigo said. "I've eaten loads of your food over the years, and most of it's been great."

"Not all of it," I muttered. "And I make Storm sick."

She shrugged. "I can have a sensitive stomach."

"Maybe you get distracted," Odessa said. "I do that when I'm making my scarecrows. I take my mind off the job for thirty seconds, and suddenly they're out of control, and I have to rip them apart and start again. It happens to the best of us."

"Although it happens to you more often than others," Storm said to me. "You should look into that."

I stuffed half a muffin in my mouth and nodded. My malfunctioning magic wasn't their problem, and I was dealing with it. My farmhouse harem just needed a tweak to get it operating smoothly.

"Let's talk murder." I could handle that better than my own issues.

"You're almost out of suspects," Indigo said.

"It wasn't me, and Regina and Atherton have been discounted, so that leaves Ulric. He spent time with Jinti the night she was killed."

"Have you spoken to him?"

I shook my head. "Not yet."

"I can't imagine a less likely killer," Odessa said. "Ulric's got such a warm aura."

"He doesn't strike me as a killer, either," Indigo said.

Storm tipped back her chair. "Let's not forget his dodgy past. When he ran that cult, he wasn't such a great guy."

"He's changed," Odessa said.

"Or he's gone back to his old ways," Storm said. "Ulric thought he could manipulate Jinti, and she turned the tables, so he had to get rid of her."

"Why pick on Jinti?" I said. "From what I know about his former cult days, Ulric went after attractive, wealthy, younger women. And no offense to Jinti, but she wasn't wealthy or pretty, and she lived in that tumbledown place the Magic

Council has been threatening to pull down for years."

"Jinti still had powerful magic, even if the supermodel body was drooping," Storm said. "Maybe Ulric needed to get his hands on it. He tried to force her to create a spell, but she refused to help him."

I finished my muffin and reached for another. "There's only one way I'm going to find out if Ulric was involved. I need to visit him."

"You do that," Odessa said. "And while you're there, get your aura cleansed. I always feel fabulous after Ulric's cleansed my aura."

Storm snorted a laugh. "Are you sure that's what he does to you? Remember, this guy brainwashed women into submitting to his every whim."

Odessa swatted Storm's arm. "I'm telling you, he's legit. Speak to him, find out if he had anything to do with Jinti, and once he's in the clear, go for a full body aura cleanse. You'll feel wonderful."

I wasn't sure I wanted my aura touched by Ulric, but I needed closure on this situation. Perhaps he could answer the questions surrounding the mystery of Jinti's murder and who wanted her dead.

"I'll speak to him tomorrow." And this time, I wasn't jumping to conclusions.

Chapter 17

"Are you sure you can handle things if I'm not here for an hour?" I said to Uncle Albert, almost tripping over Earl as he rolled by my feet.

"I'm feeling much better. And the lunchtime rush is over, so it'll be quiet for a few hours. Go out if you need to."

"I won't be long. When I get back, you can take a break. I'll get on with icing the cakes." I nudged Earl with my toe. "Are you sweeping the floor with your tail or coming with me?"

"Coming with." He rolled onto his paws and arched his back.

"I'll be fine, Luna. Most of the afternoon customers are regulars, so they won't mind if I'm slow. Off you go." Uncle Albert shooed me and Earl out the door.

After my failed attempt at discovering who killed Jinti last night, a visit to Ulric was my final option. I was hoping he could shed light on what happened to her.

Ulric lived in a small apartment above his store. He opened every day to offer free healing and counselling to any magic user who needed it. And he was always busy. Managing magic was a tricky business.

"I'm glad we're going here," Earl said. "I'm running low on supplies."

"What supplies do you need?"

"Ulric does the best quality catnip around. It's balled up and ready to go."

"You've got plenty of catnip at home."

"No, it's all gone."

"It can't be. I got you a huge bag a week ago. It was supposed to last the month."

"What else am I supposed to do other than kick back and chew the catnip?"

"Be more useful to me? You're my magical aide, and you're meant to strengthen my spells." I glanced at my fingers. "Maybe you're the reason I keep misfiring. You're too spaced out on catnip to help."

"You need more than my help to fix your issues. Besides, you've always got things under control. That's what you tell me." He sniffed. "You act like you don't need a familiar."

I frowned. Maybe I didn't have things as under control as I'd thought. "Just behave when you're in Ulric's shaman shack."

"I won't do anything to get on Ulric's wrong side, in case he cuts off my supply."

I shook my head as we reached the door and walked into the store. The air was heavy with the scent of incense, and a string of silver bells tinkled in the breeze by an open window. It was milder today, the odd freezing conditions vanishing as quickly as they'd arrived.

There were several shelves in the store, littered with charms, healing cards, and positive affirmations, and I took a moment to look around as I waited for Ulric to show.

"Luna! How nice to see you." He appeared through a multi-colored beaded curtain and walked toward me, a warm smile on his face. "And Earl, too. I can guess what you're here for."

"Hit me with your best stuff," Earl said. "It's Luna's treat."

"It's always my treat."

Ulric chuckled as he unscrewed a glass jar, scooped out a large cup of dried herbs, and placed them in a small brown bag. "Be careful with this brand. It's got a kick."

"Lay some out for me while I'm here," Earl said. "I might as well enjoy myself while I'm waiting for Luna."

"Just a small amount," I said, "or you'll be worse than useless for the rest of the day."

"I can handle my catnip."

Ulric obliged, laying out a small clump of catnip in a neat row on the floor. Earl pounced on it and started licking and drooling.

"Shall we go somewhere more comfortable?" Ulric gestured to two large armchairs at the back of the store. "We can talk there. If any other customers come in, we won't be disturbed. Everyone knows this is my private corner."

"Sure. That would be great." I walked over and settled into a seat.

"Would you like tea?" Ulric said. "I've got several excellent herbal blends."

I glanced over at Earl. He was on his back, purring and exposing his belly for anyone who wanted to tickle it. "I'll pass."

Ulric's smile broadened. "Don't worry, my herbal tea won't make you behave like Earl."

I grinned at him. "Even so, I'm not here for a social visit."

"I understand. You need some healing?"

"No, I'm fine on that front, too."

His gaze ran over me. "If you don't mind me saying, you seem troubled. Your aura is hazy and cut through with strands of black."

"Black? That sounds bad. Although it's a slimming color, so I guess that's good. Should I be worried?"

"It suggests you have conflict in your life."

"Ah! That makes sense. I don't know if you've heard what happened yesterday with Atherton and Regina?"

Ulric shook his head. "I haven't seen either of them." He settled back in his seat, crossed one leg over the other, and rested his hands against his knee.

"It has to do with what happened to Jinti."

His chin lifted, then he slowly nodded. "I heard the Magic Council looked around the bakery. I doubt they found anything."

"They didn't. But Devlin isn't letting it go. And... well, I was convinced Atherton was involved, given his history with Jinti and her daughter."

Ulric lowered his eyes for a second. "There's not a day goes by when I don't think about my beautiful Bella."

"You were seeing her before she went missing?"

"Yes, and it's no secret. Although I expect Atherton would like it to be. The man's pride is something else. I've tried several times to calm his ego with magic, but nothing helps."

"I find it strange you two are friendly. After all, Bella was cheating with you."

"It took a lot of work to get Atherton onside, and I still carry the burden of guilt with me. I genuinely cared for Bella, and she felt the same about me." Ulric's eyes misted. "It was a difficult time for her before she left. She'd been married to Atherton for several years, and things weren't going well, but she didn't want to give up on her marriage. She held her vows close to her heart."

"Did Bella join your cult? Is that how you got to know her?"

He arched his eyebrows. "You are well informed about my past."

"I asked around. I really want to find out what happened to Jinti, and when I looked into her life, your relationship with Bella came up, along with your former cult."

"My previous lifestyle isn't one I'm proud of. But no, I didn't meet Bella at my cult. We had mutual friends." He gestured at the shelves. "She's part of the reason I opened this place."

I looked around the simple room. "The store can't make you much money. You're always donating your services. And I know you undercharge for Earl's catnip."

"No, it doesn't make much money, but it's enough for a simple life. The money I obtained from running True North made me wealthy, so I don't need to earn a wage."

"It's a sort of cleansing for you, to help those in need?"

"Exactly. And I have a lot of repenting to do. When I set up the cult, I was arrogant and thought I was better than every other magic user. I preyed upon those who were weaker than me and took things I shouldn't, both material and emotional." Ulric shook his head. "I damaged people, but I'm making up for that by helping troubled magic users."

"Everyone says great things about your store."

"I'm glad to hear that." Ulric's gaze drifted over me again. "That offer extends to you. I don't like to see anyone struggling."

"I'm not struggling," I said. "But I would like to know more about your relationship with Jinti. Did she ever come to you for healing?"

"No, and she was a cut above me for restorative medicine. There was nothing she didn't know about using nature's remedies to cure illness. Even as she aged, she still had a wealth of knowledge. She'll be a real loss to the village."

"How was Jinti with you?"

He tilted his head. "We had a good relationship. Of course, we locked horns sometimes, but that was Jinti's way. She never let anybody off easy. I sometimes consulted her about unusual client maladies. She'd often have a solution."

"Considering you had an affair with her daughter, I wondered if Jinti didn't think much of you."

Ulric's smile was rueful. "When Jinti found out I was seeing Bella, I thought she'd rip my head off.

She tore into my house like a whirlwind, shouting and yelling and telling me she'd ruin me. I was terrified. But when she calmed down and Bella spoke to her, she realized we were happy together. I gave Bella something Atherton never could."

"What was that? If it's not too personal a question."

"No, it's not personal. Bella simply wanted to be loved for who she was." Ulric was quiet for several seconds. "I have a solid relationship with Atherton now, but I'm not a fan of his materialistic desires. And believe me, I know how ironic that sounds. I was just like him. I desired more wealth and power and wanted people to adore me. But after I lost Bella, none of that mattered. It seemed shallow. Bella changed me. She used to tell me about her dreams of a simple life, a cozy home full of children and laughter. It made my heart warm to hear her talk about the things that would bring her joy. I craved that as well."

"Was Bella thinking about leaving Atherton for you?"

"We talked about it, but Atherton had a hold over her, and he made her feel guilty when she expressed concerns. Bella always thought she'd only marry once. Atherton knew it wounded her to think she was failing."

"If he deceived her into marrying him, she had every right to leave."

"He didn't. When they met, Bella was young, and she had nothing. Jinti rarely charged people what she should for healing them, so they always scraped by. I think that's why Bella was so enamored by Atherton and accepted his proposal. She wanted for nothing. Atherton provided all the material things to make life comfortable. The grand apartment, a thriving business, the social events, and expensive clothes and jewelry. But it didn't take Bella long to realize those things were hollow. They didn't fill the hole in her heart."

"And you did?"

His smile was tinged with sadness. "I like to think I did. It wasn't long after I became involved with Bella that I closed the cult and changed my ways. She had a wonderful way of making me see sense and gain clarity over what mattered. That was her magic gift."

"Atherton didn't hold a grudge about that? It sounds like you were a catalyst in making Bella walk out on him."

"I wasn't a catalyst, and I never forced her to leave him. Bella needed to make that decision for herself. I was devastated the day she vanished. To walk away from everything like that, it was terrible."

"Bella never mentioned her plan to leave? Not even to Jinti?"

"From what I could find out, she told no one. I spoke to Jinti to see if she knew anything, but she was as surprised as me."

"Did Jinti ever think you could have been involved with what happened to Bella?"

"She questioned me, but she was certain Atherton was behind the disappearance."

"What do you think about that theory?"

He hesitated. "I don't know what to think. All this time has passed, and the memories get hazy. Bella was unhappy, and we all knew that, but no one could get through to her. Not even Jinti."

"Someone must know something." I spoke more to myself than Ulric.

"I'm sure they do." He leaned forward. "I have a question for you. Why the interest in Bella?"

"I had a theory about who killed Jinti. I thought her murder was linked to Bella."

He made several rapid blinks. "Go on."

I shook my head. "I made a mistake and accused Atherton of killing Jinti."

"Why would he do that?"

"Because Jinti suspected him of doing something to Bella, or she was angry because he drove her away." I hesitated in sharing my other reason then decided to keep Atherton and Regina's relationship to myself. I didn't know how many people knew about it. "I figured they fought, and he poisoned her."

Ulric nodded slowly. "You were wrong?"

"Completely wrong. And Atherton called me out. I feel like an idiot."

"You're not an idiot. You're a powerful, clever witch who has just lost her way." He smiled. "Was that why you were at the magic swap? You were there looking for something for your troubles?"

I wished he'd stop telling me I was troubled. "I promise you, I'm not troubled. I've just had a lot on my mind. And I'm determined to make sure the Magic Council no longer sees me as a suspect in Jinti's murder. That's the other reason I'm asking these questions."

"You're looking for other suspects?" Ulric drew in a slow breath. "Do you think I had something to do with it?"

"I... maybe. You were at the store that night, and you have a history with Jinti."

He laughed softly. "I understand."

I felt a twinge of guilt, but I had to keep up the questions. Ulric was my only suspect. "Were there any problems between you and Jinti?"

"No. We were healers and respected each other's craft. And Jinti appreciated I'd brought joy to her daughter's life. She didn't have many other people to turn to, and we supported each other and often discussed herbal remedies and healing treatments. I admired her and considered her a friend."

"Did you see Jinti argue with anyone at the magic swap?"

He shook his head. "I wasn't there for long and only dropped by to support Atherton. He wasn't happy because of the party at the inn. It took away his custom, and he was thinking about cancelling, but Regina said it was wrong to let people down. The customers I saw didn't pay Jinti any attention."

"What did you do after the magic swap ended?"

"I had a late dinner in the inn, along with a couple of drinks, and headed home. After that, I went out to meet Atherton."

"What were you doing?"

Ulric shook his head. "I shouldn't tell you. I was helping Atherton with something. It was nothing bad."

I repressed a groan. "Does this have to do with the reform school?"

His eyes widened a fraction. "You know about that place?"

"I visited the school with Atherton after I accused him of murder."

"Well, then I suppose it doesn't matter if you already know. Atherton often takes parcels of food and equipment to the gremlins. I join him sometimes and offer free counselling and healing. The residents find it helpful."

"What time did you visit the school?"

"I met Atherton just before ten-thirty. We were there just under two hours. There were several residents in need of support, so I was happy to stay late and give them guidance."

I wanted to weep. This didn't help me. It only strengthened Atherton's innocence and ruled out Ulric.

"Is everything okay?" he asked. "Your aura flashed red and then a dense black for a second."

"Yes, sorry. I got caught up in my thoughts. I wish I could figure out what happened to Jinti. Why did she go back to Atherton's store that night? Why was she killed there? Who wanted her dead? And how can I make sure the Magic Council doesn't keep looking at me for the crime?"

Sympathy crossed Ulric's face. "I spoke to Regina yesterday, and she mentioned the Magic Council was concerned about the food you'd supplied. If it's any comfort, I ate one of the muffins and felt fine. If you want me to, I can speak to the Magic Council and tell them."

"Thanks. It won't do any harm." Although I doubted it would do me much good.

"I shall do that." He jumped up and secured a window that had blown open before returning to his seat. "I really would like to offer you healing. I'm aware you had a difficult time during your abduction. It must have been terrifying."

I kept the smile on my face. You've got to love small places and their fine-tuned gossip networks. "It was more confusing than terrifying. Most of the time, I felt sleepy. And I always knew my friends would find me, so I had hope."

"You have excellent friends," Ulric said. "It's important to have people you can rely on. People you trust with all your problems."

"My friends are amazing. I'm lucky to have them."

He caught hold of my hands and cradled them. His fingers were soft and warm, and a gentle tickle flickered across my palms as I relaxed under his touch.

"If there's anything I can ever do, or you'd like to be healed, come back anytime. No charge. Those who are most troubled always get my help for free."

I couldn't figure out why he was so concerned about me. Sure, I had a few problems going on, but others had it worse than me. "Thanks for your time, but I'd better let you get on."

He slowly withdrew his hands and nodded. "The offer is there. No time limit."

I collected a snoring, dribbling Earl, and left the store. I was stumped about Jinti's murder. There were no more suspects left.

There was the vague possibility Regina was putting on an incredible act. She'd snuck out of

Atherton's house once he'd left, returned to the store, and killed Jinti.

I pressed my lips together and shook my head. That was me clutching at the thinnest of straws. Regina had no motive for wanting Jinti dead.

I turned the corner and froze. Devlin Goody stood outside the bakery with two large, ominous looking members of the Magic Council. One of them was holding a chain.

Backing away several steps, I tried to get my brain to function. They were here to arrest me. I'd run out of time and hadn't solved this murder or cleared my name.

Devlin's gaze lifted, and he saw me. "There she is!"

I clamped Earl firmly over my shoulder, turned, and raced away.

Chapter 18

There had to be a place to hide. I ran to the end of the road as my sensibilities kicked in. What was I doing? I had no reason to run. Racing off like an idiot would make Devlin think I was guilty. Or guiltier, if that was even possible.

It was too late now. I'd seen him, he'd seen me, and then like a donut, I'd run off.

And I kept running.

This was terrible. I needed time to think. I had to find Jinti's killer before the Magic Council whisked me away to a remote prison, and I was never seen again.

"Stop!" Devlin's voice sounded faintly behind me.

I didn't look back as I raced through the gates of the cemetery and along the gravel path. I ducked behind a large crypt, drew in a deep, shuddering breath, and wished to be invisible.

"Hey! What are you doing here?"

I looked up to see Silvaria Digby striding toward me, a long white carved stick in her hands.

"Nothing. I'm admiring the view." I poked my head around the crypt but saw no sign of Devlin chasing me. Maybe I'd given him the slip.

"Admiring the view? What's the matter with you? This isn't a holiday park."

I waved my hand at Silvaria to get her to leave me alone. "I'll only be a minute, and then I'll be on my way."

"If you're not here to pay your respects, you need to leave. I don't like people gawping at the graves. It's mawkish."

"I'm not gawping. I'm resting, and—" I stopped talking as male voices drifted toward me.

"I'm sure she came in here." That was Devlin. "You two go either side. I'll cut through the middle. We'll find her."

"Have you brought the Magic Council into my cemetery?" Silvaria glared at me. She was always overly protective in her role as cemetery guardian. "I don't want trouble. The bodies don't like noise and fuss. It unsettles them."

"There'll be no trouble from me. I just need to be left alone."

"And I want my graveyard and its residents left in peace." Silvaria raised a hand. "Over here. I found what you're looking for."

I grimaced. "Thanks for nothing."

"I don't owe you a thing. You come into my home, cause noise, and you bring the Magic Council with you. What did you expect would happen?" Silvaria turned and stamped away. "Oh and tell Indigo dance class has been cancelled this week. We'll have to make up for it another time."

I was about to race away, when Devlin appeared around the side of the crypt, gasping in breath. "Luna! Why did you run?"

I straightened my spine and kept a firm grip on Earl, who'd slept through all the fun. "You don't turn up with two scary looking guys and a chain because you want to eat one of my buttered crumpets."

Devlin sucked in several more breaths then looked around and waved his colleagues over. "This looks bad for you."

"It can't get any worse. You've made your mind up about me. You think I'm guilty of murder."

"You're guilty of something."

"You have no evidence. You just don't like me."

Devlin's colleagues arrived and flanked either side of him, looking menacing.

I glanced at the chain. "You can keep that away from me. I'm not going to fight you, but I'm also not giving up. I didn't kill Jinti."

"Then explain your strange magic." Devlin adjusted his broad-brimmed hat, sweat glistening on his upper lip.

"What do you want me to explain?"

"The samples from the bakery showed unusual results. Concerning results."

I swallowed down my panic. I knew Devlin would pick up something unusual if he looked too closely at my magic. "I'm not sure what you're talking about."

"I took six samples. Albert's magic was easy to identify. It has a pure, sweet signature. But four of the samples were confusing. We tested them several times and got the same result."

I lifted my chin. "What result was that?"

"There was an odd mix of magic in the baked goods. It looked as if several magic users had made them. Do you have other staff who assist in the bakery?"

"No, it's just me and Uncle Albert. Occasionally, my friends help box up orders when we have a rush job. Maybe you're picking up their magic signatures."

"It wasn't that. The magic was mixed in as if used in equal measure. Why is that?"

There had to be a way to convince Devlin there was nothing wrong with what I did. "Sometimes, my baking magic is a tiny bit haphazard. It's a delicate balance to get the sweet and savory just right. Baking is tricky. Have you ever tried making a souffle?"

He frowned. "Of course not."

"That could be what you're picking up on. The fine art of seasoning." That almost sounded plausible to me.

"Haphazard means dangerous," Devlin said. "You shouldn't use magic you can't control if you're giving it to other people. They could end up dead, just like Jinti."

"You already know she wasn't poisoned by my muffin. And I've talked to several other people who went to the magic swap. They all ate my muffins and had no ill effects. Ask them. I was just speaking to Ulric. He'll defend me."

"That's still not good enough. Even if you aren't behind what happened to Jinti, you're misusing magic, and that's illegal. Whatever odd blend of spells you're using is unstable. One sample exploded. What if someone had been about to eat that?"

"My baked goods never explode." They did, but I always neutralized the cakes that had a habit of going boom.

"Add this strange mix of magic to the complaints we've received about the bakery, and I have no choice but to arrest you," Devlin said.

"You can't. That's unfair."

"You must be prevented from using any magic until we discover what you're doing. And we have more tests to conduct. I'm certain that, once we've run the right test, we'll discover something in the muffin that killed Jinti."

I backed away until I hit the crypt. "I have no reason for wanting Jinti dead."

"You don't have a reason we've discovered yet, but everyone has secrets."

"You're making a huge mistake." I held up a hand as Devlin's colleague approached me. "You're not putting me in chains. It's humiliating."

"We need to make sure you're unable to use your magic. It's harmful." Devlin gestured at his chain wielding colleague. "Bind her."

"Look out! There's a wild animal on the loose."

My head jerked around at the sound of Storm's voice.

A second later, Fire Fang crashed into Devlin and his colleagues. He snarled, grabbed Devlin by the back of his collar, and dragged him away.

I stared open-mouthed as Devlin squealed. His colleagues chased after Fire Fang, who was moving with eye-blurring speed and not like he was dragging a two hundred pound plus warlock across the dirt.

Storm stopped by my side, a smile on her face. "Be careful! His bite is toxic."

"What are you doing?" I gasped out.

"Saving your behind. I heard you were being chased by Devlin, so I came to see if you needed a hand."

"Um... thanks. I was dealing with them."

"Sure you were. You didn't look at all cornered by three goons. What were they doing?"

"They were about to arrest me. Devlin thinks my magic is odd. And he still thinks I poisoned Jinti."

"I always knew the Magic Council was full of morons."

"Yeah, they are. Although Olympus is excluded."

"Even he can be a jerk."

My heartbeat slowed to under a thousand beats a minute as I sucked in air. "I appreciate Fire Fang's save. I was running out of options, and nothing I said convinced Devlin of my innocence. They wanted to chain me up."

We stood in silence for a minute. The only sounds reaching us were the snarls and growls from Fire Fang and the bellows and squeals from the Magic Council employees.

"Are you sure Fire Fang is okay? There's three of them and one of him," I said.

Storm chuckled darkly. "Don't worry. He's pretty much indestructible."

I could no longer see Fire Fang or Devlin, but I kept hearing growls and shrieks. "Should we help?"

"Fire Fang does his own thing. He's fearless, and nothing can slow him down. He has everything under control."

"Does that mean you're keeping him?" My gaze shot around the cemetery, looking for any sign of Devlin returning.

"Nope. Although it's turning into a longer term foster than I imagined," Storm said. "And I'm not sure I'll ever find him a permanent home. Fire Fang does strange things, and he has a habit of setting stuff on fire when he's angry. He gets angry a lot. He has issues."

"You sound perfect for each other."

"That's not a compliment." Storm glared at me, then grinned. "What's so strange about your magic that the Magic Council thinks you have to be taken off the streets?"

"Nothing. Devlin is making it sound worse than it is." I gripped my hands behind my back and leaned my head against my snoozing familiar to stop him from sliding off my shoulder.

"What did Devlin say about your magic?"

"He said I have an odd blend of abilities. I tried to explain that my baking magic is temperamental, but he wasn't having it. One of my cake samples even exploded when they tested it. That had to be their fault."

Storm was quiet for a moment, her gaze flitting around the cemetery. "The others would never say this to you, but your magic is strange."

My gut tightened, and I glanced at her. "What makes you think that?"

"Most of us have a stable magic pattern. I'd know Indigo's magic anywhere, just as I would Odessa's. Yours is always different. It changes."

"Changes how?" She knew. Storm was going to figure out what I'd been doing.

"Sometimes, it's so powerful it hurts my eyes. Other times, it's kitten weak, almost like you have no magic. And it changes color and smell. It's like there's a different magic user in the room. If I didn't see you, I wouldn't recognize the magic."

"It's not that different."

"It is. And we're worried about you." Storm kept her gaze forward, but her jaw was twitching.

"Have you been talking about me with the others?"

She nodded. "And before you get offended, we've not been gossiping but talking because we're concerned."

"I'm fine." If I said those words enough, maybe they'd leave me alone. I really was fine. I'd just had a few bad days.

"I don't know everything that happened with Indigo's mom, and maybe that messed you up more—"

"Yep. That's it!" I grabbed this excuse and clung to it. "I've been having problems since I was taken, but I'm sorting it. You don't need to do anything to help."

"Let me finish. This problem has been happening for a long time. Even before you were taken, I always thought your magic had a weird flair, and I never knew what power you'd bring if we did a group spell."

"We all have off days." I had to get Storm away from this topic. When she wanted to find something out, she dug her heels in and never gave up. And I really didn't want her attention on my magic issues.

"I'm saying this because we want to help. If you've got something weird going on, tell us what it is. We'll figure out a workaround."

There was a wail and the sound of something tearing.

I winced. "I have no problems or weirdness going on. We should check on Fire Fang. I haven't heard any growls for a few seconds."

"He'll come back to me when he's ready."

"I don't want him getting hurt."

"Stop deflecting." Storm turned to me. "What's going on with you? And if you say you're fine, I'm going to kill you and have this etched on your tombstone: *Luna Brimstone. She always said she was fine. She lied. Look where it got her.*"

Storm would do that, too. "I'm... distressed because of this Jinti business and the Magic Council poking around and causing trouble."

"It's more than that." The uncharacteristic worry in Storm's eyes made my heart clench. She wasn't a witch who shared her feelings, so I knew how serious this was. "We want to make sure you're safe and happy."

"I am. As soon as everything is sorted with the Magic Council, I'll be back to normal." And once I'd fixed my farmhouse harem and added Cole to the mix. When I was firing on werewolf magic, I'd be able to solve any problem.

"Luna, you've never been normal. I'm not saying that's bad, but it's odd. We're all here for you. I'm never letting go of my weird little witch buddy." Her hand skimmed my arm.

This was about as close as Storm got to telling me she loved me, and I appreciated it. But if I told my friends what was going on and how many years I'd been draining magic to get through each day, they'd think of me differently. I'd no longer have the same power as them. I'd be strange and unnatural. Who wanted a friend like that?

"I see you don't want to talk about it now." Storm turned away, her shoulders tight. "That doesn't mean we won't talk about it soon."

A sigh slid from my lips. "I can't deal with any more drama."

"I'm not causing you drama."

"You're not exactly a stress reliever. Uncle Albert's not well, I've got the Magic Council on my back, and I have to focus on work."

"Let's not forget all the guys you're seeing," Storm said. "That's another mystery I want solved."

"You and me both. And it will be solved. I promise you, everything will be back to normal soon enough."

She gave a nod but still didn't look at me. "We're here for you when you're ready."

"I appreciate that." I gave her arm a quick squeeze. "And I could do with your help."

Storm turned, her eyebrows raised. "You want to talk weird magic?"

"No, but since I've got some breathing space from the Magic Council, I was thinking about checking out Jinti's home. Maybe there's a clue there the

Magic Council missed, something to lead us to the real killer."

Her expression hardened, then she shrugged. "Sure. That sounds like a not terrible plan."

"I can't officially go in and do a search, though." I risked a smile. "What do you feel about a little break and enter?"

Storm grinned, just as Fire Fang bounded across the cemetery, Devlin's hat in his mouth. "Always. Let's go have some break and enter fun."

Chapter 19

I jogged along beside Storm and Fire Fang, still holding onto Earl. I'd never known an animal to sleep through so much. That catnip must have been super strong.

We arrived outside Jinti's quirky hut. It was set on the edge of the forest and had faded green clapboards on the front and a red door with a dried wreath hung above the knocker.

"We need to be quick," I said. "I'm on borrowed time. It won't take long before Devlin regroups and comes after me."

"I doubt he'll come looking for you here," Storm said.

"Even so, let's get in and out quickly."

"We can guarantee no one is home. Jinti lived here on her own."

We dashed to the door, and I tried the handle. It was locked.

"Let me." Storm spun out a crackle of red magic, and the door sprung open.

I peered around the corner. The door led into the living room at the front of the house. I hurried in, followed by Storm and Fire Fang.

I set Earl on the couch and looked around. The air smelt musty, with a hint of weak lemon.

"What are you hoping to find?" Storm stood beside me.

"Anything that could give us a clue about who killed Jinti."

"I doubt you'll find threatening letters or evil plots strewn around."

"There has to be something I've missed." I rubbed my forehead, a headache growing behind my eyes. I'd been using a lot of magic, and the power I'd borrowed was fading fast. I'd soon need a boost.

I glanced at Storm. She was powerful, and I was certain she could handle having a little power drained.

With teeth gritted, I took a step away and clenched my hands. I didn't take magic from friends. There were some lines I wouldn't cross.

Storm walked over to a cluttered cabinet. "These are all pictures of her daughter."

I joined her. It looked like a shrine had been set up. There were dozens of pictures of Bella, along with a photo album and newspaper cuttings about her disappearance.

"I've been doing my own digging about Jinti and heard a few rumors about her daughter." Storm checked through the cabinet drawers. "Bella might not have left the village."

"She can't still be here. Someone would have seen her." I opened a cabinet and found dozens of empty glass potion vials.

"Technically, she could be. The rumor goes, Bella was so unhappy and unable to decide between leaving her marriage or being with Ulric that she killed herself. Her body could be lying undiscovered somewhere in Witch Haven."

I paused from my search as a cold shudder ran down my spine. "There was never any evidence of suicide, was there?"

"No, but there wasn't evidence of anything. It's like Bella snapped her fingers and vanished. There was no note, all her things were left in her closets, and she took no money with her."

"What do you think happened to her?" I sifted through a stack of books.

"If I was married to a creep like Atherton, I'd escape. Everyone thinks he's so smooth and self-assured, but I find him dodgy."

"He can be smug. And he loved rubbing my nose in it when he revealed his charitable work with the gremlins."

"That doesn't sit right, either," Storm said. "He's the kind of guy who'd love to brag about his philanthropy. He brags about everything else."

"I thought the same thing. What do you think he's doing if he's not helping the gremlins?"

"Something self-serving. I can't figure out what, though." Storm shut the cabinet drawer. "There's nothing in here."

"Let's try the kitchen." I led the way into the next room. The kitchen was dark, with only a small window at the back providing natural light. The units were a dark faded wood, and a single bowl and plate were set on the dryer by the sink. Most of the surfaces were covered in potted plants or dried herbs. There was a large pot on the stove, with a pungent smell coming out of it.

"This is where Jinti worked her magic," Storm said. "Feel it. All these herbs have power."

"Sure. It's intense." I walked to a large stack of books and leafed through them. "It's strange Jinti was in Atherton's store asking for a book on herbal remedies. It looks like she has every edition ever published right here."

"Maybe she was looking for something obscure." Storm hunted around the kitchen, Fire Fang on her heels. He had what was left of Devlin's hat perched on his head.

"Jinti was the expert in magical herbal remedies. Everyone knew about her, even if they weren't local. Why would she think Atherton had something she didn't?"

"The guy is always going on about how he can get anything a person needs for the right price. Maybe he deceived Jinti into thinking he had something valuable. You said she was sick, didn't you?"

"She was troubled with something, although I'm not sure what." I walked to a crowded bookcase and studied the titles. Every single one was a herbal remedy book. "I have to find something concrete, so Devlin doesn't think I'm the killer."

"We all know you're not," Storm said.

"That's not good enough for the Magic Council."

"Devlin's floundering. I expect he's not properly examined the evidence." Storm arched an eyebrow as she glanced my way. "And you do look guilty because you're acting so weird."

"I don't think I'm acting weird."

"You ran away from Devlin so fast, I figured he'd asked you to wax his back."

"I panicked. That's natural."

She grunted. "Then there's your strange magic."

"It's not so strange. Let's keep looking. Something will show up."

"Don't eat that!" Storm grabbed a plant off the floor Fire Fang was investigating.

"What's wrong with it?" I asked.

Storm tossed the plant in the trash. "It'll give him hallucinations. He's manic enough without the addition of psychedelic plants to his diet."

Fire Fang growled and headed into the open pantry.

I grabbed an empty watering can and filled it, making my way around the plants and giving them a good drink as I continued to poke about. "I suppose this place will be pulled down. Jinti resisted calls for it to be demolished for years."

"I heard a developer has plans. Jinti's hut was the only thing standing in their way. They'll probably throw up some bland apartment block and charge a fortune for them."

"It's sad all of this will soon be gone. Jinti's knowledge and her remedies will be lost, and there'll be nothing left of her."

"Yeah, it sucks," Storm said. "Have you found anything?"

I finished watering the plants and set down the can. "I don't think there's anything here." My fingers brushed a pile of dried herbs, and my skin tingled. "Jinti's power is still active in these herbs."

Storm looked around the kitchen. "She's not ready to go just yet. Maybe she'll come back as a ghost and haunt the residents of the new apartments they put up here."

My skin continued to tingle, so I ran my hand under cold water to wash off the residue. When I examined my skin, it was bright red.

Storm looked at my hand. "Did you stick that in something you shouldn't?"

I clenched my fist a few times, and the muscles ached. "Jinti wouldn't have used damaging herbs in her remedies, would she?"

"There'd be no reason to use them. Maybe you're allergic to something in here."

"My tongue gets a weird fur on it when I eat mushrooms, and onions make me gassy, but that's about it." I sniffed the herbs.

Storm nodded. "I'm much the same with anything green and leafy."

"These are pretty." I walked over and admired a plant covered in tiny red flowers. "We should take some of these in memory of Jinti. She'd like to know her plants found good homes."

"I'm not a plant person," Storm said. "Anything I take won't survive. Fire Fang will either pee on it or chew it to death."

He gave an angry grumble from inside the pantry and then sneezed.

I picked out a large, healthy plant. "I'll have this one. Every time I look at it, I'll think of Jinti and everything she did for this village."

"Including getting you on the suspect list for her murder," Storm said.

"That's not helpful."

"And neither is this search." Storm shook her head. "There's nothing here. What do you want to do next?"

"We'll look around upstairs, then I have to head to the bakery and warn Uncle Albert what's going on. After that, I need to keep a low profile. I have to stay out of the way of the Magic Council."

"Is it a good idea to go to the bakery? They'll be looking for you. Devlin could already be at your place." Storm glanced at Fire Fang as he emerged from the pantry. "Although if the rest of him is as bad as that hat, you've got some time."

"Then we'd better hurry. I could always run some confusion spells around the bakery. They'd slow him down."

After a hunt around Jinti's tiny upstairs and finding nothing, I picked up Earl and my new plant, and we dashed away from Jinti's.

I said a quick goodbye to Storm and Fire Fang and then ran to the bakery. I was relieved to see no sign of Devlin outside. Maybe he needed medical treatment after Fire Fang had played with him. I tried to feel bad, but it was a struggle.

I hurried inside and raced up the stairs to see Uncle Albert.

His head jerked up when he saw me. "Luna! I was getting worried. Where have you been?"

I kissed his cheek, then set down Earl and my new plant. "Don't panic, but I've got myself in a little trouble. I need to lie low until I figure out what to do next."

"Trouble? Has this got to do with the Magic Council? Devlin was hanging around outside the bakery. He came in and was looking for you. When I asked what he wanted, he said it was official business. What's going on?"

I hurried to the window and peered out, expecting to see Devlin lurking in the shadows, but there was still no sign of him. "It's a misunderstanding, but he wants to arrest me. He still thinks I hurt Jinti."

"No! I won't have him arresting you. You've done nothing wrong."

"The trouble is, he thinks I have, which means I can't stay here. Until I find the killer, I need to keep my head down." I dashed into my room, grabbed a few clothes and toiletries, and then hurried back out.

"You're leaving? Where are you going?" Uncle Albert hurried along behind me as I headed down the stairs.

"I've got somewhere safe I can stay. And most importantly, somewhere the Magic Council can't find me."

"But where?"

"I can't tell you, just in case Devlin uses magic to force you to reveal where I am."

He caught hold of my arm. "Luna, are you sure this is the right thing to do? Can't you stay and face him? Won't running make you look guilty?"

"I've already tried facing him. He won't listen to anything I have to say. It's up to me to find the killer and present the evidence to Devlin." I stopped at the door. "Will you be okay on your own?"

"I'll be fine. I'm already feeling better. But I'm worried about you."

"I'll be back tomorrow. I know I have to face the Magic Council, but I need a night to clear my head and get the facts straight. I'm missing something in this mystery, but I can't put my finger on it." And I desperately needed a boost of magic. I was running on fumes.

"Stay safe and come back as soon as you can. What do you want me to tell Devlin if he shows up again?"

"That I'm looking for answers. And I'm not running because I'm guilty. Maybe cast a confusion spell if he gets difficult."

"I'll do what I can, and I'll try to talk sense into him. Be careful."

I gave his cheek another kiss before saying goodbye. I considered taking Earl with me. Witches needed their familiars by their side to strengthen them, but he'd be no use. He was too zonked out on catnip.

I hurried out of the bakery and dashed to the farmhouse. I lowered the magic barrier and raced inside.

"Is someone there?" Faye called from the front parlor.

"It's just me." I entered the parlor. Gloria and Faye sat in their usual comfortable armchairs. Gloria had her knitting out, and Faye was reading a book. Ridley was lounging on the floor, playing on his games console.

"This is a lovely surprise," Gloria said. "Have you brought us something nice?" Her gaze went to the bag.

"No. Actually, I'm staying here tonight."

"Oh, what fun," Faye said. "We can have a girls' night." Her gaze flicked to Ridley. "He can be an honorary girl if he likes."

Ridley chuckled. "I'd be happy to put on a dress for you ladies. I'll even wear some skimpy undies if you ask real nice."

I pushed up my sleeves. My hands were shaking. "Who'd like to help me out?"

"It's been a few days since you've taken my magic," Faye said. "I don't mind."

I shot her a grateful smile as I grabbed her hand. Faye's magic pulsed into me in a welcome wave, and I relaxed.

I hadn't acted sensibly when I'd seen Devlin. If I sat him down and talked to him, he'd understand why I couldn't be Jinti's killer. There had to be a way to get him to see sense.

"My dear." There was an edge of panic in Gloria's voice. "You might like to let go of Faye. She's fainted."

"Oh! I didn't realize." I yanked my hand away. "Faye, are you okay?"

Faye groaned, and her eyes fluttered, but she didn't wake.

I bit my bottom lip. I hadn't been focusing. All I'd wanted was her energy.

"Give her a few minutes." Gloria bustled over and pressed her hand to Faye's forehead.

"I'll go make coffee. That'll bring her around." I dashed to the kitchen, brewed coffee for us all, and returned to the parlor.

Faye was awake, a dazed expression on her face. I placed a mug of coffee in her hand. "Drink this, and you'll feel better. Sorry, I didn't mean to take so much magic. I've been having a rough few days."

She weakly waved a hand. "I'll be fine."

"Someone's been poking around here while you were gone," Ridley said.

"Did they get through the magic barrier?" I stretched out my fingers and rolled my shoulders. Faye's magic had felt good when we'd been connected, but it hadn't touched the sides. I still felt hollow and shaky.

"No, but he knew something was here," Ridley said.

"Do you know who it was?"

"Just some jerk. He was prowling about less than an hour ago."

"A good looking jerk." Gloria sat on the arm of Faye's seat and checked her pulse. "He had a werewolf vibe and dark brooding looks, like a muscled Rhett Butler."

"You're describing Cole." My heart skipped a beat. "What's he doing around here?"

"If he's a werewolf, he probably sniffed us out," Ridley said. "Do you want me to scare him off the next time he comes by?"

"No, he's a friend. At least, he sort of is. I don't really know him." My heart gave a thud of excitement and worry. What was Cole doing so near my hidden farmhouse?

"I didn't trust the guy." Ridley's top lip curled, and red sparks of magic danced around him.

"You should trust him. I'm hoping he'll move into the farmhouse. He's got a lot of power. I've had a brief taste."

"You've kissed him!" Gloria bounced off the arm of the chair. "What a treat. I remember kissing my first werewolf. It's not something you forget. Although be careful. I had bruised lips for days when we went out on the full moon. Not that you'll hear me complaining."

Ridley made a gagging noise.

"Thanks for the tip, Gloria. How's Faye doing?" I headed to the window and peered outside.

"She's already got a glow back in her cheeks. She'll be talking in full sentences in no time."

I nodded, but my attention was on a shadowy figure outside. Was that Cole?

"I'll be back in a minute." I hurried out the front door and around the side of the house. No one could see through this magic barrier unless I wanted them to, so I was safe.

On my tiptoes, I snuck closer to the barrier where the shadow lurked, being careful not to tread on anything that would give away my position.

"I can smell you," Cole said.

My breath caught, and I froze.

"And even though I can't see you, I can hear you moving around. Where are you, Luna?" Cole's voice was low and too close for comfort.

There was no hiding from him. If he could smell me, he wouldn't leave. I dodged back around the front of the house, passed through the magic barrier, and made a pretense of walking through the trees.

Cole appeared in front of me a few seconds later.

I jumped back. "Oh! You scared me."

His eyes narrowed. "You knew I was here."

I glanced over his shoulder to make sure the farmhouse was still hidden. "What are you doing out this way?"

"Hunting."

I licked my lips. "Not cute bunnies, I hope?"

"Nope, cute witches."

I did an unsexy snort-laugh. "That's nice. I was taking a walk."

"Why here? There's nothing here."

"Which is why I like it. It's peaceful. I'm surprised to see you, though. Don't you have business with Atticus?"

"It's in hand." His gaze shot around the clearing. "What are you hiding?"

"What makes you think I'm hiding anything?"

"Your heart's racing, and you're sweating."

"Because you surprised me! That'll make a girl's deodorant fail."

"I can sense the magic. It's all around me. I don't know what it is, but it's a tangle of messy spells." Cole inhaled deeply, and his eyes flared amber. "Some of it's your magic, but there is other power in the air."

"This village is full of magic users. Some local kids have probably been doing spells around here."

"Hmmm, I don't think so."

This was an opportunity for me. I could introduce Cole to my magic harem. He might like the idea of living in a secluded farmhouse with wide-open spaces to run around in any time he wanted to go all werewolf.

"It's not kids." His gaze settled on me, and my heart sped up even more. "What's on your mind, Luna?"

"I... I was thinking about your family. I've never asked you if you have anyone special. Mom, Dad, a big pile of puppies at home?"

"I'm a lone wolf. I'm loosely affiliated to the Cumbria pack, but my ties aren't official. It helps I'm not confirmed in any one pack because of my negotiating role. No one can accuse me of playing favoritism when disputes come up."

"And no female werewolf or pups in your life?"

He grinned. "Why do you want to know?"

I had rules about who joined my team. I didn't want anyone to be missed. "Well, you kissed me. I assumed you were available. I don't want to tread on any lady werewolf's paws, or she might tear off my head."

A flash of warm amber lit his gaze, and I almost felt bad for my deception. "I'm available. There's no one in my life."

I stepped closer. "Doesn't it get lonely, not having anywhere to call home? Not having someone looking after you?"

"I can look after myself. Why? Have you got an offer for me?" Cole turned around and tilted his head. "Who else is here?"

I grabbed his arm, trying to keep his attention. I could imagine Ridley, Faye, and Gloria on the other side of the magic barrier listening in. "What makes you think there's anybody else here?"

"I can hear them breathing. And you didn't answer my questions." The heat in his eyes was gone, and the suspicion was back. "What are you doing? Why is there strange magic in the air?"

Should I show him the farmhouse, or cut my losses? "Can you keep an open mind?"

"Usually. Werewolves get in all kinds of trouble, and I don't judge until I have all the information."

"I don't want you jumping to the wrong conclusion about me."

His eyes were full of questions as he nodded.

My inner coward leaped forward before I lowered the magic barrier. This was too risky. I'd figure something else out and recruit someone who was more in need. Although Cole's energy had tasted like warm honey, and I wanted it so badly. My throat ached for another gulp of his power.

"Luna, what's going on?" he growled out.

I shook my head and backed away from the barrier. "I was messing with you. You're so serious."

"I need to be."

"It's nothing. Forget about it." It was better this way and safer for everyone.

"That won't happen. And I can't be friends with someone who keeps secrets," Cole said. "That's not how I roll."

An ache flared from the center of my heart. "I'm not keeping secrets because I want to."

He shrugged, his expression shuttered. "It doesn't matter. We don't know each other. I'll get out of your way, then you can do whatever you need to without me getting under your feet."

Another pang of regret hit me, but I nodded. Cole was too independent to be part of my group. He asked too many questions, and I wasn't sure I'd be able to keep someone that powerful under control.

"Take care of yourself, Luna. I hope you figure things out. I'm sorry I couldn't be here to help."

So was I, more than I should have been. "You take care, too. Drop by the bakery the next time you visit Witch Haven."

He nodded, turned, and walked away.

I waited until Cole was out of sight before lowering the magic barrier and stepping through. As expected, Ridley, Gloria, and Faye were watching, their eyes wide.

"Look out!" Ridley yelled.

A pair of solid arms wrapped around me, and I hit the ground. I rolled over and discovered Cole on top of me.

His arms were either side of my head as he pinned me down with his chest. His eyes glowed amber as he stared down at me. Cole glared up at the others and growled a warning.

"What are you doing?" I tried to get out from under him, but he growled again, and my knees shook.

"Finding out your secret." His gaze cut to the farmhouse and then the small group watching. "Why are you hiding this place? Who are these magic users?"

"We're Luna's harem," Gloria said. "We'd love for you to join us. And I can make you a scarf to match your lovely eyes."

His gaze shot back to me. "Harem? What is this? Weird sex games with old ladies?"

"I'm not an old lady. Luna can play weird sex games with me any time she likes." Ridley glared at Cole.

Cole shifted off me an inch, his anger pulsing toward Ridley.

"No! No fighting. And definitely no sex games, weird or otherwise."

"So, what's going on?" Cole demanded.

I couldn't tell him, so I grabbed his head with both hands and kissed him like my life depended on it.

Cole struggled for several seconds, grazing my bottom lip with his teeth and drawing blood. He almost got free, but I clung to him until he relaxed and sank on top of me, pressing me to the ground with his broad chest.

His magic was glorious. It filled me from head to toe with a hot, delicious energy that erased my headache and made me feel like I could run for miles without getting out of breath.

"Hey, is he bothering you?" Ridley appeared beside me.

I broke off from the kiss, the initial flash of joy fading as I realized what I'd done.

I eased Cole off me and rolled away, accepting Ridley's outstretched hand as I stood. "I didn't mean for this to happen. I made a mistake. He can't join us."

"This isn't your fault," Faye said. "He snuck up on you. He waited until the barrier was down. Is he dangerous?"

"Isn't this the werewolf you wanted to join us?" Gloria said.

"Yes! But he won't. I got things wrong."

"But... he knows about us." Gloria grasped Faye's hand. "We aren't safe."

"You are. I won't let anything bad happen to you. You'll always be safe here." My veins were heating with Cole's energy. I felt guilty and elated in equal measure.

"We can't let him leave," Ridley said. "What if he tells people about us? The Magic Council will snoop around and find me. They'll arrest me for murder. And what about Gloria and Faye?"

I sucked in a breath. Cole's energy still flooded through me, making it hard to focus. "We'll keep him here. I've got strong chains in the basement. And I'll take more magic, so he's sedated."

"How long will that work?" Gloria whispered.

"Long enough for me to figure out what to do next." I couldn't let Cole go free now he knew about the farmhouse and what I did to keep my magic stable.

"I'll help you get him inside," Ridley said.

Between the two of us, we hauled an unconscious Cole into the parlor.

Gloria and Faye no longer seemed scared of the new arrival and twittered around excitedly as I chained him to the wall.

I knelt in front of Cole and brushed his hair out of his eyes. "I'm sorry, but you left me with no choice."

I pressed my hands against his cheeks and drained more magic.

"Be careful, my dear," Gloria said. "You don't want to grow fur and a tail."

I broke away from Cole a few seconds later, feeling full of warm, intoxicating werewolf juice.

"Is he always going to be difficult to handle?" Faye said.

"He might. He'll have to stay like this for now until I figure out a way to convince Cole not to reveal this place."

"We'll help you convince him," Gloria said. "If he wakes up, we'll talk to him and tell him how wonderful you are. He'll want to stay when he learns all about you."

"Thanks. I hope he does." Although I wasn't sure it would be enough. I needed fresh air and time to get my thoughts together.

"I'll make sure he doesn't cause any trouble," Ridley said.

"Be nice to him. Cole will be confused if he does wake."

"We'll look after him." Faye had a worryingly lecherous look in her eyes.

"I'll be back soon." I went to the door and then turned and looked at Cole. Though I was glad to have such a strong magic asset, regret filled me. We could have had something special, but I couldn't risk Cole telling everyone I was a fraud.

It would take some convincing, but he was now mine. It was the right thing to do to keep him here. Although what he'd think about that was a whole other problem to figure out.

Chapter 20

After a bracing run outside, thanks to werewolf energy, I'd spent the night pacing the farmhouse, getting barely any sleep as I'd puzzled out my next move.

I looked out the window at the yellow snow clouds and frowned. The weather wasn't supposed to turn bad. A sharp wind whipped the clouds along, so maybe they were passing through.

After making sure Cole was still sedated and the others happy, I snuck out of the farmhouse just after dawn broke.

Werewolf energy pounded through me, and I was practically bouncing as I hurried along. I broke into a jog which quickly turned into an all-out sprint. I laughed. It felt amazing to have werewolf energy coursing through my veins. I needed a whole pack of werewolves. Imagine me, queen alpha, to willing werewolves who'd submit to my every whim.

I snuck in through the back of the bakery and peered out the front windows. There was no sign of Devlin. Excellent. Maybe Fire Fang had scared him off for good.

The stairs creaked as I snuck up them and peeked into Uncle Albert's room. He was asleep, with Earl laying on the pillow next to him.

Despite the twisty situation I found myself in, I felt positive. I wasn't sure whether it was the werewolf magic or the fact it was a new day and I'd survived the night, but I had a good feeling. The Magic Council hadn't staked out the bakery, and there was no sign of Bram chasing after his debt. All I needed to do was hold things together for a bit longer, and I'd figure this out.

With a flick of my fingers, I cast a spell around the building to alert me if Devlin or Bram showed up.

I pulled out a tray of muffins and brewed a pot of coffee before sitting at the kitchen table. One thing I hadn't anticipated was that werewolf magic would make me starving hungry. I'd soon demolished six muffins and half the pot of coffee, and I could eat more. I had to hope I also developed a high running metabolism alongside the werewolf energy to burn this all off.

Once my early breakfast was cleared away, I pulled out baking supplies and was soon whisking a huge batch of caramel chocolate sponge batter as I mulled over my next move.

I was all out of suspects for Jinti's murder. Everyone had an alibi or no motive for wanting her dead. I could almost understand why Devlin was desperate to pin this on me. But it was just a coincidence my muffin was found by her body.

I filled three tins with the batter and placed them in the oven.

My gaze flicked to the plant I'd brought back from Jinti's hut. Uncle Albert must have moved it to the kitchen table after I'd gone.

I didn't have much knowledge about herbal remedies but wanted to know how to keep this beautiful plant alive, and I had time to kill while the caramel chocolate sponges baked.

I settled at the table with a book of herbal plants and flicked through it until I found a picture that looked like the plant on the table.

Earl ambled into the kitchen, yawning.

"Busy night?" I said.

"Yes. I've been sleeping. It's exhausting."

I grinned at him. "Thanks for keeping Uncle Albert company."

"Why wouldn't I? His pillows are softer than yours."

I shook my head as I continued to flick through the book. I read through a few descriptions of plants, but none matched the one on the table.

"Where did you go, yesterday? The last thing I remember is being at Ulric's. It gets fuzzy after that." Earl hopped up and mooched over for a tickle under the chin.

"You really don't remember?"

"Nope. What did I miss?"

"Ulric's innocent, Devlin still thinks I'm guilty of Jinti's murder, and Fire Fang and Storm saved me from being arrested." I kissed his head. "You don't remember that?"

"That catnip was strong. Where is it?" Earl lifted his nose and sniffed.

"You should have a few days off that stuff. I need my magic focused. You should be helping me stay centered."

"I always help." He sat on the book and washed himself.

"That's the opposite of helpful." I eased his fluffy butt off the page.

"I never understand your fascination with books."

"They're useful."

"Are there pictures of cats in there?"

"No, it's all plants."

"Then it's not useful. And it's boring."

"I'm working out what this is." I pointed at the plant. "I brought it back from Jinti's and thought I'd keep it as a memorial to her. Her place was full of plants, and they'll all die." I continued flicking through the pages, then stopped and looked at the picture in front of me, then studied the plant. "This is a match."

Earl walked over to the plant and sniffed it.

I read through the description of how to take care of it. It needed natural light, and watering three times a week. I also needed to change its soil once a year and feed it in the spring. And I needed to wear gloves when I handled it.

I glanced back at the plant. It was the right one. My finger traced to the bottom of the page where two words were written in red. *Extremely poisonous.*

I looked up and gasped. Earl was about to take a bite out of a leaf. I leaped out of my seat and grabbed him. "You didn't eat any, did you?"

"I was about to. I thought it might be a substitute for catnip." He hissed as I slid my finger into his mouth and felt around. "What's the matter with you?"

"That plant is poisonous. Don't eat it. It'll kill you." I returned to my seat with him in my arms and read through the rest of the information. Every part was dangerous, from the cute flowers to the sap.

Earl struggled out of my arms and hopped onto the table.

"Jinti had several of these plants," I said. "And she'd been drying them. I think I got some on my skin. The tips of my fingers are still tender."

"What's she doing growing a plant that could kill me?" Earl wrinkled his nose. "You should throw it out."

"There must be a reason Jinti had such toxic plants in her collection."

"Not for healing. Maybe she didn't like cats." Earl hissed at the plant.

A screeching noise, followed by the sound of breaking glass, had me leaping to my feet. Something had triggered my magic alert.

I clutched Earl to my chest as I raced out of the kitchen and into the bakery.

Bram was behind the counter, grabbing money out of the till.

"Hey, stop that! That's not yours to take."

He jabbed a finger at me. "I've tried being nice, but you won't listen. The boss needs this money now, so I'm taking it."

"That's not my money." I set Earl down and raced over. "Give it back."

Bram shoved me away. "You need to watch yourself. I've been good to you. I kept your secret, so your friends didn't find out about your troubles, but it's time to pay up. And remember, you owe me double."

I grabbed his arm. "Please, my uncle can't know what's going on. I said I'd pay, and I will."

"Yet I'm not seeing any evidence of payment. You keep making excuses." Bram stuffed a wad of notes into his jacket pocket.

I grabbed money out of his hand. "I will pay. You'll get it all. I just need a few more days."

He shoved me against the counter and yanked the money back. "It's too late. And don't come crawling to Sylvester when you want more magic. He doesn't work with witches who don't pay their debts."

"But... I need that as a backup resource."

"That's not my problem."

I raised my hands and sparked magic across my fingers. It crackled alarmingly and glowed orange.

Bram scowled at me. "Don't make threats you're not prepared to follow through on."

"I'll... I'll hurt you if you don't leave this store. This is my business and my family, and I will protect them."

"With whose magic?" Bram sneered at me. "That spell doesn't belong to you. I bet you don't even know what it does."

"You won't need to find out what it does, so long as you leave now." The magic wavering on my fingertips was out of control.

He smirked and continued pulling money out of the cash drawer.

I blasted out the spell. It shot out in a hot wave, tingling down to my toes, as a jagged line of bright magic rushed at Bram.

He blasted out his own spell, slamming into my chest. Then he was looming over me, his eyes blazing. "Time is up, little witch. You've pushed me too far." He raised his hand, gray magic sparking on his palm.

A screech echoed around the bakery, making Bram pause. It was my alert again.

"What's going on?"

I'd never been so glad to hear Devlin Goody's voice in my life.

Bram looked over his shoulder, then leaped over me and raced into the kitchen.

A few seconds later, Devlin appeared at the counter and looked at me. "What are you doing on the floor?"

"Get him! Bram just broke into the store. That warlock robbed us."

Devlin's forehead wrinkled, then he gestured behind him. "You two, go see where that warlock went. I'll stay with the suspect."

"Suspect! You're still after me?"

He didn't offer to help me up, so I staggered to my feet and stared into the empty cash drawer.

"Of course I'm still after you. But following your attack in the cemetery, I realized you were far more dangerous. I needed stronger enforcers to back me up." Devlin looked strange without his hat. His hair was thin, and I could see his shiny forehead.

"That attack wasn't my doing. That was a wild animal."

"An animal that bears a remarkable resemblance to the beast I've seen stalking along beside Storm Winter." Devlin brushed a hand over his hair as if he missed his hat. "Storm's a friend of yours. Should I bring her in for questioning in relation to what happened to Jinti?"

"She had nothing to do with that." I winced as I touched my chest. The skin burned where Bram's magic had hit me.

Devlin shook his head. "It seems you've gotten yourself into all kinds of trouble."

"You will arrest Bram, though? He broke in."

"My colleagues will deal with him. I'm more interested in you." Devlin pulled back his shoulders. "Luna Brimstone, you're under arrest for the murder of Jinti Calrook."

My mouth went dry. I'd done everything I could to find the killer, but it hadn't been enough. My time was up. There was nothing I could do but submit to Devlin's chains and allow him to lead me out of the bakery.

He was joined a moment later by his two colleagues. "Where's the warlock?"

One of his colleagues scratched his head. "He escaped out the back door."

"Find him!" I said. "He has our money."

"We'll ensure the break-in is recorded," Devlin said. "But that's not the reason we're here."

"I know. You think I'm a cold-blooded killer, even though I have no motive."

"We'll find your motive."

"Stop! You can't take Luna away." Indigo raced over with Olympus not far behind her.

"Stay out of this," Devlin said. "I have every right to arrest this witch. She's been behaving suspiciously, and she fled the last time we tried to question her. That suggests she's guilty."

"All it suggests is that you terrified her," Indigo said. "Are you okay?" she asked me.

"Not really. The bakery got broken into, and these jerks let him get away with the cash in the till."

Indigo touched my burned clothing. "Luna's been injured. She needs treatment, not an interrogation."

Olympus caught hold of Indigo's shoulder as she advanced on Devlin. "Devlin, explain what's going on. I've had no communication to say this arrest was about to happen."

"This isn't your case," Devlin said. "And I know what you've been doing. You sent me off on that wild goose chase to the mines, but it was for nothing. You've had me wasting my time, when I should have been investigating this witch. Jinti's murder would have been solved by now if you hadn't interfered."

"Olympus, I need you to listen to me," I said. "I didn't do this."

"Back off," Devlin said to Olympus. "You're not taking the credit for this arrest."

"I don't want the credit. And you're wrong about Luna. She's a good witch. She'd never hurt anyone."

"You need to let her go," Indigo said.

Devlin glowered at her. "No, I need to question her."

There were a few seconds of tense stand-off, where no one gave an inch.

Olympus sighed. "Use my office. You can question Luna and then let her go."

"I'll decide when to let her go." Devlin scowled at me. "Although the use of your office would be useful. I want this matter quickly resolved."

"Indigo, can you get someone to stay with Uncle Albert?" I said. "He doesn't know about the break-in or the money being stolen. He'll be worried."

"Of course. I'll see if Storm's free. I'll join you as soon as I can." She gave me a quick hug, then raced away.

I walked in silence to Olympus's office, my head down as shame ran through me. If other villagers saw what was going on, they'd think the worst, so I was grateful we didn't meet anyone.

I hurried into Olympus's office, to be met by Monty, who bounded over, wagging his tail. "Hey, Luna. What's going on?" He sniffed my feet. "Oooh! You smell like werewolf."

"Keep your familiar out of this." Devlin cast a sharp look at Olympus. "He's trouble."

"Monty won't get in the way."

"I never get in the way of an investigation. I'm helpful and ready to take down an enemy at a moment's notice." Monty's eyes flashed to Devlin. "Are you a friend or a foe?"

"That's debatable," Olympus said. "Luna, take a seat. And Devlin, unchain her. She's not going anywhere."

Devlin scowled, then took off the chains. "If you make one wrong move, these go back on."

"I won't. But you need to listen to me. I found something in Jinti's hut."

"What were you doing there?"

"Looking for answers. Jinti's murder has never made sense to me."

"It should make sense, since you did it," Devlin said.

"Let Luna speak. You said you wanted to question her, but you need to listen, too. And stop looming over her. Take a seat. All of you." Olympus gestured at the two enforcers standing in the doorway.

After a second of hesitation, Devlin sat behind the desk in the office, and his two colleagues took visitors' seats by the wall.

The door burst open, and Indigo raced in. "Have I missed anything?"

"You shouldn't be here," Devlin said.

"She's my representative," I said. "I'm allowed that, aren't I?"

Devlin pursed his lips. "Indigo doesn't have legal training."

"I have life training, bozo, and that's more important." Indigo nodded at me. "Storm's going to the bakery. She'll get everything sorted."

"Thanks." I blinked away tears. My friends were always looking out for me.

"Luna, let's start with the basics," Olympus said.

"I'm leading this." Devlin tapped the desk. "We already know most of the information. Luna was seen arguing with Jinti shortly before her murder."

"About a stale pie," I said. "That's hardly worth killing over."

"Perhaps there were other arguments," Devlin said.

"I had no problem with Jinti." I looked around the group. "And you need to hear me out before you blame me for this murder. I've been doing my own investigation."

"More like interfering with evidence," Devlin said.

"That's enough," Olympus growled out. "Let her speak."

"Thanks, Olympus." I sucked in a deep breath and took a few seconds to get my thoughts in order. I had to lay this out clearly, so there was no misunderstanding. Once Devlin saw how everything fit into place, he'd know I was right.

"There weren't many suspects in this murder. I was one, and there was also Atherton, Regina, and Ulric." I left out my earlier concerns about Ridley. They didn't need to know about him.

"Those were our main suspects." Devlin's tone was grudging. "We've eliminated everyone except you. You have no alibi."

"That doesn't mean I killed Jinti. And if you're going down that route, Regina also doesn't have an alibi. She was home alone."

"It wasn't her."

"Did Atherton tell you to say that?" Indigo said.

I shook my head at her. I didn't need Devlin any angrier than he already was. "I don't think it was anyone."

"What do you mean?" Indigo said. "Someone murdered Jinti."

"Jinti was heartbroken. Her only daughter, Bella, was missing, and that was impossible for her to move on from. Jinti was alone, she was old, and she wasn't well. She was suffering and had no one to help her."

"I don't see the point of this," Devlin said.

"You will soon enough. Bella vanished, and Jinti blamed Atherton for what happened to her. Jinti was convinced he had something to do with her disappearance."

"That's still not relevant," Devlin said.

"You said you don't think anyone killed Jinti," Indigo said. "What do you think happened to her?"

I looked around the group again. "I think Jinti broke into Atherton's store the night she died. She had it all planned out and brought what she needed with her to end her own life."

No one spoke for an uncomfortably long time. Devlin didn't look impressed, while Indigo and Olympus looked shocked.

I continued. "Jinti had the means to kill herself. When I visited her hut, I found several deadly plants. I mistakenly took a deathcap rose home and discovered just how poisonous it was."

"You stole from the victim's home?" Devlin said.

"It was a plant," Olympus said. "And you're missing the point."

"Luna shouldn't have been there."

"I took the rose, so I had something to remember Jinti by," I said. "I didn't realize I'd picked up the plant she used to poison herself with."

"You really think she killed herself?" Indigo said.

I nodded. "It's the only explanation that makes sense. Jinti never got over losing Bella and blamed Atherton for her going missing. She used a combination of deathcap rose and hemlock to end her life."

"So... did Atherton hurt Bella?" Indigo looked at Olympus, and he shrugged.

"Of course he didn't," Devlin said. "That's a closed case. Bella left him."

"I'm not so sure about that," I said. "Bella was in an unhappy marriage, and she was having an affair with Ulric. She was torn between the two men, but Atherton decided for her. He must have been humiliated his wife was so openly cheating. Perhaps Bella even made the decision to leave, and he reacted badly. Atherton can be a proud man."

"He's a pillar of this community," Devlin said.

"He's an asshat," Olympus said. "Go on, Luna."

"Jinti was certain Atherton had killed Bella but couldn't prove it. So, she did the next best thing. She was already sick. Maybe she didn't have long to live. Jinti killed herself in his store in an attempt to frame him. She made her suicide look like a murder in the hope the finger of blame would be pointed at Atherton."

"But it was pointed at you because of the muffin found by her body," Indigo said.

I looked at Devlin, and he nodded, although he still didn't look happy.

"Maybe Jinti decided to have one last meal. Or she needed something sweet to wash down the bitterness of the poisons. Whatever the reason, she left half a muffin beside her when she died. That ruined her plan."

"What poisons did Jinti use?" Olympus asked Devlin.

He sat up straight in his seat. "We don't know for certain it was a suicide."

"Humor me. What killed Jinti?"

Devlin's nostrils flared. "It was the plant toxins Luna mentioned."

"Which proves she's right," Indigo said.

"Not exactly," Devlin said.

There was doubt wavering in his eyes. I was getting through to him. "Jinti wouldn't have cultivated those plants for use in her herbal remedies. They're too dangerous. She must have been thinking about this for a while, since she had several large, healthy plants."

"Wow! A suicide." Indigo shook her head. "Jinti must have hated Atherton to do that."

"There's something else," I said. "Something that's been on my mind. Atherton likes to keep visual memories of big events in his life. You go to his store, and there are pictures of him with influential people and trinkets from his trips to other countries. And there's that creepy box of bones he keeps on display."

"I know what you're talking about," Indigo said. "Why is that important?"

I looked at Olympus. "If you take me to see Atherton at his store, I'll explain everything."

Olympus glanced at Devlin. "I see no harm in doing that."

"I do. And I have more questions," Devlin said. "This isn't just about what happened to Jinti, anymore. We completed our tests on the samples taken from the bakery, and there's no doubt about it, you're using unauthorized magic."

I dry swallowed and glanced at Indigo. "Your tests are wrong."

"They're never wrong. Where does your power come from? We've identified four different sources of magic in that food."

I had no explanation I was willing to give, so I clasped my hands together and wouldn't look at him.

"Luna, what's going on?" Indigo said.

I shrugged. "Devlin is desperate to arrest me. If not for murder, he's finding fault in my baking."

"It's a lot more than a simple fault. Your magic is dangerous."

"Could the tests be wrong?" Indigo said.

I glanced at Olympus to see him shake his head.

"It's unlikely," he said. "But there'll be an explanation. Luna, have you been working with another magic user in the bakery?"

"Only Uncle Albert," I whispered.

"This is unacceptable," Devlin said. "I have enough evidence to hold you."

"But not for Jinti's murder," Indigo said. "Luna's solved the case for you. Jinti poisoned herself and tried to frame Atherton."

"I'll look into that claim." Devlin gestured at me. "For now, Luna Brimstone, I'm detaining you for the illegal use of magic. And I'll be asking questions about why you're associating with Bram Vexx."

"Who are we talking about?" Indigo said.

"It... it doesn't matter," I muttered.

"This matters. Is Devlin trying to frame you?" Indigo's brow furrowed. "Aren't you dating a guy called Bram? Is that who he's getting confused about?"

I shook my head, defeat hitting me in the gut and leaving me breathless. The Magic Council had found me out.

I let Devlin attach the restraining chains to my wrists and take me to the cell at the back of Olympus's office.

Everything felt lost. And my secrets were about to be exposed.

Chapter 21

My eyes felt gritty after a sleepless night in the cell. I stared at the ceiling as I lay on the single cot, my mind racing as I failed to figure a way out of this disaster. I'd messed up this time. I'd let down Uncle Albert, the bakery was in ruins after Bram broke in and stole from us, and the villagers would be gossiping about my arrest. They'd think I was a killer.

I couldn't see a way out. And Devlin had evidence that I'd been illegally siphoning magic for my own use. He hadn't figured out why I was doing it, and I'd had no opportunity to convince him what I was doing wasn't so bad. I needed that magic, and I had people who were willing to give it to me.

I groaned as I covered my eyes. And I still had the Cole problem to untangle. He'd soon wake and be raging mad to find himself chained up in the farmhouse. My plan had been to go back today and talk him into joining my magic harem. He had to see the benefits of being in the group.

That wouldn't be possible now. Even if I could convince Devlin to let me go, the Magic Council would be watching my every move, which meant I couldn't go back to the farmhouse.

If I got out of this, I needed to be more discreet about using other magic users' abilities, but there was no way I could block the magic signature I emitted when channeling it into my baking.

Perhaps I should only recruit other witches and not go after werewolves for my magic boosts. But even that would be a problem. Witch magic was diverse, and I wouldn't know what would be easy to blend into my own spells.

If only I'd been born with the right magic, then I'd have no trouble creating delicious treats that everyone loved. I wouldn't have to face the daily struggle of not knowing if what I baked would turn out delicious or disgusting.

I squeezed my eyes shut to stop tears from leaking out the corners. I'd make this right. Uncle Albert would be so worried about me, but I'd convince him the break-in was a one-off and had just been a desperate individual in need of money. It had nothing to do with me.

The problem with that was Bram didn't get all the money I owed, so he'd be back.

My stomach lurched. Maybe he'd go after Uncle Albert. I sat up on the cot. I had to get out of here and make sure my family was safe.

And I'd figure out a way to hide my problem and ensure the Magic Council didn't keep coming after me. I could do this. I had to get the magic balance right, and everything would work itself out.

The main door leading into the cells opened, and Olympus appeared.

I jumped to my feet and hurried to the door of the cell. "Have you got news?"

He pressed a finger to his lips and beckoned over his shoulder.

Indigo hurried in. She kissed Olympus's cheek. "Thanks for doing this."

"You'll be in so much trouble if you get caught," he said. "I won't be able to protect you. Neither of you."

"I know. But we've talked about this, and we can protect ourselves. I'll say you had nothing to do with this and I be-spelled you into opening the cell." Indigo gave him another kiss, then hurried over to me.

"Opening the cell? What are you doing?" I said.

"I'm breaking you out." Indigo waggled her eyebrows.

"What about the Magic Council guards? Devlin left his two enforcers to watch me overnight."

"Odessa is charming them with muffins and smiles. She's got them wrapped around her little finger."

"I can't get you involved in this. This is my mess." I badly wanted out, but not if my friends got in trouble.

"I'm already involved. I'm your representative and your best friend." Indigo winked at me. "And I believe you. I talked it over with the others last night, and it makes sense. Jinti killed herself. It's kind of genius, in a warped sort of way."

"You really believe I didn't do it?"

"I never did. You're not a killer. And once Devlin examines the poisonous plants, he'll see Jinti administered that poison to herself."

"Is he doing that?"

"Yes. I gave him no choice," Olympus said. "He wasn't happy, but he's checked Jinti's home, and the plants have undergone testing."

"I have to speak to Atherton," I said. "I didn't finish what I needed to tell you yesterday, but he's not innocent."

"I'd figured you weren't done. Although I can't work out how Atherton's involved in a suicide," Indigo said.

"I'll explain everything once we get out of here."

Indigo glanced over her shoulder. "Olympus is giving us a head start."

"A small one. If I don't notice your escape quickly, we'll all be in trouble."

"Sure. Thanks, Olympus," I said.

He smiled. "You have a very persuasive best friend."

"Olympus will join us at Atherton's store," Indigo said. "He'll bring Devlin with him."

My eyes widened. "Devlin hates me. And he won't listen to a word I say."

"Devlin can be an idiot, but when he sees the facts laid out, he'll accept the truth." Olympus slipped through the door. "Hurry!"

Indigo used magic to break open the cell door. She gave me a quick hug. "You still have explaining to do, though. What's going on with your baking magic?"

"Not now." I wasn't willing to face that tangled problem. "Let's get to Atherton's store and end this."

"Wait here. I'll check the coast is clear and Olympus is in position." Indigo poked her head out the door and then gestured me to follow her.

We tiptoed out of the cells and through Olympus's office. He stood with his back to us, pretending to look through a filing cabinet.

"If he can't see us, he can't be involved," Indigo whispered. She pressed a finger to her lips as Monty stood and wandered over to us.

The sound of male laughter in the kitchen had me tensing, and I hurried to the door with Indigo.

A few seconds later, we were out and raced away, speed walking, so not to look too suspicious.

My teeth chattered as a blood chilling wind slammed into me.

"Have you got a plan to deal with Atherton?" Indigo said.

"Sort of. It involves the bones in his magic store."

"You mentioned them last night. What do they have to do with Jinti?"

"You'll find out in a few minutes how important they are." My gaze darted around, hoping desperately no one would see us and report me to the Magic Council.

We got to Atherton's store without incident, and Indigo hammered on the door.

A moment later, Regina appeared, surprise in her eyes as she unlocked the door. "We're not open for another hour. Is everything okay?"

"Is Atherton here?" Indigo said. "It's important. It has to do with Jinti's murder."

"Um, of course. Come in. He's meeting with Ulric." Regina opened the door and allowed us inside.

"Olympus and Devlin will be along in a couple of minutes," Indigo said. "They need to be here, too."

"Have you found out what happened to Jinti?" Regina glanced at me. "I was surprised to hear you'd been taken in for questioning."

"That was a misunderstanding," I said. "Can you get Atherton? He needs to hear this."

"I... yes. I'll go get him." Regina hurried away.

I walked to the bones sitting in the glass cabinet. "You're the answer to my problem. I can finally get you resolution."

"Those bones had better not talk back," Indigo said from behind me.

"Can you sense the magic coming off them? I think Atherton's put a blocking spell around them, but it's not quite strong enough to trap everything."

Indigo placed a hand against the glass. "I feel something faint. If I had to describe it, I'd say it felt like misery."

"You're mistaken. You can't feel anything coming off those bones." Atherton's voice sounded behind me. "They're just decoration."

I turned and faced him. "I don't think that's true. And these bones will explain what happened to Jinti."

There was a thud on the door to the magic store, and Regina opened it. Devlin pushed his way in, followed by Olympus.

"I just heard you'd escaped custody and were seen heading this way. No doubt, you had help." Devlin shook his head as his gaze went from Olympus to Indigo. "My apologies, Atherton, but this witch is out of control."

"I'm very much in control," I said. "And I know what happened to Jinti."

"Who killed her?" Regina hurried to Atherton's side and caught hold of his arm.

There was no time for subtlety. "She killed herself."

"What makes you think she did that?" Atherton said after a short pause.

Ulric ambled out of the back room with a mug in his hand. "What have I missed?"

Regina's face was pale as she looked at Ulric. "Luna thinks Jinti committed suicide."

Ulric's mouth fell open, then he sighed. "I'm actually not surprised to hear that. She was gravely ill. Maybe the pain got too much for her. But why did she do it here?"

"I'll explain," I said.

"You'll go back to the cell," Devlin said.

Olympus shook his head. "We're here now. We should listen to Luna. Maybe this mystery can be solved."

"Two mysteries. Jinti might have been in pain, but I don't think that's the main reason she killed herself." I tapped the glass cabinet containing the bones. "The reason is sitting here. Jinti always knew something bad happened to Bella."

"Devlin, take this witch away," Atherton said. "She's making no sense."

"Let her explain," Olympus said. "Luna has already figured out Jinti used her own plants to poison herself."

"Why do you think something bad happened to Bella?" Regina said.

"I expect Luna's been listening to gossip," Atherton said. "And you must remember, Jinti went through a period when she was convinced I hurt Bella."

Ulric patted him on the shoulder. "That's been resolved. We know you'd never do that, even with the difficulties you two had."

Atherton arched an eyebrow. "Of course. We're all adults, and we all know mistakes happen."

Ulric's face blanched, but he nodded. "That's right. It's in the past. Bella would have wanted us all to be happy."

"And I've found happiness with Regina." Atherton slid an arm around her shoulders.

Ulric looked at the bones. "What do you think they have to do with this?"

Devlin made a step toward me, but Olympus caught hold of his arm.

I had barely any time left. "Jinti planned her own suicide. She grew toxic plants, knowing they'd kill her when she ate them. She killed herself here in the hope Atherton would be blamed for her murder. After all, they had a troubled history, and he has a cabinet of poisonous herbs that was broken into on the night of her death."

"That's been dealt with. All the herbs were accounted for," Atherton said. "And Jinti didn't blame me for what happened to Bella."

"She did for a long time," Ulric said quietly. "She even talked to me about it. I gave her healing sessions to cleanse her aura and help her find a resolution to losing Bella."

"But Bella was never lost. Or rather, she didn't simply walk away from her unhappy marriage and her complicated love affair with you, Ulric," I said. "Bella was killed. And she was killed by Atherton."

Regina's face paled, and she looked up at Atherton. "That's not true. She left you. You told me that's what happened."

"She did leave me." He glanced at the bones. "Bella decided she'd had enough of the marriage and her tawdry affair and wanted a fresh start. She left everything behind."

"That's because Bella had no choice," I said. "I'm not sure how you killed her, but your love of keeping trophies meant you needed a reminder of your triumph over Bella. You hated that she cheated. She'd seen through your facade and realized you were wrong for her. I'm guessing you didn't want to let her go. Or maybe it was revenge because she found love with Ulric."

Ulric set down his mug, his hard expression fixed on Atherton. "Is this true?"

Atherton's laugh sounded forced. "No! It's a desperate fantasy created by this witch. A witch who's about to be charged with murder and is desperate for a way out. But it's too late for Luna."

Devlin cleared his throat. "Possibly not. We found a match for the poisons in Jinti's home. And after another look at the autopsy results, she could have administered them herself. There were traces of poison on her hands."

Ulric looked uncertain, his fingers flexing. "We should hear what else Luna has to say."

Atherton's head snapped around. "So you can believe Bella really wanted to be with you? If you do, you're fooling yourself."

"Atherton, we should tell them about the keys." Regina's voice was almost a whisper as she moved away from him.

His jaw clenched, then he shook his head. "They're not important."

"What keys?" I said.

Regina licked her lips. "I was tidying the counter after the Magic Council allowed us back in the store, and I found a spare set of keys tucked away. I don't remember putting them there, and Atherton said they weren't his."

"They must have been yours," Atherton said. "You made a spare set and forgot about them."

"Do you think they belonged to Jinti?" I said to Regina. "She could have made an extra set to get into the store when she was ready to frame Atherton."

"I... I don't know for certain," Regina said, "but if that's what she did—"

"Jinti didn't kill herself." Atherton glared at Devlin. "You need to do your job. Arrest Luna and remove her from the store."

Although Devlin didn't look impressed with me, he was listening. "Have you still got those keys?" he asked Regina.

She nodded. "They're under the counter where I found them."

"We'll take them away as evidence," Devlin said. "We should be able to find out where and when they were made."

"This is ridiculous. Those keys aren't relevant. Your killer is right there." Atherton jabbed a finger at me.

"You should take the bones, too," I said.

"Don't touch them." Atherton dashed over and stood in front of the cabinet.

"They still have energy in them. If you test the bones, you'll find they belong to Bella," I said.

Regina covered her mouth with a shaking hand.

"It's not true!" Atherton was almost shouting.

"Where did you get those bones?" Devlin said.

"I don't remember. I picked them up years ago."

"Three years ago," Regina said. "Not long after Bella went missing. I remember you bringing them to the store. You took ages finding the right case to display them in."

"That's a coincidence," Atherton said. "Regina, you're supposed to be on my side, yet you're looking at me as if you think I'm guilty."

She bit her bottom lip. "I care for you, but I won't hide things from the Magic Council. And I won't let Luna get in trouble."

"Perhaps we should examine them, just to eliminate this possibility," Devlin said.

"You can't have them." Atherton turned to the cabinet, a fireball appearing in his palm. He aimed it at the bones.

Without thinking, I thrust out my hands and blasted magic. Water poured over Atherton, extinguishing the flames, and a loud rumble of thunder shook the building. Then I was running at him, Indigo alongside me. She grabbed Atherton and yanked him away, while I stood in front of the bones in a pool of water, making sure he couldn't get to them.

My elbow nudged a case of preserved beetles, and it toppled to the floor and smashed, causing the beetles to tumble out.

"This is assault and the reckless use of magic," Atherton yelled. "I'll have you both arrested. There are two members of the Magic Council who witnessed this unprovoked attack and damage to my precious collection. Get off me!" He tried to shove Indigo away, but she clung on tight.

"I'm restraining a dangerous murder suspect," Indigo said. "A suspect who was about to destroy evidence that will convict him." She looked at Olympus. "Are we good?"

"You're fine. But we need those bones. Don't you agree, Devlin?"

Devlin gave a swift nod.

"They belong to me." Atherton was pinned against the wall by Indigo's magic.

"A simple test will show who those bones belong to," Devlin said. "If you have nothing to hide, there won't be a problem."

Atherton glowered at Indigo and then at me. "You'll be sorry about this."

My gaze shifted to the floor as something brushed my foot. The beetles were shivering.

Sparks exploded out of them as they tripled in size, and large, sharp mandibles sprouted from their jaws.

I squeaked and leaped in the air. The building was rocked by another growl of thunder, and hail beat against the glass, so hard it sounded like it would crack the window.

Devlin hurried over. "Stay back! They're flesh eaters."

I stared at him. "How do you know that?"

"I collect bugs. But these beauties are the biggest I've ever seen."

"Ignore the bugs! Devlin, Olympus, get this under control, or you'll both lose your jobs," Atherton snarled. "I've done so much for this village, and this is the thanks I get."

"I know someone who'd say thank you if she could." I side-stepped a huge beetle as it lunged for my foot. "You murdered Bella, and Jinti was determined to make sure you paid for that crime. She gave her life to ensure that would happen. She'd be grateful the mystery has been solved."

Devlin scooped the beetles into a large plastic container and stared at them. "These things are stunning."

"You said they're flesh eaters?" I said.

He nodded. "They eat almost anything."

"Stop staring at those evil critters and put a lid on that box," Indigo said. "I don't want my face chewed off. Olympus, a little help over here." She shoved Atherton against the wall.

Olympus dashed over and assisted her with Atherton.

"Would those beetles eat the flesh off a corpse?" I said.

Devlin's eyebrows shot up. "Oh! Sure. They'd enjoy that."

"They could eat a whole body?" I pointed at the bones.

Devlin stared at the beetles and then the bones. "You think... these beetles disguised Atherton's crime?"

"You tell me. You're the bug expert."

He studied the beetles again. "You'd need more of them and a couple of weeks, but they would pick a corpse clean."

"They were Atherton's willing little helpers in getting rid of Bella," I said. "That's why she was never found."

Devlin covered the beetle box with a book. He took down the glass cabinet and stared at the bones. "I think you're right. Olympus, please detain Atherton and take him to your office. We can press charges there."

"Charges! Are you insane?" Atherton still couldn't move, thanks to the combined power of Indigo and Olympus holding him down. "Those bones are mine. You can't test them."

"They aren't yours, and I can. And I want to discuss these super-sized carnivorous beetles. Is your magic affecting them?" Devlin glared at Atherton.

He spluttered out several half-sentences. "Bella belonged to me. I had every right to keep her."

Regina gave a small sob and hid her face against Ulric's shoulder.

Olympus nodded at me as he led Atherton out of the store.

Devlin picked up the beetle box and the bones. "Luna, I expect to see you back at the office, too."

"Of course." I let out a sigh as he left before turning and hugging Indigo. "Thanks for your help. I could never have done that on my own."

"Any time." Her gaze shifted to the water on the floor. "Nice spell, by the way. And was that thunder yours, too?"

I glanced outside. The hail and thunder had stopped. "Nope. No clue where that came from."

Regina hurried over with Ulric beside her. "I'm so sorry the Magic Council thought you were guilty. But... I still can't believe it. All this time, Atherton had a trophy of his kill on display. And those beetles..." She shuddered.

"I can believe it," Ulric said glumly. "Atherton wasn't always kind when he spoke about Bella."

Worry crossed Regina's face, but she nodded. "He could be bitter, although he hid it well."

"I tried to give him healing magic to help him move on, but he wasn't interested," Ulric said. "He said there was no point, and everything had been resolved."

Regina shook her head. "I'd sometimes catch him talking to those bones when he thought no one else was around."

Ulric wrapped his arm around her shoulders, and Regina leaned against him. "Now we know why. He murdered the woman I loved. He took Bella from me. I always hoped she'd come back. Now, that'll never happen."

"At least you know the truth," I said. "I hope you get comfort from that."

"And poor Jinti." Regina dabbed at her eyes. "She knew the truth but could never prove what Atherton did. She sacrificed herself to reveal Atherton's true nature."

"He did an amazing job of hiding who he really was for a long time," I said.

"Atherton never fooled me. I always thought he was too smarmy." Indigo touched my elbow. "We should catch up with Olympus and Devlin. We'll have questions to answer."

I nodded. I'd face my punishment, although I was hoping to get off lightly since I'd helped find a killer.

We said goodbye to Regina and Ulric and left the store.

Indigo tucked a hand through my crooked arm and grinned at me. "Nice work."

"It was too close for comfort. If Devlin hadn't believed me, or Atherton destroyed those bones, my escape would have come to nothing."

"But you did it. You're in the clear." Indigo lifted her gaze to the sky. "And the bad weather is clearing up."

I glanced at the brightening sky. "It must have been a freak weather event."

"We rarely get those. We have enough weather witches to keep things stable. Maybe there's someone new in town we need to watch out for."

"So long as they don't cause me trouble, I'm not bothered," I said. "Let's go deal with the Magic Council, and then I'm looking forward to doing nothing for a very long time."

Chapter 22

Uncle Albert placed a tray of delicious scones and sandwiches in front of me. I was sitting at a table in the bakery with Indigo, Storm, and Odessa. They'd joined me for a late lunch and were eager to hear what was going on with Atherton.

"I'm still surprised it was him." Odessa helped herself to a strawberry scone. "He was always so charming. And attractive for an older guy."

Storm smirked. "It doesn't surprise me. Atherton always chased after anything pretty and shiny and wanted to claim it as his own. I remember when he got together with Bella. He was always showing her off and dressing her in new things like a doll. Atherton always had to have the latest and the best of everything, whether that was an object or a person."

"I bet Regina's regretting getting involved with him," Indigo said. "She was shocked when the truth came out."

"Regina came good, though. She helped strengthen my argument when she revealed the keys Jinti used to get in the store," I said. "And add in the flesh-eating beetles, and Atherton won't get away with this."

"I'll have to take her a basket of treats," Odessa said. "And make sure she's doing okay. She's lost her man and her job."

"I wouldn't worry about that. Ulric was doing a great job of comforting her," Indigo said. "I reckon she'll land on her feet just fine."

Olympus entered the bakery and walked to the table. "Mind if I join you?"

"No, we were just talking about Atherton," I said. "Have you got news from the Magic Council?"

He smiled as he settled in a seat next to Indigo. "You were right about the bones. I rushed through the testing. They're what's left of Bella. Plus, there were traces of dermestid fecal matter on the bones."

"That's beetle poop," Indigo said.

"Eurgh! That's nasty." Odessa sank her teeth into her scone.

"Which is more proof those little snappers were used to get rid of Bella," I said.

Olympus nodded. "Beetles, bones, and magic. It all adds up."

"And Atherton?" Indigo said.

"He's confessed. At first, he kept claiming it was a coincidence that he had his missing wife's bones in his store, but with some prodding and after laying out all the evidence, he admitted what he'd done."

"How did he actually kill her?" Indigo said.

Odessa shuddered as she chewed on her scone. "He didn't set those beetles on her, did he?"

"No, the beetles weren't involved until Bella was dead," Olympus said. "They fought, and Bella threatened to leave and start a new life with Ulric. Atherton struck her on the head. He said he didn't mean to kill her, but that blow ended Bella's life."

"What did he do with her body?" I asked.

"He took her to the forest and stored her in a box with the beetles. Once they'd done their work, he took a few trophies and buried the rest."

"That's cold. To kill your wife and then go back and dig up some bones so you can always see her," Indigo said.

"We're taking the scent bears into the forest to find the rest of Bella's remains," Olympus said. "If we can find the skull and evidence of the injury that killed her, we'll have even more evidence against Atherton. Not that we need it, thanks to Luna."

"Fire Fang can help with the search," Storm said. "He's got a great nose for anything rotting or foul smelling."

Olympus tensed. "I'll give it some thought. The bears will most likely handle it."

Indigo laughed. "That's a no. Olympus knows Fire Fang will terrify the scent bears and then rampage through the forest."

"That's him letting off steam. Fire Fang can sniff out anything. He even found an old glove I'd lost three years ago. He ripped up a carpet to get to it, but there it was. I've no clue how it got under there."

I rested my elbows on the table. "Jinti almost got away with framing Atherton."

"But her efforts weren't perfect. She left behind too many clues," Olympus said.

"Not that Devlin noticed," Storm said. "Jinti should have planted those poisons on Atherton. Then he'd have gone down for her murder, too."

"It's sad she had to go to such extremes before anyone realized Atherton was a killer," I said.

"Jinti was a very sick witch, so she had nothing to lose," Olympus said. "I got a report from a specialist she'd been seeing. She was dying of an incurable stomach tumor. She got the diagnosis six months before she killed herself."

My heart lurched. "Jinti figured, since she was dying, she'd use it to her advantage to frame Atherton."

"It makes sense," Olympus said.

"Although that is sad news," Odessa said, "it's great for you, Luna. You didn't kill anyone with your food."

"Not today, anyway," Storm muttered.

I laughed along with my friends, but I mainly felt relief. I'd cleared my name, and the crime Atherton had committed years ago had been discovered. He'd soon be behind bars.

"I need to get back to work. I just dropped by because I knew you'd be interested in an update." Olympus grabbed some sandwiches as he stood.

"How's Devlin behaving himself?" Indigo asked.

"He's being difficult. He hates being proven wrong."

"I don't know what he's complaining about. He solved a murder no one else could. With a little help from Luna."

"I'm sure he'll come around," Olympus said. "And I'll make sure he gets the credit, so he won't hold anything against you, Luna."

"I guess he'll want to talk to me some more about breaking out of my cell?"

"He will, but I'm working on him so he goes easy on you. We might be able to negotiate community service, since you've been such a help in this investigation."

"I can handle that. Thanks, Olympus." I didn't believe for a moment Devlin would leave me alone as I nodded and said goodbye to Olympus.

"Now that fun is over, we need to talk." Odessa's gaze was fixed on me.

I swallowed my piece of sandwich, my gaze flicking around the group. "What do we need to talk about?"

"Your weird magic," Storm said.

"There's nothing to discuss. Besides, we've already talked about this."

"No, I talked, and you avoided my questions. And Indigo told us about that spell you did in the store to stop Atherton. I've never seen you produce weather magic before."

"I didn't even think about it, I just reacted. Atherton's fireball had to be extinguished. Of course, I'd create a spell like that." I went to grab a scone, but Odessa caught hold of my hand.

"We want to make sure you're okay. We're your best friends, and we're worried about you. You would tell us if anything was going on, wouldn't you?"

"Of course. I'm sure my misfiring magic has to do with all the stress I've been under. Being accused of murder doesn't help a witch sleep easy at night. Plus, Uncle Albert has been ill, and—" I bit my tongue. I couldn't mention my debt issue or my farmhouse.

"And?" Storm said.

"Are you worried about your relationships?" Odessa said. "Maybe dating so many guys at once is too much for you."

"It must be exhausting," Storm said. "It's why I don't bother with any guys."

"It hasn't helped." I grabbed onto that excuse. "I'm better sticking with the single life, too."

"No, I didn't mean that," Odessa said. "But pick one guy and stick with him."

"Don't go for the werewolf," Storm said. "They're too intense. They always make unreasonable demands and get dominant and predatory."

Odessa fanned her face. "Now you're talking. Keep the werewolf. Although the half-naked guy was cute. He had a sweet smile."

"He's just a friend."

"What happened to Bram?" Indigo said. "And why did Devlin get him confused with that other guy?"

"No idea. Devlin was under a lot of pressure." My heart was beating so loudly, I was certain they'd hear.

"Huh! I guess. Although he seemed to think Bram was trouble."

"He was wrong. Bram is fine." And still on my list of problems to solve.

"What's this all about?" Odessa said.

Indigo narrowed her eyes. "Nothing. Just Devlin being a jerk."

She didn't believe that, but Indigo was letting me off without more interrogation.

"Anyway, Bram's not going to work out." I really hoped I'd seen the last of him. I needed to make things right with Sylvester and pay off the debt. I could focus on that now I didn't have a murder charge looming over me.

"Are you sure there's nothing we can do to help?" Odessa said.

"No, I've just had too much nervous energy, that's why my magic was odd when I attacked Atherton. Life will get back to normal, and so will my spells."

Odessa glanced at the others.

"I'll get more cake." I hurried to the counter and stared at the desserts. It felt good to have my name cleared, Jinti's death solved, and the Magic Council off my back. I was even feeling mildly optimistic about dealing with Bram. Life felt good again.

I finished my lunch with the others and watched them leave. Then I walked around the counter and gave Uncle Albert a hug.

He kissed the top of my head. "You've had an adventure these last few days. We don't want to see the Magic Council back here soon. Although I'm sure they're happy with their findings and will leave you alone."

"I hope so." I bit my bottom lip. I still needed to answer questions about my baking magic and my cell breakout. Devlin was busy with writing reports and checking evidence on Jinti's murder. But he'd be back.

"Are you doing okay, Luna?" Uncle Albert said. "I thought you'd be pleased all this is over."

"I'm fine. If you're okay here, I'm going to take a break. I could do with some fresh air." I spotted Earl's butt poking out from under the warming cabinet and gently pushed him in so he wouldn't get trodden on.

Uncle Albert looked out the window. "You go out and enjoy the sunshine. I'll be fine."

After giving his cheek a quick kiss, I went into the kitchen, made up a large basket of treats, and then snuck to the farmhouse. I was overdue a visit, and my magic harem wouldn't be happy I'd left them alone.

I approached the magic barrier and slowed. Something felt weird. The magic was hazy, and there were small holes in it. When I looked through one, I could see the farmhouse.

After lowering the barrier, I dashed to the farmhouse. I opened the door and almost walked into Ridley. He was wandering around with a dazed look in his eyes.

I caught hold of his shoulder. "Ridley, where's your chain?" His ankle was free of the chain that kept him tethered to the house.

He scratched the back of his head. "I don't know. Everything went weird. The new guy, he's crazy."

"Cole? Where is he?"

Ridley simply shook his head.

I hurried past him into the parlor. Gloria and Faye were in their usual seats, but they weren't smiling. My panicked gaze dropped to the chain Cole should have been attached to.

I raced over and picked it up. There were traces of blood on it. I turned to Gloria and Faye. "What happened in here? Where is Cole?"

Gloria's face was pale as her sad eyes fixed on me. "He woke up. And then he got angry."

"I've always been cautious about werewolves," Faye said. "He wouldn't listen to reason. And last night was a full moon. He ruined his chains."

I groaned. Of course, a full moon. I'd been so wrapped up in dealing with Jinti's murder that I hadn't paid attention to the lunar cycle. Cole would have been at his strongest last night.

"He didn't hurt you, did he?" I dropped the chains and hurried over to Gloria and Faye.

Gloria shook her head. "He wasn't angry with us. We told him how wonderful you were and how you look after us, but he didn't agree. He claimed we were prisoners and tried to make us leave with him."

"He's left the farmhouse?" I looked out the window. It made sense now why the magic barrier felt so odd. Cole must have used his power to break through and escape.

"After searching the place, he insisted we leave, but we stayed put, just like you always tell us to do," Gloria said proudly.

I swallowed slowly as my gaze scanned the trees outside the window. Cole could be anywhere, and he knew my secret.

"We didn't want to go with him," Faye said. "We're happy here. This is our home. It always will be. But he didn't like that answer."

Ridley ambled into the room. "Cole said it wasn't right what you were doing. I told him he hadn't a clue what he was talking about."

"Did Cole say where he was going?" I said.

"No, but he left a message for you," Gloria said.

"Where is it?"

She lifted a shaking hand to the wall behind me.

I turned, and ice dripped down my spine. Smeared on the wall in what could only be blood were four terrifying words. *I'm coming for you.*

I sank to the floor and dropped my head in my hands. How was I supposed to stop an angry werewolf from hunting me down?

About Author

K.E. O'Connor (Karen) is a mystery author living in the beautiful British countryside. She loves all things mystery, animals, and cake.

If you want to be part of the Witch Haven crew, practice spells, solve a few murders, spend time with amazing witches and their talking familiars, and get a **free** book, join her weekly newsletter.

Sign up today.

Newsletter:
https://BookHip.com/QKGDWJW
Website:
www.keoconnor.com/writing
Facebook:
www.facebook.com/keoconnorauthor

Also By

Spells and Spooks
Hexes and Haunts
Curses and Corpses
Muffins and Moonlight
Cupcakes and Cauldrons
Pancakes and Potions
Hauntings and High Jinx
Hauntings and Havoc
Hauntings and Hoaxes
The Case of the Screaming Skull
The Case of the Poisoned Pumpkin
The Case of the Cursed Candy
Fire Fang
Silvaria

If you enjoyed

Muffins and Moonlight

turn the page to read an extract from the next Witch Haven mystery.

CUPCAKES AND CAULDRONS

ISBN: 978-1-915378-32-3

Chapter 1

"Don't stick that rolling pin in your ear!" I dashed over and grabbed the floured rolling pin from Zek, a teenage gremlin with a chipped front tooth and bright green spiky hair.

He growled and hung onto the rolling pin before swinging it at my head.

I ducked and fell, bumping into two other gremlins on my way down as they carried cupcakes to the counter. Two dozen pale yellow cakes flew in the air and splatted to the floor of the reform school classroom.

Warm cupcake slid off my cheek as I stared at the ceiling. No one told me community service would be this challenging.

"Are you okay, miss?" Zek peered down at me. "You've got icing all over your face."

Vak, another of my teenage students, grabbed my arm and yanked me into a seated position.

I struggled up, careful not to stand on any cupcakes. I turned to the gremlins I'd bumped into. "Sorry about your cakes. They looked perfect."

They looked at the scattered cupcakes and shrugged.

"They'd have been gross," Vak said. "My mate replaced the sugar with salt to make you puke when you tried one."

The gremlins lunged at each other, growling and snarling as they rolled on the floor.

I left them to it as I scooped up squashed cakes. It took me most of my first day on community service trying to stop these fights before I learned that was how they settled their differences. No amount of reasoning or pleading did any good. And once the gremlins got it out of their system, they were fine.

A quick check of the time revealed class was almost done for the day. I clapped my hands together. "Everyone worked so hard today. I'll make sure that goes down on all your assessments."

The fighting gremlins pulled apart and grinned at each other before leaping up.

"We passed?" Vak said.

"You've all passed your domestic science course."

"Whoa! I never passed nothing."

"Congratulations."

He grinned at me, several of his teeth missing. "I liked it. Some of the others thought it was rubbish being forced to learn to bake, but I can use my skills to get girls. I'm now a master of lifting purses and making treats. I'll have them eating out of my hand."

"Um, maybe stick with the baking skills when you go wooing. Not all the ladies love light fingers."

He chuckled. "The ones I hang around with do."

"Everyone gather around with your cupcakes," I said. "We'll do a taste test to finish."

The group of six gremlins I'd been supervising over the last eight weeks bustled to the table. This was always their favorite part.

Four of them clutched trays of cupcakes. They placed them on the table, and after much shoving and growling to figure out where was the best place to put the cakes, they looked up at me expectantly.

"There's a lot of delicious cake here."

"I'm not touching anything Zek made," Vak said. "He picks his nose all the time and never washes his hands."

"I don't." Zek shoved his friend.

"No more shoving, or no one is eating cake! And no more picking noses when you're baking. Remember, clean hands at all times." I stared at the cakes. My students tried so hard, but their efforts looked as bad as mine when I'd had a terrible day using my baking magic.

I divided the cakes into six small piles then picked up one that was iced in brilliant green and sprinkled with something I hoped was chocolate and took a small bite. I chewed cautiously.

"That's mine," Cal said. "What do you think? It's rubbish, ain't it?"

It had an odd, sour taste, but it was edible. "Excellent work on the icing. The base is a little heavy. Cupcakes are usually lighter, but it's a solid six out of ten."

His face brightened. "I got a six. That's a pass?"

"It is. Well done."

He grabbed a cupcake, chewing it with a smile on his green face.

"I did way better than Cal." Zek shoved a cake at me. "You'll want to marry me after you've tried this."

I took a bite of the chocolate cupcake, and my eyes widened. "Zek! This is excellent."

"He cheated," Cal said. "I saw him."

Zek lobbed a cupcake at Cal's head. "Keep your lying mouth shut!"

"You did! You snuck in a packet mix this morning. He thought he got away with it, but I saw him tuck it under the kitchen counter. Miss, you should disqualify him."

The gremlins lunged at each other, snarling and snapping their sharp little teeth.

I ate more cake, waiting for the fighting fever to die down. "I'll have to fail you if you keep challenging each other. Fighting isn't allowed in class. You know the rules. They're on the wall if you need a reminder." Gremlins were almost as hierarchical as werewolves, always fighting for the top spot.

Vak snorted a laugh. "Zek can't even read."

"Can so." Zek broke away from the fight and glared at Vak. "It says no fighting. No swearing. No unauthorized magic."

"And no bringing in pre-made cake mixtures." Cal jabbed him in the ribs with a clawed finger.

"Did you bring in a packet mix?" I said to Zek.

He shrugged and looked defiant, although his cheeks colored pink. "There's no harm in it. I was using my initiative. You told us to be inventive."

"With the icing and the finished design." I looked at his too good to be true cupcakes. "Still, you get a mark for using your initiative."

"That's not fair!" Cal said.

I raised a hand. "But I'm deducting six marks for not using your own recipe. That gives you a two out of ten, Zek."

The gremlin scowled and swiped a cupcake off the counter before stomping away and glaring out the window.

I sampled more cupcakes, glad all of them tasted normal, although there was a hint of fried pickle in one. Maybe that was the cake from the nose picker.

"Who wins?" Vak said.

"I'm calling it a draw," I said. "You're all winners."

"That's not right. Zek cheated. He can't be a winner," Cal said.

Zek made a strange wheezing noise and staggered to the side, bumping into a table.

"Ignore him," Cal said. "He's angry because he came last."

Zek wheezed again and thumped his chest.

"Are you okay?" I hurried over to Zek. He was pale, and his green lips had lost their color.

He coughed and struck his chest again.

"He's choking!" I stood behind him, put my arms around his middle, and squeezed hard.

Cal gathered around with the other gremlins. "That's what you get for cheating."

"Don't be a horse's butt." Vak shoved him. "He's got cake lodged in his throat, dummy. It's probably one of yours."

"He stuffed a whole cupcake in his gob. That's why he's choking. It's not my fault he doesn't know what his teeth are for!"

It took me several hard squeezes before a large lump of slimy cake shot out of Zek's mouth and landed on the floor.

He gasped in a breath and slumped forward, resting his hands on his knees.

I patted him on the shoulder as he got his breath back, while his classmates examined the ejected piece of cake.

Zek lifted a hand and waved it in the air. "You saved me. No one's ever saved me before."

"Oh, Zek, I'm sure that's not true."

He kissed my cheek. "I owe you. I'll be in your debt until I save your life."

"There's no need. I'm happy to do my job."

Someone clearing their throat had me looking up. Devlin Goody, a meddling compliance auditor from the Magic Council, stood in the doorway, a sour expression on his face.

The gremlins froze for half a second and then scattered.

"Was that one of your cakes this young gremlin was choking on?" Devlin asked.

I stared at the gooey lump on the floor. "It's hard to tell. I don't think so."

"It had better not be. You've been in enough trouble with your dubious cake offerings."

I opened my mouth to protest. Devlin and I had history, and none of it good.

"Leave Miss Brimstone alone. She's a great teacher." Zek stood in front of me, his teeth bared at Devlin.

Devlin scowled at him. "Move back, unless you want your privileges taken away."

"I don't care about no privileges. Don't pick on Miss Brimstone." Cal joined him and was quickly followed by the rest. They surrounded me like a small, scaly army of righteousness.

I fought hard not to grin smugly at Devlin. "It looks like I'm getting a gold star for my teaching."

He walked over and slapped papers on the table, staying out of the reach of the snarling gremlins. "That's why I'm here. It's your final day of community service."

"You're signing me off?"

Devlin's thin lips pursed. "I was considering extending your sentence. Two months of teaching hardly seems a suitable punishment for your crimes."

"She's no criminal," Zek said. "Miss Brimstone is awesome. She's an inspiration. When I get out of here, I'm opening a catering van. I'll travel the world, selling gremlin snacks."

"Zek, that's a great idea," I said. "And I'm glad I inspired you."

"Hopefully, your time here will have inspired you to keep your nose out of things that don't concern you." Devlin scratched his signature at the bottom of the piece of paper.

"My brush with murder isn't something I plan to repeat."

"Did you kill someone, Miss?" Cal stared at me with excited eyes. "Who'd you whack?"

"No! I definitely didn't kill anyone. It was all a misunderstanding." I leaned down to my captive audience and lowered my voice. "Although Devlin thought I was guilty. And he worked hard to get me put in jail."

"Then he's a giant dirty horse's butt, thinking a nice witch like you could go around slaying people," Vak said.

"I heard that." Devlin pointed a finger at Vak. "You watch your manners, unless you want your file reviewed and your stay extended."

"I don't mind staying if Miss Brimstone is teaching. She's more fun than the others." Vak sneered at Devlin. "And you do look like a horse's butt with that tiny puckered mouth." He mimicked Devlin's expression.

Within seconds, six gremlins were leaping around with pinched faces as they brayed and trotted about the room.

Devlin gathered up the papers and checked my signature. "I can see your influence in these reprobates."

"Thanks. I take that as a huge compliment." I grinned as Vak whinnied so loudly it made Devlin jump.

"That's your copy." Devlin flipped me a piece of paper before stalking out.

"Horse Butt Face doesn't think much of you, does he?" Cal trotted past.

"He doesn't. But I've seen the last of him." I waved the paper in my hand. "I'm a free witch."

Cal trotted back to me. He dropped his chin to his chest. "Does that mean you won't be coming back? I mean, not that I care. You can do what you like, but your lessons aren't terrible. I don't hate you teaching us."

"They're a million times better than those boring woodwork lessons they insist we do." Zek cantered over.

I looked around the group as they assembled in front of me, and my heart felt warm. "Have you really enjoyed learning to bake?" It felt great to be wanted. And even though my baking skills were far from perfect, the gremlins didn't mind.

"You could teach us to make other stuff," Vak said. "We could come up with ideas for a three course meal. Starters, main course, and then pudding. We'd get to stuff our gobs."

"I want to do the pudding," Cal said. "I've got a sweet tooth."

I didn't hate the idea of carrying on the lessons, and I didn't want to let the gremlins down. It had been fun when I discounted the fighting, squabbles, and nose picking. "I'll speak to Sinbad and see what he has to say. Maybe they can move your schedule around and we can fit in a weekly cookery class."

"Then we can all go off and be world-class bakers," Zek said.

"You'll be a world class butthead." Cal ducked a punch from Zek.

I moved in between them. I had a genuine pang of affection for these little guys. "I love the way you always shoot for the moon, Zek. Never stop doing that."

He flashed his teeth at me. "One day, I'm gonna stick a pin in that sucker and claim it as mine."

The gremlins helped me clear up, and once the equipment and cakes were dealt with, I said goodbye to my class and headed out. I stopped by Sinbad's office and tapped on the door.

He looked up and smiled at me. "You survived your last day."

"It was touch and go a few times, but I've enjoyed myself." I stepped into his office. "And the gremlins asked if they can continue their cookery classes with me. Would that be possible?"

His grin widened. "You really want to do that? I know they can be a handful, and I've been in the class a couple of times and seen them be cheeky to you. A lot of teachers won't stand for that."

"I'm used to it. And if I can help them, I'd love to." I lifted a shoulder. "I know I'm not a proper teacher, so I'd understand if it doesn't work for you."

"You're a real teacher to them, no matter how you came to be here." He scratched his head as he glanced through a calendar on his desk. "We even have a small budget for lessons, so I can supply you with the ingredients. So long as you don't make Lobster Thermidor every week."

"I promise, it'll be simple home cooking. Recipes they can use every day once they're released. Knowing how to make a nutritious meal will be useful for them."

"Then consider it done. Life skills are crucial for our residents. Give me a few weeks to juggle things around, and I'll find the space. How does that suit?"

"That sounds great. I'm looking forward to it."

We said goodbye, and I headed out of the reform school and walked back to the center of Witch Haven. It felt good to get back to normal.

Well, things weren't quite normal.

I glanced around, relieved to see there was no sign of an angry werewolf stalking me. Ever since my misadventures with Cole Kellam, I'd been on the alert after he left a worrying message in my farmhouse.

I'd have to tackle him soon. That was, unless he tackled me first and chewed my arm off.

My forehead wrinkled as I spotted a large truck outside Fandango's, my Uncle Albert's bakery, where I worked when I wasn't doing my community service. The back was open, and people were carrying equipment out of it into the empty store next door.

Uncle Albert emerged from the doorway and hurried over the second he saw me. "They're early!"

"The film crew? I didn't think they were getting here until tomorrow."

"They've pushed everything forward." He clasped his hands together, his wispy hair blowing in the breeze. "We're not ready."

I caught hold of his shoulder and gave it a gentle squeeze. "We are ready. You've been making preparations for weeks."

"I wanted to run through everything one more time. What if I've forgotten something important? Will they want to interview me?"

"I don't know. But if you have, we'll fix it together. And you'll be a huge hit. Everyone will love Fandango's when they learn about the bakery."

My uncle's expression remained anxious. "I don't want anything going wrong. This is a once-in-a-lifetime opportunity to promote us."

I nudged him out of the way as two members of the film crew walked past with a large box between them. We'd been contacted three months ago and asked to take part in the prestigious baking contest, *The Bewitching Bakery Showdown*. It was a huge event in the magical baking community. Each year, the sponsor picked a venue to promote and live filmed the show in the area. It was a great platform to promote our desserts, and the orders would come flooding in.

Uncle Albert had almost fallen off his seat when he got a request for Fandango's to star in the show. It was hardly a surprise it was picked. My parents were world-renowned bakers, and Uncle Albert wasn't far behind, although he preferred to keep things small scale. I was a Brimstone, and he was a Black, but both bloodlines came with a hefty dose of natural baking magic. At least, that was the theory. I was the wonky reality.

"Albert, I've been looking for you." Mrs. Henriette DeVere, a tall witch with long white hair and brilliant amber eyes, strode over. She wore an expensively tailored black suit with a red blouse underneath.

"Mrs. DeVere. It's good to see you again." Uncle Albert stepped forward and shook her outstretched hand.

"Please, call me Henriette." She turned her attention to me and smiled. "I hope you've both been looking forward to this."

"Of course. We're glad to have you at Fandango's." Henriette had been to visit the bakery twice while making plans for the show.

"We're thrilled to be here. And I'm so looking forward to your father being a judge. We were delighted when he accepted our request to head up the judging panel. It's a treat."

"I'm looking forward to him visiting, too. Dad hasn't been to Witch Haven for a year."

Her eyebrows shot up, then she nodded. "His work must keep him busy. I saw the marvelous eight-tiered cake he made for Viscount Hornsbill. It was a work of art. It deserved its own private viewing gallery in an exhibition."

I grinned. My dad was a show-off with his cakes. "He's always enjoyed making unique designs."

"I'm hoping we can press him into making us something special for the show," Henriette said. "Nothing elaborate, because I know how many weeks it takes to make the decorations and come up with the concept, but something that will delight our viewers. It would be a ratings smash."

I glanced at Uncle Albert and bit my bottom lip. My dad hated surprises. He loved order and routine. He wouldn't be pulling any last minute surprises out of his chef's hat, but I didn't want to dash Henriette's hopes. "Maybe we have something in Fandango's you'd like to showcase? Uncle Albert is also an incredible baker. He comes from the Black family line."

"Of course. And they're excellent at what they do. I've already tried three of his cakes." Henriette smiled at Uncle Albert. "And I hope you don't mind us turning up early. We heard the venue next door was empty, so we decided to get ahead of ourselves. We're setting up live cooking stations with state-of-the-art equipment. Nothing but the best for our talented bakers."

I glanced at the store the crew hurried in and out of. It had once been a used book store and small café, but it had shut down months ago and stood empty ever since. "It's a perfect location."

"And we'd love to get shots of you and your uncle in action in your kitchen. You can wow the viewers with your special Brimstone baking talent."

I gulped down panic. "You should focus on Uncle Albert. He'll be a natural in front of the camera."

"You must be included, too," he said. "I'm sure your dad wants to see your baking star shine."

I hid a grimace. I didn't want my baking star appearing on screen. It was wonky and dull. My plan was to stay below the radar. Uncle Albert loved baking, so he was welcome to take center stage and show off Fandango's.

There was a yelp, and something crashed to the ground.

I looked up and gasped. Earl, my lazy black cat familiar, was flopped in the pathway of the crew. I raced over and scooped him off the ground, muttering apologies to everyone.

Earl grumbled and flipped himself up onto my shoulder.

"What are you doing?" I hissed at him.

"I don't like all these people hanging around." He booped his damp nose against my cheek and yawned fishy breath in my face. "They're making so much noise. I was having a nap in the empty store when they barged in. Who are they?"

"You can't have forgotten the baking show starts tomorrow. Uncle Albert has been talking about little else for the last few weeks. And this will be big business for the bakery. Imagine what'll happen to Fandango's when we get national exposure."

"It sounds like a lot of extra work." He wrapped himself around my neck and began snoring.

"I'm looking for Luna Brimstone and Henriette DeVere." A bike messenger stopped by the store.

"I'm Luna." I pointed over my shoulder. "And that's Henriette."

Henriette walked over to join me. "It's probably paperwork for the show. There's always last minute admin to deal with."

I took a letter and signed for it, and so did Henriette, before the bike messenger cycled off.

Henriette opened her letter first. She glanced at me. "It's good news for you, my dear."

I tore open my letter, and my heart sank to my boots as I read the contents. "Dad's not coming. He got an urgent commission he couldn't turn down."

"To bake for the royal family in the Elven kingdom." Henriette sighed. "He'll do such a wonderful job."

"Yep, I'm sure he will. It would have been great to see him, though." But that was my dad. Work was his life, and his family was an afterthought. I tried not to take it personally, but it stung that he always picked pudding over me.

"I'm disappointed he can't make it, but his replacement is almost as good."

"Oh! Who's his replacement?"

"Didn't he say in his note to you?" Henriette said.

I flipped it over. "Nope."

She smiled at me. "He nominated you to take his place as head judge. Congratulations."

Cupcakes and Cauldrons is available in e-book and paperback

ISBN: 978-1-915378-32-3